KATERINA

KATERINA

James Frey

SCOUT PRESS

New York   London   Toronto   Sydney   New Delhi

Scout Press
An Imprint of Simon & Schuster, Inc.
1230 Avenue of the Americas
New York, NY 10020

First Scout Press trade paperback edition July 2019

SCOUT PRESS and colophon are registered trademarks of Simon & Schuster, Inc.

For information about special discounts for bulk purchases, please contact Simon & Schuster Special Sales at 1-866-506-1949 or business@simonandschuster.com.

The Simon & Schuster Speakers Bureau can bring authors to your live event. For more information or to book an event, contact the Simon & Schuster Speakers Bureau at 1-866-248-3049 or visit our website at www.simonspeakers.com.

Manufactured in the United States of America

10 9 8 7 6 5 4 3 2 1

The Library of Congress has cataloged the hardcover edition as follows:

Names: Frey, James, 1969- author.
Title: Katerina / James Frey.
Description: First Scout Press hardcover edition. | New York : Scout Press,
   2018.
Identifiers: LCCN 2018018077 (print) | LCCN 2018023185 (ebook) | ISBN
   9781982101466 (ebook) | ISBN 9781982101442 (hardcover) | ISBN
   9781-982101466 (ebook)
Subjects: | BISAC: FICTION / Literary. | FICTION / Coming of Age. | FICTION /
   General.
Classification: LCC PS3606.R488 (ebook) | LCC PS3606.R488 K38 2018 (print) |
   DDC 813/.6—dc23
LC record available at https://lccn.loc.gov/2018018077

ISBN 978-1-9821-0144-2
ISBN 978-1-9821-0145-9 (pbk)
ISBN 978-1-9821-0146-6 (ebook)

A while back, if I remember right, my life was one long party where all hearts were open wide, where all wines kept flowing.

One evening I took Beauty in my arms - and I thought her bitter - and I insulted her.

ARTHUR RIMBAUD, *A SEASON IN HELL*, 1873

Los Angeles, 2017

It started with a message request on Facebook. Someone named Jente Paenbenk. No picture, no friends. A blank profile. It started again. After twenty-five years.

Do you ever think of me?
I responded:
Maybe.

And so it went.

I think of you every day.
Good.
Sometimes it is, sometimes it's not.
That's life, right? Sometimes it is, sometimes not.
Yes, Jay, that has certainly been the case. For both of us.
Who is this?
I want you to think of me every day.
Who is this?
I want you to think and smile and remember.
Who is this?
Think and smile and remember, Jay.
Who?
For me. Do it for me.

Paris, 1992

I'm living at rue Saint-Placide. The floor is covered with empty wine bottles and ashtrays, my mattress is on the floor in the corner. The paint on the walls has been chipped away and the windows don't close. It's the end of the twentieth century and we are living in what is supposed to be an advanced society. Our desires, though, our desires are the same. The same as they have been since the first day one of us stepped out of a fucking cave. Love fuck eat drink sleep. And this is what I do here, in the most beautiful, most civilized city on earth. Love fuck eat drink sleep.

Last night Louis tied a red scarf on the door handle. Louis likes Arab boys, as close to eighteen as he can find them. The scarf means stay out, though I could hear them through the door and knew without seeing the scarf. I went for a walk and bought a couple bottles of cheap wine and sat on a bench in Saint-Germain and watched pretty girls walk by and imagined what it would be like to be with them, to kiss them, make them smile or laugh, flirt with them, fuck them, fall in love with them. Some I knew would never happen. Some I knew could be mine. I sat and drank and watched and imagined until I couldn't think and stopped remembering and I woke up under a tree on Quai Voltaire and I walked back to the apartment. The red scarf was gone.

Louis is making coffee. He thinks of himself as a philosopher, a weatherman, an astronomer, a speaker of languages, an artist. We live on a little ball, he says, a little blue ball in a minor solar system in a small galaxy in an infinite universe. Nothing I do or you do or anyone does means a goddamn thing. We should be happy and spend our days in pursuit of pleasure and pain and every form of lust and desire that exists. We should make sure our cocks are hard and our pussies are wet and our hearts are beating fast, fast, fast. But we don't, because we're stupid, and because we all think we're important, that we matter, that what we do matters, so we spend our time working meaningless jobs and struggling and fighting and trying to be something or someone other than what we are, which is animals. Everyone does it, all of humanity, the whole teeming, silly, idiotic mass, everyone does it except me. I, Louis, the Prince of Saint-Placide, know better. I follow my heart and my cock, and the only things that matter to me are the things that make them sing. So listen to me, boy. And learn from me. Follow your heart and follow your cock. And remember that none of this means anything. And you will be as happy as me.

I've been in Paris for a month. I'm twenty-one, I came here alone, didn't know anyone, didn't speak a word of French, packed a bag and walked away. From my friends, my family, from America. Whatever my life was or was supposed to be is gone. I was born and raised to be part of a machine. A spoke. A little gear. An obedient cog locked in fucking place forever. Go to school, follow the rules, get a job, work save vote obey, get married buy a house have children, work save vote obey teach your children to do the same, work save vote obey, die and rot in a fucking hole in the ground. Fuck that machine. Fuck the people who built it. Fuck the people who run it. Fuck the people who choose to be a part of it. I am here, in the most beautiful, most civilized city on earth. I believe in Louis, in his crazy eyes, shaking hands, bellowing voice, in his view of the weather and the stars. I follow my heart and I follow my cock. When they want to sing, we sing. When they want to smile, we smile. When they want to dance, we dance. When they want to be broken, we break. Whatever they want, wherever they want to go, however much pleasure we find or pain, we will never work save vote obey. Fuck that machine. The only goal should be to burn it down. Light it on fire and dance in the fucking flames.

And so I go through ancient streets filled with people speaking a language I do not know seeking something that I will never find, I could call it freedom but it's more than that, I could call it enlightenment but I want to feel more than enlightened, I could call it everything because it is everything to me, loving fucking eating drinking sleeping feeling living living living. It is everything. I want to burn that machine the fuck down. I want to live.

Los Angeles, 2017

My grass is green. I can see the ocean from some of the windows and a yellow haze above glittering steel towers from the others. There are trees and birds and a swimming pool. Three cars in the garage, two children in bedrooms, a wife who sleeps next to me. My mortgage is paid on time every month, as are the rest of the bills that arrive. A housekeeper is here every day, and men who take care of the lawn and the trees and the pool and pick up the dogshit our family pet leaves everywhere. I have a little barn, or cottage, or studio, whatever you want to call it, on the back of our property, away from the house, away from the noise, away from people, away from the world. I spend my days in that little building in front of a computer, listening to music and watching TV, reading books and playing video games, sometimes working, supposedly doing things that matter, that are important, that people want to read and that other people give me money to produce. They give me stupid amounts of money. I do what they want and give them what they pay me for and I hate myself. And when I stop long enough to think about what I'm doing and how I got where I am and how much I have and how much I've wasted, when I think about how lost I feel every second of every day, how completely fucking lost I am and I feel, I want to buy a gun and blow my fucking brains out. But I'm not brave enough for that. So I walk through my grass and I stare at my trees and I listen to the birds and I look at the ocean and the skyscrapers and I smile for my children and I sleep next to my wife and I pay my bills and I do my work. And I hate myself. Every single minute of every single day. Hate myself.

Paris, 1992

Open the door.

Step outside.

Life is waiting.

Sex and love and books and art. The sun rising or setting. Laughter and music. A quiet place to sit. To read or think or watch the day go by. Or not. To walk. Amidst the chaos, the people, the noise. A car horn. A motorcycle. People talking. Bells on doors as they open and close. A couple fighting, a baby crying. Walk or dance or skip or run, do whatever you want to do, go wherever you want to go. You can find something magnificent or terrible or nothing at all. Ecstasy or heartbreak. Adventure or boredom. Open the fucking door.

Life is waiting.

Step.

My day always starts the same way. I go to the bakery. Whether I wake up at home, or in an alley, or a park, in someone else's apartment or on someone else's floor or bed or bathtub, I go to the bakery. It's on the ground floor of the building where I live, directly below the apartment that Louis and I share. It's a standard French bakery, a *boulangerie* as the French say with their beautiful words, and they have one on every block. They sell bread at the boulangerie, though in France bread is more than bread. It's life, it's spirit, it's blood, it's identity, it's art. Every French I know takes their bread seriously, like Americans take their guns, or Christians take their prayers. They argue over who makes the best baguette, the best pastries, the best pain au chocolat, what time of day is best to buy the bread, if it should be eaten warm or cooled, what kind of butter to put on it and how much, if one could survive on bread alone. If you're ever with a French and you don't have anything to talk about, just bring up bread. They'll tell you how good it is in Paris, and that the bread everywhere else is terrible. And for whatever the reason, they're right, the bread is better in Paris. It tastes better smells better feels better looks better. When you break a piece off, it sounds better. I eat baguette bread every day, and most days it's all I eat. Five francs, which is about a dollar, and I don't have to worry about food. I can spend my money on more important things, books or pens or cigarettes or coffee or wine, sometimes flowers for old ladies or random beautiful girls I see walking down the street. The old ladies always smile, sometimes the girls do. Sometimes they just turn and walk away. It's a simple idiotic thing to do. Give flowers to someone you don't know. Whatever happens, it's money well spent.

The bakery below me has a simple blue sign and a simple steel counter and cases with fancy pastries and bins behind filled with the various forms of bread. You can see the ovens and tables behind the bins, the flour, the dough, the rollers, the organized chaos that produces the goods. An old French couple owns the bakery. I imagine they got it from one of their parents, who got it from their parents, who got it from their parents, and on and on back to the Gauls with butter in their hair. The couple is there every day, the old couple, they open at dawn and close at 5 p.m. The husband does the baking, the wife runs the cash register, they wear matching white aprons with trim the same color blue as the sign outside. They smile at the customers, exchange pleasantries and laughs with regulars, sell them baguettes, croissants, pain au chocolat, hand them things that have names I don't know and can't pronounce, fancy French concoctions that taste delicious and cost almost nothing. They do not like me, despite the fact that I am here every day. I enter, wait in line, say hello and ask for a baguette in French with my shitty French accent, hand them the five francs. The woman does not say hello to me, or acknowledge me in any way, aside from taking my money and handing me a baguette. Sometimes I wave at the man, who either scowls or looks away. As far as I know, and have seen, I'm the only American who buys bread from them, and I assume that's why they don't like me. Generally I've found, despite the French reputation for hating Americans, that if you attempt to speak French, and you're not an asshole, the French are cool. They're aloof and distant and cold and somewhat rude, and they will let you know if you're doing something stupid, but they're that way with everyone, including each other. There is a directness I appreciate, a lack of bullshit. Be cool, the French are cool. If you're a dick, expect it back.

The bakers, though, the cute little old people in their white aprons with blue trim who sell me my bread, they do hate Americans. Or maybe just this American. Most days I make the transaction as simple and painless as possible. Order the bread hand over the money take the bread walk. Some days, however, I try to speak to them, ask them questions about politics, if they're fans of Paris Saint-Germain, if they prefer Manet or Monet, if they've read Victor Hugo and Gustave Flaubert and if so, who they prefer, if they've ever challenged other local bakers to a baguette showdown. No matter what I say, they ignore me. Dismiss my every word. Sometimes the other customers laugh, sometimes they turn away, uncomfortable and embarrassed. Whatever happens, I hand over the money take the bread walk.

Open the door.

Step outside.

Life is waiting.

And so I walk. With no destination, no plan, nothing to do. Nowhere to be and no one to meet. There is no better city in the world to walk in than Paris. On every block there is food and wine and art and beauty. The buildings all soft white or deep gray. High windows on every floor. Single twelve-foot wooden doors with

discreet numbers embedded into stone. The streets are crowded.
There's no grid and they move and turn as they please. The Grands
Boulevards dominate the city. Les Champs-Élysées with its wide
sidewalks and giant cafés and lights, the Times Square of Paris,
contained by the Arc de Triomphe on one side and place de la
Concorde on the other. Saint-Denis with its criminals and whores,
openly hawking their wares and their bodies, dead during daylight
but when the sun drops it pulses with sex and danger, desire and
violence. Montparnasse with intellectuals and academics endlessly
debating and smoking, taking three hours to drink a coffee.
Haussmann and its department stores and old ladies with fancy
hats and handbags that cost more than a house. Beaumarchais,
Filles du Calvaire, Temple, Saint-Martin. Clichy with the ghosts
of Picasso, Dalí, Modigliani, and van Gogh. Saint-Germain,
where Hemingway and Fitzgerald drank and fought and pissed
themselves. I walk and I look and I listen. I sit on benches outside
of cathedrals. I lie in the grass of parks. I drift through museums
and watch people as much as I stare at the art. I think and I dream.
I carry a small notebook made of thick brown paper bound with
string, a pen, whatever book I'm reading, a pack of cigarettes and
a lighter, a small wad of bills in my back pocket. I sit in cafés and
write, drink coffee, read. I go to bars in the morning and have
a drink, I have wine for lunch, cocktails to celebrate the arrival
of the afternoon. I look through the stacks of bookstores, even
though most of the books are in French and I can't read them. I
look at the names on the spines, the words on the pages, smell
the paper, feel the weight of them. I walk and my mind wanders
and I dream. I dream of art and food. Enough money to have as
much of whatever I want whenever I want. I dream of an endless
supply of wine and cocaine, of sex and having it with almost every
woman I see. I stand outside of restaurants and read the menus in

the windows. I look at pictures in the magazines at the newsstand.
Sometimes I just stop and stare at a building, imagine it being
built, its history, the lives of the people who live in it, the pain
they feel, the joy, the struggles they have, the occasional triumph
and relentless failure. I walk and I wander and I dream. More than
anything, I dream of love, crazy crazy mad love. Not the love of
rings and white dresses and churches, but of lust and insanity, the
love where you can't stop touching, kissing, licking, sucking, and
fucking. The love that breaks hearts, starts wars, ruins lives, the
love that sears itself into your soul, that you can feel every time
your heart beats, that scorches your memory and comes back to
you whenever you're alone and it's quiet and the world falls away,
the love that still hurts, that makes you sit and stare at the floor
and wonder what the fuck happened and why. I dream of crazy
crazy mad love the kind that starts with a look, with eyes that
meet, a smile, a touch, a laugh, a kiss. The kind of love that hurts
and makes you love the pain, makes you want the pain, makes
you yearn for the fucking pain, keeps you awake until the sun
rises, stirs you while you're still asleep. The kind of love you can
feel with every step you take, every word you speak, every breath,
every movement, is part of every thought you have every minute
of the day. Love that overwhelms. That justifies our existence. That
provides proof we are here for a reason. That either confirms the
existence of God and divinity, or renders it utterly meaningless.
Love that makes life more than just whatever we know and see
and feel. That elevates it. Love for which so many words have been
spoken and written and read and cried and screamed and sung and
sobbed, but is beyond any real description of it. I've known much
in my short, silly, unstable, sometimes wonderful sometimes brutal
always reckless wreck of a life, but I've never known love. Crazy
crazy mad love. Fear and pain, insecurity, rage, occasional joy,

fleeting peace, they are all friends of mine. Kindness and familial love have always come my way. Disdain, contempt, and rage are constant companions. But never love.

So I open the door.

Step outside.

Walk.

Think.

Read.

Write.

Sit.

Watch.

Drink.

Eat bread.

Dream.

Life is waiting.

Life and love.

Life.

Love.

Los Angeles, 2017

Two weeks later, another message. I respond. And so it goes.

How is your heart, Jay?
Beating.
Not singing.
Not for years.
It used to sing so beautifully. A bit off-key, but loud and with such joy.
It's silent and black now.
It was always black, but there were stars in that blackness. Big bright beautiful stars.
Just black now. And silent. No stars.
I read you're married, children?
Where did you read that?
A magazine, I think. Or maybe I saw it on TV.
Ah yes, magazines and TV.
True?
Yes.
I never thought you would be.
Neither did I.
What happened?
I met someone I wanted to marry.
Happy?
I'm generally happy. At least in that part of my life. I love her, and I love our kids. I've been lucky in that way.
It's good you recognize it.
I guess.
Why is your heart black?
I'm old.

You're 45.

They've been long years.

By choice.

Most of the time, yes. But not always.

That heart of yours, it sang, but I also know it hurt, it always hurt.

One thing feeds the other thing.

Singing and screaming.

It's a fine line between them.

Tell me what hurt you the most, Jay.

No.

Tell me.

No.

Why?

I don't know who you are.

Yes you do.

I don't.

Have there been that many of us?

There were enough.

Where am I among them in your memories?

I don't know.

You do.

Nope.

You will.

Maybe.

I want your heart to sing again, Jay.

So do I.

Off-key, but loud and with joy.

So do I.

My Favorite Spots in Paris
After Living Here For Two Months

Le Polly Maggoo, rue du Petit Pont. A shitty bar filled with derelict drunks they keep absinthe behind the counter. There are chessboards on some of the tables and Turkish bathrooms, which means there is just a big hole in the floor. I have never seen a napkin there, or toilet paper, and the drinks are strong and cheap and they don't care if you yell or fall down. They ask that fights take place on the sidewalk outside, and the bar always empties when a fight begins, and everyone goes outside and watches and cheers, and the combatants often hug and have a drink when they're done. Most of the customers are Turks and Algerians who like to get drunk, but can't do it in their own neighborhoods, and old Americans who came here for some reason but don't remember what it was and now spend all their time getting drunk. The girls aren't particularly beautiful, but they aren't there looking for husbands, and after ten drinks, it doesn't really matter what they look like.

The Film Room at the Musée Picasso, rue de Thorigny. Sit on a bench and watch movies of Picasso making paintings. I'm young and naïve enough to still believe I'm going to be great at something. I'm old and wise enough to know I'll never be as great at anything as Picasso was at making art.

The Grave of Alexandre Dumas. Panthéon. Motherfucker wrote *Count of Monte Cristo*. Much respect.

Cactus Charly, rue de Ponthieu. They claim to have the best cheeseburgers in Europe. I've had three. Each was worse than the last, and in a life filled with eating cheeseburgers, I've never had

one as bad as the Cactus Charly Burger, a mass of meat and cheese
and chili and bacon and BBQ sauce that should be called the
Abomination Burger. But they serve gigantic drinks for cheap and
five-franc shots of Southern Comfort at Happy Hour and there
are often drunk American and English girls willing to fuck in the
bathroom.

Musée de l'Orangerie, Jardin des Tuileries. I always thought
Monet and the *Water Lilies* were boring as fuck. And most of them
are. I've seen them in museums in America and they always remind
me of stale farts. But one day I was wandering around and ended up
in the two large oval rooms that hold eight large paintings Monet
made right before he died. He said the goal was to make something
that would make people forget the outside world existed. And he
did. They are fucking magnificent. Breathtaking. Serene. A vision of
the real world somehow made more beautiful, more overwhelming.
But what sucks is other people in the room. For some reason they
always want to talk, want to make sure everyone within a hundred
yards knows how much they love the *Water Lilies*. They need to
learn to shut the fuck up and look and feel and disappear. Shut. The.
Fuck. Up. And let themselves disappear.

Texas Star, place Edmond-Michelet. A dumb American bar with a
Texas flag flying out front. Every human from Texas who's in Paris
seems to be there. Discovered it coming out of le Centre Pompidou.
They serve Lone Star beer and make edible tacos, which don't really
exist anywhere else in France, at least as far as I know. I met, drank
with, and threw up on a former US president's niece one evening.
We were doing shots of tequila, and I was doing two for every one
she did. She could drink like a fish, I got sick, puked all over the
table, in our drinks, on her lap. We made out a couple hours later,

and I woke up on her floor the next morning without my pants on. She was not there and I never saw her again, but whenever I want to listen to people talk about guns and oil and football and how cool they think it is to wear cowboy boots, which I absolutely believe it is not, I go to the Texas Star.

Maison de Gyros, rue de la Huchette. A street lined with Greek restaurants. Some fancy, some less so, some shitty fast-food gyro joints. All of them have those spinning spits of piled lamb chunks in the window. Maison D is around the corner from Le Polly Maggoo, where I often get blindingly drunk. It's open late. It's cheap as fuck. I found it one night when I was stumbling around, drunk off my ass, I bought their specialty, a third of a baguette filled with lettuce and tomato, a huge stack of incredibly fragrant gyro meat, red sauce and white sauce, and topped with French fries. It's a massive, delicious, and incredibly unhealthy meal. I have a Maison D (which is what I call both the sandwich and the restaurant) fairly often, though I rarely remember it. I have also woken up with full and partial Maison D sandwiches in my pockets, in my bed, all over my floor, and in and on any number of random apartments and park benches.

Pigalle. Sex. Sex sex sex sex. I like sex. Actually I love sex. Whether it's sweet and tender, or hard, fast, and dirty, or both or somewhere in between, I'm down with it. I want it every minute of every day. Be nice if it came with love, that crazy crazy love, but it rarely does. So I take it however it comes. There's sex in Pigalle. Sex shops, strip joints, adult shows (folks fucking each other), burlesque shows, hookers, hustlers, swingers, random people walking around looking to fuck. Some want money for it, some have money and are willing to pay for it, some just want it. Boulevard de Clichy is lined with shop after joint after show palace after theater after peep show after

discreet door leading to some magnificent perversion. I wander
Pigalle drunk, sober, half-drunk, during the day, the night, in the
morning, whenever I want to cum, and want to feel some shame
after it happens. I don't hide from my shame. It comes with my life.
Sometimes I yearn for it, look for it, need it, have to fucking have
it. The intense blinding joy of an exploding orgasm, the can't look
in the fucking mirror because I'm a dirtbag piece of shit shame that
follows. So be it. I know where to go to get it. And go I do.

**Le Jardin du Luxembourg, multiple entrances, 6th
arrondissement.** A huge fancy palace, surrounded by mammoth
fancy gardens. The most luxurious wide stretches of grass in the
world. Old marble sculptures of dead Kings and Queens and Princes
and Princesses scattered around. A couple kiddie playgrounds
(which I avoid), some fountains, bunch of benches, some quiet
areas of shade where old dudes read books and drown in their
memories and their regrets. I often go to the park to sleep when I'm
hungover, to read when I'm not, to lie in the grass and drink wine
and daydream about some stupid future filled with madness and
fame and controversy. Lots of couples and families have picnics in le
Jardin. I watch them. Imagine what they are thinking about, if they
are as happy and content as they seem. I respect them. Their choices
are different than mine. But we are all living our dream in some way.

Le Bar Dix, rue de l'Odéon. A shitty old bar in the basement of
a shitty old building. It's small, maybe twenty feet wide and forty
feet long. Walls are stone and the ceiling, also stone, is arched, some
shitty old paintings hanging around. It's dark, the music is loud,
and they only play French music, so I don't know what they're
singing about, though I do know it's not about being a respectable
citizen or paying your taxes. Around the edges of the room are

padded benches, there are table and chairs in front of the benches. Everything is sticky. Not sure with what and don't want to know. But the tables and chairs and benches and walls and glasses and bottles and pitchers are all sticky. The only drink I have ever had in Bar Dix is sangria in a pitcher. It's strong and cheap and tastes good, but also hurts a little. Kind of like French Mad Dog, or French Thunderbird. I sit alone with my journal and write and drink and look at the girls, who are also often alone, usually dressed in black, with sad eyes, also writing in journals and drinking alone. Heaven it is not.

The Grave of Victor Hugo. Panthéon. Motherfucker wrote *The Hunchback of Notre-Dame* and *Les Miserables*, both of which are abysmal musicals but amazing books. Much respect.

Berthillon, rue Saint-Louis en l'Île. In France they call ice cream shops *glaciers*. It's a beautiful word. *Glacier*. There's an elegance to it, like so many French words. *Glacier.* I like ice cream, and I like glaciers. This glacier makes the best ice cream in Europe or so they say. And it's on a small fancy little island tucked behind Notre-Dame de Paris. Ice cream tastes good and feels good going down your throat, nice and cold and sweet. And it reminds me of being a little kid, when life was simple and everything was big and important and incredible, when I had a sense of awe and wonder. So I eat it often, because it feels good, and it makes me think of simpler, happier days. *Glacier.*

Shakespeare and Company, rue de la Bûcherie. There have been two. The first one, the one where Hemingway and Fitzgerald and Gertrude Stein and James Joyce hung out, got shut down by the Nazis in 1941. The Nazis loved killing Jews, but they didn't like cool

bookstores. The second, the one where I go, was opened in 1951 by
an American serviceman named George Whitman who kicked some
bookstore-hating Nazi ass in WW2. It's had Allen Ginsberg, William
Burroughs, Anaïs Nin and James Baldwin and Sartre and Lawrence
Durrell. The store itself is a charming little shitbox. Right on the water
across from Notre-Dame. A little stone square out front. Bright-green
exterior with ramshackle sign. Inside is filled with books, beautiful
books in English that I can read. Shelves overflowing with them,
tables covered with stacks of them, a maze of words with little nooks
and hidden recesses also filled with them. There is very little crap,
no cheesy thrillers or steamy romances. It's just great books, classics,
or newer shit that comes with a serious reputation. It's a literature
store more than a bookstore. Anyone there is interested in reading,
in words, in the history of them, the future. Upstairs there are living
quarters, and most of the people who work there, live there. They take
in wanderers, misfits, let them sleep for a night or two, or a month
or two. There are always pretty girls in the store, or in the little plaza
outside it. I spend more money here than anywhere else in Paris. It's
the best little weird beautiful crazy bookstore in the world.

Stolly's, rue Cloche Percé. Tiny shitbox bar. In the Marais. Tables
and chairs out front. Serves English beer, French beer, all sorts of
liquor. Mix of people, unlike most other joints in Paris, which tend
to be entirely French, or entirely American, or entirely something
else. I almost always sit outside, regardless of the weather, watch
people walk by, read, write, think, and dream. Other customers tend
to be interesting people, writers or artists, academics. A joint where
smart people get drunk.

La Basilique du Sacré-Cœur de Montmartre. A church. At the top
of Montmartre, the highest point in Paris. I'm not usually a big fan

of churches, but this church. I dig it. Stairs up are endless, feels like I'm climbing Everest. I stop at least three times for cigarette breaks. Once up, the view is spectacular. There are sections of grass where you can sit and stare or have a smoke or drink. Directly out front there is a stone plaza with a viewing deck. There are tourists with cameras, young couples meeting, true believers going to worship, sometimes there are Africans selling souvenirs, sometime the police chase them away. I usually go up with a bottle of cheap red wine and a pack of smokes, walk to the edge, look out over the city, the most beautiful, most civilized city on earth. The view is magnificent. It calms me, silences me, tells me stories, takes the thoughts out of my mind, or focuses the ones that are there. I sit and stare and write in my notebooks, sometimes read, drink, smoke. I often see an old man there. He's probably eighty, well-dressed, usually in a black suit and shirt and tie, white hair perfectly combed, face heavily lined. He's always in the same place, at the edge of the plaza, just off the center, staring out over the city. He looks sad, alone, sighs deeply, sometimes looks down and stares at the stones. I wonder what's in his mind, his heart, his memories. Wonder what he lost and when and how much it took from him, how much damage it did to his soul. I wonder what kind of pain he feels, what kind of joy he once felt, whether his life was what he wanted it to be, whether it was worth it. Who he loved and whose hearts he broke, and who and what broke his heart. I wonder if he could go back, would he change it, wonder what mistakes he made and whether they matter anymore. I never talk to him, or acknowledge him, or disturb him. He's nearing the end. I hope he goes peacefully. I hope when my time comes, I do as well.

Le Refuge des Fondus, rue des Trois Frères. Fondue is cool. You get a vat of boiling cheese and dip stuff in it. Or a vat of boiling oil and a plate of raw steak and you cook it as you please. All this place serves is fondue. Simple and delightful and delicious. Fondue and wine, which comes in baby bottles, so you feel kind of stupid and kind of wonderful when you drink it. It's a tiny place. Music is loud. Customers are rowdy. I went once, alone. I ate both kinds of fondue and got drunk as fuck. Thought about my ex-girlfriend, who is somewhere in America. We went to school together. I always thought love at first sight was some silly bullshit until I saw her. And I fell in love. Deep and hard and immediately. I didn't talk to her for a year. Just stared at her when I saw her. And looked away when she glanced at me. It hurt me to look at her. Made my heart beat faster, made it feel like it was going to explode. Made my hands shake. If she had tried to talk to me I wouldn't have been able to talk. She didn't seem real. And I didn't feel real when I saw her. When we met, amongst a group of people at a bar, I ignored her. Not because I was trying to pull some bullshit, but because I was scared of her. We saw each other again, and again, and eventually I could talk to her, tell her silly stories, make her laugh, make her blush, and she fell in love with me, and life wasn't real for a while. But it always returns. The cold brutal reality of existence. And so I ate fondue alone. And thought of her. And watched the other couples on dates in Le Refuge. And hoped they didn't end up like we ended up. That the smiles stayed on their faces. And I got fucking drunk. And I left and bought three more bottles of wine at the first shop I found. And I woke up on a sidewalk late the next morning.

The Gates of Hell, Musée Rodin, rue de Varenne. Rodin was the greatest sculptor in the world. The only one in history on the level with Michelangelo. The museum is his old house, where he worked, where he drank and raged and fucked, and where he made the most beautiful things on earth. It's a huge French mansion, with huge grounds, and giant gardens. The house is filled with drawings and sculpture, as are the grounds: *The Kiss*, *Balzac*, *The Thinker*, *The Three Shades*, *The Burghers of Calais*, *The Secret*, and the most magnificent of them all, *The Gates of Hell*. The apartment where Louis and I live is about ten minutes away. I come here most days. At some point I'm drawn and I come. Walk through the front garden to a path that leads to *The Gates*. As you move along green hedges, *The Gates* looms in front of you, twenty feet tall, fifteen wide, 180 figures swirling around and on two massive doors, doors that lead to a hellfire of eternal damnation. It's made of bronze, weathered from being outdoors for eighty years, set on a stepped pedestal against a giant stone wall. Conceptually based on the beginning of Dante's *Inferno*, it's Rodin's vision of beauty and love and terror and eternity, men and women screaming, reaching, kissing, begging, crying, dying, being tortured, tortured by love and pain, regret and sorrow, the prospect of burning in Hell forever. Every time I see it, it moves me, scares me, thrills me, humbles me, makes me feel small, inspires me. I can't imagine the mind that envisioned it, the hand that made it, the mad horrible wonderful state Rodin was in while he did it, the labor involved, the intensity of focus, the virtuosity with which each figure and each element of it was made. There are two simple wooden benches in front of *The Gates*. Each large enough for two people, three if you don't mind being crowded. They are usually both empty. People stare at *The Gates*, but not for long. They are disturbing, unsettling, menacing, and there are many other sculptures at Musée Rodin that are more user-friendly, more pleasing to both the eye and the soul. I love *The Gates*. For whatever reason, they calm me, settle me, hold me. I always sit on one of the benches. I read, write in my notebook, stare at the sky, take naps, talk to myself, talk to God, even though I don't believe in God. *The Gates of Hell*, though, I believe in them. On the rare occasions someone sits next to me, or on whichever bench I am not on, I don't acknowledge them or speak to them. I keep reading or writing or doing whatever I'm doing. This is my spot. *The Gates of Hell*. One of the few places in my life where I have ever found any peace. I don't know what that means, that *The Gates of Hell* bring me peace, and I don't care. I'll take what I can, wherever it may come.

La Closerie des Lilas, boulevard du Montparnasse. Fancy restaurant. Or it's fancy to me. On a corner. Covered with vines so you can't see inside. It is said Hemingway wrote most of *The Sun Also Rises* on a stool at the bar. Picasso, F. Scott Fitzgerald, Modigliani, Breton, Sartre, André Gide, Oscar Wilde, Samuel Beckett, Man Ray, Ezra Pound, and Henry Miller, my beloved Henry Miller, all hung out here. The entrance has a green vined arch, a menu under glass next to it. I've never been inside. Never walked under the arch, sat at the bar, had a drink. I don't deserve to step inside. Maybe someday, but not now. For now I will stand outside and imagine a future where I can sit among the echoes of my heroes, where I will have earned my rightful place. For now I will read the menu and peer through the arch and dream.

The Mona Lisa, **Musée du Louvre.** It actually kind of sucks. There are a hundred more interesting paintings in the same hall. But I went and took the picture and stood there with all the other fools and pretended to think it was amazing. And I believe the conspiracy that the painting on the wall isn't even the real one. Just a good copy, that the real one is in a vault somewhere covered with a tarp, away from lights, away from flashbulbs, away from all the idiots, myself included, gawking at it, away from the world, protected. But the

Louvre itself is amazing. The most magnificent building in existence.
The idea that it was someone's house is absurd to me. Like telling me
the Empire State Building or the Sears Tower was someone's house.
Kind of makes you understand the Revolution. If I had to eat rats
and mud every day and I saw someone living in a building as vast
and beautiful as the Louvre, I'd want their fucking head as well.

The Grave of Charles Baudelaire. Montparnasse Cemetery.
Alcoholic, opium addict, whoremonger, maniac. Wrote *Les Fleurs
du mal*. Wrote *Paris Spleen*, which crushes me every time I read it.
Wrote *The Painter of Modern Life*. The utmost respect.

Los Angeles, 2017

Lunch with my agent. We're at the restaurant next to the pool at the Beverly Hills Hotel. The sun is out, sky is blue. The walls and awnings are pink and the tables and umbrellas are white. Everyone is beautiful and rich and they're all having a wonderful time, picking at tuna tartare, drinking lemonade (also pink), taking selfies, doing incredibly important things and taking them very seriously. My agent is thirty-five years old, wears a $5,000 suit and a $50,000 Rolex. He works for a big, fancy agency, and he represents me and my company, which publishes commercial fiction and creates intellectual property for large media companies. He's smart and cool and works hard and has the patience of a saint. I'm in a pair of light-blue pajama bottoms and a white T-shirt. We meet here once a month, talk about my *business*. I like him, and appreciate how hard he works and how much he cares, but the idea that I'm a *business* makes me sick to my fucking stomach.

How'd the Spielberg job go?

I think well. Ask the producers.

Next steps?

Ask them.

The studio read it?

Yes.

Like it?

They said they did.

Network read it?

They have it now. Waiting.

I'll follow up, set a call.

Can't wait.

He laughs, takes a sip of lemonade.

What's next?

What's out there?

What do you want to do?

Nothing.

I don't believe that.

It's true.

Company have any new IP?

We have two books coming out this month. Doing a video game. Working on a bunch of new series treatments.

You going to the office?

A couple times a week.

You should be there every day.

They don't need me.

Yes, they do.

They really don't.

The books any good?

Usual.

You write any of them?

You know how it works.

I know sometimes you write parts of them, or rewrite them.

In the beginning. Now I just come up with the ideas, the editors find the writers, I don't even read them.

You should.

I know.

There's business to be done with them.

If they sell.

Even if they don't. Plenty of massive franchises didn't sell at first. You never know when something will hit.

I'm tired of talking about franchises.

That's our business now.

I miss the old days.

When everyone was an *artist*?

When everything didn't have to make a billion dollars or it's a failure.

The world has changed. You changed with it.

I didn't become a writer to talk about franchises and business.

I didn't become an agent to listen to rich writers complain.

I laugh.

Touché, David.

He smiles.

Go write one of your books.

Is that really what you want me to do?

No. I want you to talk to me about the offers we have for you, and after you decide which to take, go create a huge fucking franchise.

I don't think I could write a book now anyway. Not a real one.

Why?

I wish I knew.

You know.

You my fucking therapist now?

It's definitely part of my job description.

I laugh.

Maybe I've lost confidence. Maybe I lack motivation. Maybe I'm just tired. I know I don't feel shit the way I used to feel it, don't really feel anything anymore. And I need to feel to write.

You scaled that mountain, Jay. You were the most famous writer in the world. The Bad Boy of American Letters. You did it and grew up and moved on to other things. You became an adult. What I think you actually miss is being young.

No, I was terrible at being young.

He laughs.

You sure?

I nod.

I miss the struggle. I miss not knowing. I miss the being alone and lonely and desperately wanting something and being willing to hurt for it. I miss the climb up the mountain. Getting there wasn't the point. And I didn't give a fuck once I got there. It was going up that meant something.

So go write a book, go struggle, go be an *artist*. Or we can go over the offers I have and you can make yourself some money. It's your call.

I take a deep breath, look across the restaurant, past the pool and all the beautiful people in it, at the sun, at the sky so perfect and blue. Sisyphus spent eternity pushing a boulder up a hill. If the legend is true, he's still pushing it. A good part of my life I did the same. Push the fucking rock, every day, day after day, push the fucking rock. Unlike King Sisyphus, I got my boulder over the hill and I rode it down, rode it until it crashed, rode it through the wreckage of the crash until it stopped, once it stopped I got off. I had a choice, walk away or do it again. I made the wrong choice. I walked away. I should have found a new boulder, a bigger boulder, the biggest boulder I could fucking find, and I should have started back up the fucking hill.

History

I was born in Cleveland. My father was a lawyer, my mother stayed
at home to raise my brother and me. We weren't rich, but we weren't
poor. We lived in a nice house on a nice street in a nice town. The
first suburb on the border of East Cleveland. The town was half
black, half white, half of the white kids were Jewish. We were all
friends, played together, went to school together, fought together,
and fought against each other. I didn't learn until I was older that
we were all supposed to hate each other. That in America you stick
with your own. When I did learn it, like many of the things I have
learned in my life, I thought it was stupid. Blood is blood and it's all
red. Show me what's in your heart and your eyes. I don't give a fuck
about the color of your skin or the God you worship.

My parents were good people. They both worked hard. My dad
worked for a company that made steering gears and auto parts, my
mom cooked and cleaned and played tennis and bridge. They loved
each other and us. Tried to instill morals and values in me. Tried to
make me go to church and become a productive member of society.
My brother was a good kid. Four years older than me. He did well
in school, listened to our parents, never got in trouble. He was a
great brother. Never beat me up or bullied me. Always included me
in things he did with his friends. Helped me when I needed help,
stayed out of my way when I didn't. I was not a good kid. I went
to school but didn't pay attention. I didn't care about grades. I got
into fights, with both my fists and my mouth. I talked back and
said no. Starting at a relatively young age, my favorite activity was
vandalism. There is joy in destruction, great joy. Be it with a spray-
paint can or a bat on a mailbox or an overturned garbage can or
ten of them. Other joys were girls, cigarettes, stolen liquor, drugs,
reading books, and sports. I was a good athlete. Good enough that

kicking a ball into a goal got me into college, despite my 2.2 high
school grade point average. My college career was unremarkable.
I viewed it as a long vacation. As long as I showed up at class I
would pass. I didn't want to be a lawyer or a doctor or a teacher or a
businessman. I didn't want to market anything. Or make anything.
Or sell anything. Or buy anything. I didn't want to wear a suit or
get quarterly review reports. I played ball and read books and chased
girls and got drunk and snorted cocaine. In the summers I mowed
lawns and pulled weeds and went to the beach. Three years in I
broke my leg, and my sports career ended. It was a relief. No more
practice, no more pretending I cared about it. I went to class, read
books, though rarely the ones assigned. I spent my free time with
Kerouac and Bukowski and Hunter Thompson. With Knut Hamsun
and John Dos Passos and William Saroyan. Ken Kesey and Allen
Ginsberg and Tom Wolfe. Tim O'Brien and John Kennedy Toole
and William Burroughs. I kept drinking, kept doing blow, started
doing enough of it that I started selling it to support my habit. I'd
buy half an ounce, which is 14 grams, for $1,000. Sell 10 grams
for $100 each and have 4 for myself. Sometimes I'd cut the drug
with NoDoz and 14 grams would become 18 and I'd keep the extra
$400, buy drinks for my friends, books, flowers for girls I liked, I'd
take a car full of people to Taco Bell and order one of everything on
the menu. I kept reading. James Joyce and Oscar Wilde and Henry
James. I read *The Awakening* by Kate Chopin and it made me cry.
I read *Don Quixote* and howled with laughter. I read Hugo and
Dumas, Tolstoy and Dostoyevsky and Gogol. My senior year started.
I didn't think about what I was going to do when it ended. My
father wanted me to go to law school or get a job on Wall Street. He
suggested a job in advertising because I was *creative*. My brother had
gone to law school and become a lawyer and gotten married and was
well on his way to becoming a productive and respectable citizen.

I was happy for him. And I knew the same was expected of me. It
made me want to drive into a tree. Or snort cocaine until my heart
exploded. Or walk into the water and keep going.

I read and drank and used cocaine and dealt cocaine and ate tacos
and bought flowers for girls and occasionally fell in love with one
for an hour or two or a night or two, occasionally had one fall in
love with me for an hour or two or a night or two. I met *her* and fell
in love for real, or what I thought was real, and life was simple and
beautiful and all-consuming. I stopped dealing and slowed down my
drinking and the books I read took on new meaning, as I felt like
I was living in one, some great romance, some love story deep and
true. I loved everything about her. Her voice, her eyes, the words
she choose when she spoke, her handwriting, how she laughed and
smiled, how she smoked, the books she read (as many women as I
read men), and the conversations we had about them, the clothes
she wore, how she was when she wasn't wearing them. She was as
respectable and decent as I was not. Her father was an executive
at a defense company, she had grown up in San Francisco, had
gone to private schools. She was going to go back and work in tech
and wanted to start her own company. I imagined going with her,
imagined, for the first time, that I could be normal, get a job, wear
a suit, go to the office every day, pay taxes. Be a husband. Be a man,
or be our society's definition of a man. Love is a crazy thing. Can
give you life or take it. Make you something you aren't, for better or
worse. Make you dream and think and speak and act in ways that
aren't normal for you, or at least for me. We had two great months.
Falling asleep and waking up together, quiet dinners and long talks
about the future. Eyes, hands, lips, and tongues. Bodies. Hearts. I
thought they were great, but maybe I was just delusional. We kissed
good-bye and each went home for Christmas break. We spoke on
the phone every day. We sent each other presents, a pair of earrings

for her, a first edition of *Executioner's Song* for me. We planned our
spring break, a couples trip to the Bahamas with a few of her friends
and their boyfriends. I stayed in and stayed mostly sober, which
shocked my parents. They had never met her, but loved the effect
she had on me. I went to church with them on Christmas morning,
and though I didn't pray or sing any songs or take communion, I
went. I put on a sport coat and went to their country club. I smiled
and greeted their friends when they came over. I went to bed early,
woke up early. I talked about a career, and maybe going to business
school, my dad said he had a friend on the board of UC-Berkeley
and could help me get in. It was a long month. I just wanted to get
back. To see her again. Kiss her, taste her. Feel her breath against
my neck in the morning. Hear her say my name in the dark. Watch
her get dressed. Listen to her thoughts on whatever she was reading,
or watching. Smile when she teased me about the shitty food I ate,
or about smoking too many cigarettes. I left a day early. Drove my
truck through a snowstorm. A five-hour trip took eight, but at least I
was closer. And I would be there when she arrived. I got to the house
I lived in, went inside, I was the only one back. I went to my room
and there was a book on my bed, a note on top of the book from my
roommate Andy, who was from Los Angeles, it said
Merry Christmas.
I meant to give you this before you left.
I think you'll enjoy it.
It was a battered old hardback, a sky-blue dustjacket, bold black
lettering across the front, it read:

<u>Henry Miller</u>

Tropic

of

Cancer

I set down my bag, kicked off my shoes, lay down on my bed,
picked up the book, opened it.

And from the first sentence.

I am living at the Villa Borghese.

First paragraph.

*There is not a crumb of dirt anywhere, nor a chair misplaced. We are all
alone here and we are dead.*

First page.

*Last night Boris discovered that he was lousy. I had to shave his armpits
and even then the itching did not stop. How can one get lousy in a
beautiful place like this? But no matter. We might never have known
each other so intimately, Boris and I, had it not been for the lice.*

I was transfixed.

*Boris has just given me a summary of his views.... There will be more
calamities, more death, more despair. Not the slightest indication of a
change anywhere. The cancer of time is eating us away. Our heroes have
killed themselves, or are killing themselves. The hero, then, is not Time,
but Timelessness. We must get in step, a lock step, toward the prison of
death. There is no escape. The weather will not change.*

I couldn't believe what I was reading. What Henry Miller said, how
he said it.

*It is now the fall of my second year in Paris. I was sent here for a reason
I have not yet been able to fathom.*

*I have no money, no resources, no hopes. I am the happiest man alive.
A year ago, six months ago, I thought that I was an artist. I no longer
think about it, I am. Everything that was literature has fallen from me.
There are no more books to be written, thank God.*

It felt like a lightbulb was turned on, a lightbulb in my mind, a
lightbulb in my heart, a lightbulb in my soul.

*This then? This is not a book. This is libel, slander, defamation of
character. This is not a book, in the ordinary sense of the word. No, this*

*is a prolonged insult, a gob of spit in the face of Art, a kick in the pants
to God, Man, Destiny, Time, Love, Beauty...what you will.*

I smiled, read the page again, again, again. It made me laugh,
shocked me, spoke to me. Simple and direct. No pretension. No
bullshit. Where most writers tried to impress with their brains, with
their skill, with their virtuosity, Henry Miller did not. It felt like he
was talking, talking to me, sitting inside me telling me things I had
always wanted to hear but never had. All the books I had read in my
life, I had never imagined I could write one. The writers were always
smarter than me, more gifted, went to better schools, had traveled
more, experienced more, seen and felt and done more. They had
some magic that I did not have. They did things with words that I
never believed I could do. They sat and worked day after day after
day after day telling stories that I didn't think I could tell. They were
something I was not. They were writers. Mysterious and talented
and educated and beyond me. I was a fuck-up. A punk and a vandal
who got shitty grades and liked to get drunk and snort cocaine. I
never believed I could be one of them.

Until.

Until.

Until.

I kept reading. A book about fucking walking eating reading writing
wanting, about the beauty of rage, the serenity of loneliness, the
power of not giving a fuck, and the nobility in deeply caring. I kept
reading a book about love, love of everything and nothing, love
of women, of art, literature, friends, a hot meal a strong drink a
cigarette on a sunny day, an empty park bench, a full bar, a couple
bucks in your pocket or nothing at all. I kept reading this book
about a man who freed himself from the bullshit of society and did
and said and lived and loved and wrote as he felt and as he pleased
and as was right for him and him alone, without regard to rules,

laws, conventions, or expectations. If it felt right he did it. If it felt wrong he walked away, never looked back, didn't apologize for who he was or how he lived, didn't regret anything. I kept reading throughout that day, I smoked and drank a bottle of cheap wine and the world disappeared, there was my bed my pillow my hands turning pages my eyes on the words my mind spinning my heart beating my soul lit.

My soul was lit.

Lit.

I fell asleep reading. Woke up with the book in my hand. Made some coffee lit a cigarette kept reading. My mind was filled with Paris, with women, with loneliness, with heartbreak and hunger and joy and rage, with a life unhinged, away from everything we are supposed to be and part of everything we want. Henry said:

I made up my mind that I would hold onto nothing, that I would expect nothing.

Henry said:

I've lived out my melancholy youth. I don't give a fuck anymore what's behind me, or what's ahead of me.

Henry said:

Do anything, but let it produce joy. Do anything, but let it yield ecstasy.

Henry said:

For a hundred years or more the world, our world, has been dying. And not one man, in these last hundred years or so, has been crazy enough to put a bomb up the asshole of creation and set it off.

Henry said:

And God knows, when spring comes to Paris the humblest mortal alive must feel that he dwells in paradise.

When the phone rang I ignored it. When I had to piss I read as I walked to the bathroom and I read as I pissed. When I heard people outside I ignored them. When someone knocked on the

door I didn't respond. I read and smoked and drank and laughed
and burned and dreamed and knew. When I read the last word on
the last page I knew. I finished my second bottle of wine. Took a
shower. Came back to my room. Got dressed and went for a walk
and took deep breaths of freezing air and smiled in the darkness
and whispered to the stars and I knew. When I started shaking from
the cold and my legs were aching I walked toward the building
where she lived, I went to see her. She was with friends. Sharing
stories about their breaks. They met a guy, they went to Hawaii,
they finished their graduate school applications, they got drunk
and hooked up with an ex, they got in a fight with a brother sister
mother father. She smiled when she saw me stood up and put her
arms around me, I smelled her hair kissed her neck her lips took her
hands in mine and whispered I missed you, I missed you. She asked
where I had been she thought I was coming earlier, I said I went for
a walk and stared at the sky and the stars, she laughed and asked me
if I was high.

I smiled.

In a way.

Coke?

Nope.

You don't like weed.

No, generally I do not.

Santa bring you something weird?

I nodded.

He did.

What?

A book.

She laughed.

Porn?

Some people think it is.

Really?

Yeah, though it's not.

I told her about *Tropic*, how I got it, read it, how it affected me, about Paris, about my plan. She was surprised, confused.

You're moving to Paris?

Yeah.

To be a writer.

Yeah.

But you don't write.

I will.

You think it's that simple.

Yes.

Why not go to writing school?

Who went to writing school?

Everyone who wants to be a writer goes to writing school.

Maybe now. But not a single writer I love went.

I bet some of them did.

You can't teach what they do.

So how'd they learn?

They just sat in a room alone and wrote and learned.

Do that in San Francisco.

Paris.

San Francisco.

Come with me to Paris.

You finished this book when?

Couple hours ago.

You'll probably move on by next week.

I won't.

I'm not going to change my life to go to Paris so you can be a writer.

If you had a dream, I'd go with you.

My dream is San Francisco.

It's different.

Why?

There are a million people who go to business school.

There are even more who are aspiring writers.

It's not going to be that way.

What way is it going to be?

I'm going to be better than everyone else who's trying.

Better than people who go to Harvard or Princeton or Stanford?

Yes.

I'm not going to Paris, Jay.

I'm not going to San Francisco.

I was looking forward to seeing you.

So was I.

I thought we'd smile, kiss, hold hands and walk to the bar, have a few drinks, come back here.

We still can.

My friends all thought I was crazy for being with you. They warned me, he's a drunk and a fuck-up and he'll fuck you over somehow. I never thought it would be over a book, but I guess it is.

I'm not fucking you over.

I fell in love with you, we made plans, we talked about a future.

We can still have one.

On a writer's salary? We going to buy a house, have kids?

You say you want a career? You'll make money.

I don't want to marry an aspiring writer who spends his life scribbling away in some room while I pay his bills.

Wow.

I'm sorry.

You're not, though. That's what you think. Cool. You made a mistake, I'm an asshole, I'll never be shit.

She didn't speak, just stared at the floor. I stood.

I'm gonna go.

She looked up.

I'm sorry.

Yeah.

I am.

Me too.

I smiled, a sad smile, we both knew we were done, whatever we were was gone, this was it. I leaned over, kissed her, let it linger.

I turned and left, didn't give her a chance to say anything, don't know if she would have anyway. I walked out of her house I could hear her roommates getting ready to go out I went back into the night. It was cold dark I could see my breath feel my heart beating feel my heart breaking. Because as much as I loved her, and I loved her more than anyone or anything in my life, and as much as I wanted her, and as much as I might have been able to imagine a future with her, it wasn't going to happen. Whatever dreams there were had just vanished. I was going to Paris alone. To find my way or destroy myself. To become a writer or fail as spectacularly as possible. To feast to starve to wander to die to become, to scream at the sky and sleep in the gutter and dance on the graves of my heroes. And maybe she'd be right, and I would end up a piece-of-shit failure, but maybe she was wrong, and I'd actually do something. Whatever it was, I knew what would happen with her. She'd finish school and go home and go to business school and get a great job and meet a great guy and go on great dates and great trips and she'd take him home to meet her parents and they'd think he was a great guy and he'd buy her a beautiful sparkling ring and get on one wonderfully healthy and successful knee and she'd act surprised and say yes and cry and they'd get married in a great Napa wedding and live in a great apartment in the city until she got pregnant, at which point they'd move to Marin and they'd join a club and have a couple

great kids and the kids would go to great private schools and they'd
vacation in Hawaii and Aspen and they'd be some kind of happy and
some kind of completely fucking miserable and it would all be great.
And I'd go to Paris and roll the fucking dice.
I went to my room and looked at the book again, blue cover sitting
on my bed. I opened it read the first page and laughed when I
finished and I knew knew knew. I fucking knew as much as I had
ever known anything. Paris. Alone. As soon as I could.
As soon as I fucking could.

Los Angeles, 2017

I'm lying in bed, Jay, thinking about you.

Wonderful.

We used to spend so much time in bed.

Yeah?

Yes.

Was it fun?

Most of the time.

Most of the time?

Sometimes you were so drunk your cock wouldn't work. That wasn't much fun. Or your breath smelled like vomit. That really wasn't fun. Or you had been sleeping in the streets and smelled like a garbage can. Not fun either.

So that gives me a timeline.

It does.

You knew me when...

Yes.

I apologize.

No need.

There probably is.

I owe you one as much as you owe me.

For what?

So many things.

Such as?

Another time. We can talk about this another time.

Okay.

Where are you now?

In my office.

What's your office like?

It's a little barn behind my big house.

What's on the walls?

Nothing.

They're bare?

Painted white. But otherwise, yes.

You used to cover them with pictures and sayings and write on them and draw on them. I remember you wrote *You Are a Chump Loser Motherfucker* on the wall. It made me laugh.

Yeah, that phrase traveled with me. Made me want to be better than I am.

And why no more?

Don't know.

Yes, you do.

Don't care anymore.

Yes, you do.

I am what I am.

There's a desk?

Yeah, it's an office. There's a desk.

Couch?

Yeah, big one. Comfortable one.

Still listen to punk and metal?

And love songs from the '80s.

LOL!

I'm not gonna lol you back.

What would you do if I knocked on your door right now?

Call 911.

Seriously?

I still don't know who this is, or if I actually know you.

Why do you chat with me?

It's something to do.

I saw you a couple years ago.

Where?

You didn't see me.

Would I have recognized you?

Yes.

Where were we?

I came to one of your readings. It was crowded, and I sat in the back.

Where?

It was in a theater.

They're all in theaters now. What theater?

If I told you, you would know who I am.

So tell me.

No.

Guess that's your choice.

I'm surprised you don't know.

I have a timeline now.

I wonder sometimes what it would have been like.

What?

Everything.

If you knew me then, probably not very good.

Maybe, maybe not.

You would have changed me?

Inspired you.

No, you wouldn't have.

You never know.

And that is why you wonder.

Yes.

Yes.

Yes.

Yes.

I wonder.

Time for me to go, old mysterious friend.

Why?

I got shit to do.

What?

Stare at an empty screen and hate myself.

Sounds fun.

It's what I do.

Good luck.

Enjoy your bed, your thoughts, your wonder.

Let me know when you start wondering.

Yes.

History

I needed money for.

A plane ticket.

Food.

Rent.

Booze and drugs.

Books.

In no particular order.

I didn't know how much, but I knew it was more than I had, which
was two thousand dollars. I thought fifteen or twenty would last
a year or two. I didn't plan on living in the Ritz or de Crillon, or
eating at Le Voltaire or Chez Georges. I didn't plan on traveling.
Find a cheap place live simply. Twenty-five would last longer.
It was winter in a college town. I could get a job but it would take
too long. Dealing was the only way. Buy the white, sell the white. It
was cold and people stayed inside and got drunk and did drugs. Buy
the white, sell the white. It was the only way.
I took my two grand to my dealer and bought 40 grams. I cut in 10
grams of NoDoz and sold all 50 grams for five grand. Bought three
ounces, which is 84 grams, and cut in 20 of NoDoz, and sold it for
ten grand. There wasn't enough demand at the school I attended, so
I went to three others that were nearby. I took the ten and bought
six ounces, which is 168 grams, and cut in 40 grams of NoDoz and
sold it all for just over twenty grand. It took three months. I kept the
money in a safebox. A huge pile of dirty green bills.
When I wasn't dealing, I was reading. The French. Hugo and
Dumas, Baudelaire and Rimbaud. When I wasn't reading I was
getting drunk. School didn't matter anymore. What the fuck would
I ever do with a degree. Stick it on my wall? Bring it with me when
I went to apply for shitty jobs? Wipe my fucking ass with it? Deal

read drink sleep. It was simple and focused. I needed money. I
needed release. I needed to feed my brain. Deal read drink sleep. She
found a new boyfriend, went on her couples spring break, I heard
they were perfect for each other, he was from New York and wanted
to be an investment banker. Whenever I saw her I turned and
walked away. If we were in the same room or same bar I wouldn't
acknowledge her. She tried to say hello a couple times and I ignored
her. I wasn't trying to be a dick, or play some game, I just couldn't
see her or speak to her because it hurt me. Despite the decision I
had made, I loved her. And it hurt me more that she moved on so
quickly, seemingly so easily. I wanted to hate her, but I didn't, and
I couldn't hate her, I loved her and it hurt me to think about her,
remember, imagine her with someone else, seeing her or hearing her
voice made me want to curl up in a ball and cry. I loved her and it
hurt me.

The end of the school year was coming. Everyone was making plans.
Move to NY get a job, move to Los Angeles get a job, go to law
school, medical school, business school, move to Chicago get a job.
The closer it got the more I felt it. I wanted out. To get the fuck out.
Three weeks left. More or less had enough money to go. I went to a
bar with some friends. The bar was crowded, loud, dense with smoke.
I didn't want to be there. I didn't have anything to say to anyone.
Though I had spent the last four years with many of the people in the
bar, their world wasn't mine anymore. They were going on to bright
futures and careers and degrees and accomplishments, money and
mortgages and responsibilities and retirement plans. I was going to
Paris, to walk and read and drink and smoke and write and dream and
starve and rage and scream and smile and laugh and fuck and hurt and
get lost and sit by the Seine and watch the world go by.

I saw her. She was with her friends, boyfriend nowhere to be seen.
I hadn't been with anyone since her, felt in some way that if I was

good she might come back, even though I knew she wouldn't. I saw her with her friends and I wanted her, more than I ever had wanted her, more than I had ever wanted anything. Wanted to kiss her, press myself against her, taste her, hear her moan as I moved inside her. Our sex life had always been sweet, simple. Lots of candles and soft music and clean sheets and quiet tender moments. It was loving and respectful and boring. In that bar I wanted to take her, ravage her, devour her. I wanted to fuck her. Long and deep and hard and wet. For the pure physical pleasure of it. For the blinding moment when I'd cum. I sat and watched her talk to one of her friends, laugh, move a lock of hair from her eye, take a sip from her glass, I watched her lips, her tongue.

I wanted.

Wanted.

Wanted.

I stood and walked over, she saw me coming, and she looked surprised, but smiled. Before she could say anything, I leaned to her ear and whispered.

I want to fuck you right now.

She laughed.

I do. Right now.

She looked at me, slightly confused, embarrassed. I kept going.

If I could, I'd wipe the bottles and glasses off that table and take you on it.

She kept looking at me, still smiling, still surprised.

Are you high?

I am.

Blow?

Yep.

Go away.

Let's go outside.

Why?

Because I want to fuck you.

I stepped toward her, kissed her, slowly and deeply, and after a
brief moment, she kissed back. When I pulled away she smiled,
and I took her hand and without a word we walked out of the bar
together. She asked me where we were going and I didn't respond.
We walked around the back of the building to the parking lot. It
was dark, quiet, the lot was full, four rows of cars every spot taken.
I saw her car a black European SUV in the back corner of the lot I
walked toward it, holding her hand. As we neared it she reached into
her pocket for her keys, I shook my head and took her other hand.
We went around the back of the SUV and I started kissing her.
She kissed me back, I pressed her against the back hatch, my hands
wandering. She pulled away.

What if someone sees us?

My hands kept wandering.

They won't.

The inside of her thighs.

What if they do.

Up her shirt.

Who cares.

The small of her back.

I do.

Her ass.

I leaned forward, kissed her, lips and tongues and breath. She was
wearing a button-down shirt, a short skirt, my hands went into
them, beneath them, pulled them open, lifted them. I kissed her
neck started softly biting her nipples through her shirt my hands
pulled her thong off one of her legs. I guided her hand to my cock,
she opened my pants took it out, I put both hands on her ass and
lifted her against the car and moved forward inside of her.

Deep.

Hard.

Wet.

We both moaned. I started moving slowly inside her kissing her tasting her pressing her deep hard wet inside of her faster harder deeper dripping moaning lips tongue nipples hard faster harder deeper her hands on my chest my neck one of my hands on her ass the other on her tit faster harder deeper.

Dripping.

Moaning.

It was dark and quiet and we were in a parking lot fucking against a car I opened my eyes she was looking at me I looked at her our lips and tongues brushed she started to shake I smiled looked into her eyes faster harder deeper and as she shook, I came inside her, my brain exploded into a blinding white wave of

Joy

Pleasure

Peace

And God

It moved through me

Inside her

Deep hard and wet

Throbbing

Shaking

She moaned and I moaned and we came, we came, we came.

We came.

Joy

Pleasure

Peace

And God

We stood there for a moment. I was still hard inside her. My arms were around her, her arms around me. I kissed her neck. I whispered I love you. She whispered back I love you, we stood for a moment together, she set her head on my shoulder stood and breathed, we stood and breathed on each other's necks, both still feeling, still feeling, still feeling, hard and wet and deep. She moved me from her and closed her shirt. When she was done, I smiled and I kissed her one more time and I turned and walked away.

I walked away walked back to the house where I lived I went to my room and I packed a bag. I went to my friend Andy's room the friend who gave me the book and I left a note on his bed that said come visit sometime. I got in my truck parked outside a bank I slept in the truck. As soon as the bank opened I went inside the bank and did what I needed to do I left after twenty minutes. I sold my truck at a used-car lot and went to the airport. I had a passport, some clothes, $18,000 in traveler's cheques and $1,200 in cash.

I got on a plane to Paris.

Chicago, 2017

I'm sitting in a crowded room. Chairs in rows, all of them full. I
know a few people in the room, but not many. Some are speaking in
hushed tones, others are crying, many, like me, are staring silently at
a box on a short pedestal in the front of the room. A friend of mine
is dead in the box. He's wearing a suit and his hair, which was long
and blond and unruly in life, has been cut and styled and brushed
away from his face in death. Someone, an undertaker of some kind,
has put makeup on his face and his eyes are closed and his hands are
folded at his waist, the silver watch he always wore still gleaming on
his wrist. In my mind I can hear him laughing, imagine him looking
on at this scene and saying what the fuck is this. He died three days
ago. Heart failure. He was forty-two years old.

We met as kids at summer camp, my friend and I. It was a
traditional boys' summer camp in the middle of the woods in
Wisconsin, somewhere parents sent their unruly children for some
wholesome outdoor midwestern fun. I was a couple years older than
him. The resident camp smartass. When he arrived he became my
junior smartass associate. We'd pull pranks on counselors and other
campers, make fun of people, say smartass shit. A couple cocky little
punk fuckers who didn't know any better. After our first summer
together, he cried when we got on our buses home, said he'd miss
me, that I was the only older kid he'd ever met who was a jerk like
him and who didn't want to beat him up. I punched him on the
arm and told him I would if he acted up and we laughed and went
home. We had two more summers of fun and secret handshakes
and filling people's shoes with shaving cream and hiding all their
underwear and swearing under our breath at our elders, at which
point I thought I was too cool for summer camp and spent my
summers sneaking cigarettes and stealing booze and smiling at girls

from the seat of my BMX bike. I never thought of my friend again. Or if I did, it was a quick wondering of what ever happened to him. Smartass little fucker. With his blond hair in his face. Always fucking laughing and ready for trouble.

I found out what happened to him when I was thirty. I was living in New York, in SoHo, in the years before bankers and hedge fund managers overran it, before it became America's most expensive mall. I had sold a couple film scripts, one of which got turned into a miserable romantic comedy starring a nerdy sitcom star, and I had some money in my pocket. I had been sober for a few years. I was single, living alone, spent most of my time reading and writing and walking, I was just starting to write, after many failed attempts and hundreds of pages of unreadable crap, the first book I would publish. I was focused, ambitious as fuck, still believed I could burn the world down with words, fell asleep thinking about it, woke up thinking about it, spent my days trying to make it a reality. It was a simple existence. Nobody knew who I was and nobody gave a fuck, which was cool with me. I had work to do. And I believed in it. And it mattered to me. I had faith in what I was doing and in myself and in my life. After almost ten years of trying, I still believed. Though I spent most of my time, aside from when I was walking, alone in my apartment, I ate dinner every night at the same place, a diner on Prince Street that's gone now, replaced by a boutique that sells fancy handbags and shoes and sunglasses designed by a reality TV star. Sometimes my neighbors, all artists or writers or weirdos who lived on the same floor of the building I lived in, would join me, but most nights I ate alone with a book. Sit read eat think. Drink diet soda finish with an ice cream sundae and a cup of coffee. I was sitting, reading, a cheeseburger in front of me when I heard his voice, the smartass singsong still in it, he said

JayBoy you motherfucker, there you are. I knew I'd bump into you again someday, fuck yeah, I knew it!

I laughed, looked up, and there he was, all grown up, wearing yellow pants and a bright blue sport coat with ducks all over it and a pink ascot, a pink fucking ascot, I laughed. He was tan as fuck, hair still blond, still long, still in his face, though now it was elegant instead of goofy. I stood and hugged him and he sat and joined me for dinner. He was a success, kind of a big one. And as bad as I had gone, as far as I had wandered, as lost as I had been and damaged as I was, he had moved the opposite way. At fourteen his parents sent him to boarding school, thinking it might be good for him, even though they couldn't really afford it. While he was away he learned about Park Avenue, Greenwich, and Brookline, about summers in East Hampton and Nantucket and Newport, he learned about Palm Beach and Aspen and Santa Barbara, trips to Europe, Jaguars and Aston Martins and Porsches, tailored suits and Italian sheets. He decided he wanted to be rich. Rich enough to go anywhere and do anything, drive whatever car he wanted, wear whatever clothing, eat whatever food, drink whatever wine. He was smart enough to know that he wasn't a genius, would never be a banker or trader, wasn't a computer whiz, would never win a Nobel Prize. He knew his greatest gift was his charm, his wit, his smartass nature. So he nurtured it, learned everything about everything related to money and society, how to speak and act, which fork to use, how to make every drink known to man, how to dance, he read the books, learned what clothes to wear and when and how and where to buy them, made a friend of everyone he met, remembered all their names, remembered everything about them. When he went to college, he went to a party school, one of the schools where smart wealthy kids who didn't get into Ivy League schools went to drink and snort and fuck for four years. He joined a fraternity and dated sorority girls,

went to formals and met parents, became everyone's best friend.
When he finished, he went to work for the father of one of his
girlfriends, where he learned the great secret of business, which in
his words is:

Find smart people who can do everything for you. Make sure you
thank them and reward them. Make most of the dough for yourself.
And that's what he did. He had an idea to sell colored water with
a tiny bit of sugar in it and make people believe that it made them
smarter, thinner, and healthier. He came up with a memorable
name and a snappy logo and wrote a business plan, got the parents
of his friends to invest in it. He seeded the business by sending
free supplies of the colored water to his friends in all of the fancy
places where they spent their time and encouraging them to mix
it with vodka and serve it at parties. He outsourced production,
hired a marketing firm, made a distribution deal. The only thing
he controlled was sales, and after years of preparing himself, he was
a master at it. He'd show up with his hair and his smile, wearing
some crazy, bright, colorful outfit and a pair of purple or pink or
bright-blue Hush Puppies, he'd have a few samples, by the time
he was done whoever he was working would absolutely believe
they were smarter, thinner, and healthier because of his ridiculous
bottled water, and they would have bought several truckloads of it.
The company grew and grew, he poured all of the profits back into
it, and after six years, at age twenty-eight, he sold it for a fucking
fortune. He was rich. And he was free. And he devoted the rest
of his life to, as he put it, *wonderful times.* He bought a house in
Aspen, another in Palm Beach, an apartment in New York. He
played golf and skied and went fly-fishing and sailing. He bought
rare wine and rarer art, drove fast cars, ate delicious food. He
joined clubs. Flew private. Stayed up until dawn, slept until the
late afternoon. And unlike some rich dudes, he wasn't an asshole

or a show-off. He shared everything he had. He wanted everyone he knew and loved to enjoy it all with him. He didn't live the way he lived to impress anyone, or flaunt his wealth, or because he was insecure or had something to prove, he did it because it brought him real joy and true delight, and he spread that joy and delight everywhere he went.

We finished our dinner that night and had a big hug, exchanged contact information, and stayed in touch. He never was my best friend, or even one of my closest friends, and we only saw each other once or twice a year when we happened to be in the same place, but I loved him. He was kind and generous and funny and cool. He was someone I had known for most of my life, even when he wasn't in it. It didn't matter if it was four months or six months or a year, whenever we did see each other it was as if it were yesterday. We'd laugh, tell old stories about dumb shit we did as kids, new stories about whatever was going on in our lives. He'd tease me about the khakis and white T-shirts that I always wore, and had been wearing since I was a teen, and he'd offer to take me shopping, I'd make fun of the fancy shoes and shirts and pocket squares and watches that he'd always have on, offered to find the nearest Dumpster so he could deposit them into it. He met my wife and children, brought them gifts, charmed them. When my books started coming out he was always the first to buy them, read them, send me a note, when trouble followed the books, he was always the first to call and offer support. When social media arrived, we followed each other, stayed in touch using it, I saw his adventures and they always made me smile. Motherfucker had pulled it off. Rather magnificently. He was the happiest person I knew, and I was happy for him, and proud of him, and felt like I was lucky to know him.

I was in my office when I got the call. A friend who was close to both of us. I answered the phone and said hello, he said Matty's dead, collapsed while he was hiking in Aspen, heart failed. The world, or at least my world, stopped spinning. I stopped breathing, heart felt thick and heavy like it was going to fall out of my chest, my stomach empty, my soul empty. I bit my lip shook my head. My friend asked if I was there I said yeah. We were both silent, I was staring at the empty white wall in front of me, trying to process, to comprehend, trying to believe what he'd just told me. I didn't want to process comprehend or believe, wished I hadn't picked up the phone, wished I could somehow rewind the last two minutes and not push play again. I asked what happened, how the fuck did this happen, he said he went hiking by himself, was supposed to meet a friend for lunch and never showed, didn't answer texts or calls, the friend had a bad feeling and went looking for him and hiked the route he knew he liked to take, found him dead on the trail. His phone was lying next to him, twenty-two missed calls. His water bottle was lying a foot from his outstretched hand. I stared at the wall, wanted to rewind time, not answer the phone. I didn't want to talk anymore, so I thanked our friend, asked him to send me the information on services, hung up.

Now I am in this room, sitting, staring at my friend Matty in a box a few feet away from me, his hair done and out of his eyes, makeup on his face, his hands folded at his waist, his watch gleaming. I'm thinking about those last moments. His last moments. What he felt, how fast it took him, if he knew what was happening, if he was scared, if he had time to be scared, if he said anything before he went. If his life flashed before his eyes, and if it did, was he happy with what he saw?

Was he happy with what he saw?

Was he happy?

I think about my own life. When it will end and how. By my own hand, in a wrecked car on the side of a road, will one of the threats I get sent turn out to be real, will my heart fail or an artery in my

brain break, will it be cancer or ALS or a stroke or liver or kidney
disease, where will I be, alone or with people who matter to me,
when and how, when and how will it end for me. I think about what
will flash before my eyes, and whether I will be happy with what I
see. I think about the pain I've caused, the lies I've told, the messes
I've created, the words I've used in anger or sadness or spite, the
apologies I've never made, I think about all the time I've wasted, all
the precious fucking time I have wasted doing nothing, being mad
over stupid shit, obsessing over the irrelevant and the meaningless.
We are told every moment is precious and valuable, but somewhere
along the line we forget. And every moment becomes just another
moment. To be passed, to be taken for granted, to be discarded
To be wasted.

And I have wasted so much. With laziness and ego, on drugs and
alcohol, chasing shit that doesn't matter, money and fame and
recognition and approval. How many times should I have called a
friend to say hello. How many times should I have reached out to
someone that I knew needed it. How many times should I have said
I love you and I stayed silent. How many times could I have made
the right decision, but knowingly and willingly made the wrong
one. How many times have I committed acts that shamed me, even
if no one but myself knew, how many times and how much shame,
so fucking many and so fucking much. There have been days weeks
months years when I couldn't look at myself in the mirror and feel
anything but hatred and disgust. And almost every one of those
times I knew why, and didn't do anything to change it. I didn't do
anything. I just stared at myself, stared into my pale-green eyes until
I couldn't do it anymore, until I turned away. In hatred and disgust.
I make accounts in my mind of whatever good I have done and
whatever good I've accomplished and I measure them against all the
hurt and wreckage and waste and squander. To see if they balance

each other out, to see if one exceeds the other. To imagine what my life will look like in that moment when it flashes, to imagine if I'll smile, or if I'll die hating myself. I know the answer. Know it all too well, know it without any real debate. The accounts aren't balanced. They're not even close. Not even fucking close.

I look up at my friend and imagine what he saw and what he felt and what he knew and what he did as the lights went out, as he said good-bye to his life, as his heart failed and he died. I look up at him and smile and I start to cry. Smartass little fucker. Sugar-water mogul man. Dancing fool in your pink-and-blue madras suit. You went way too young, way too fucking young. But I'm happy for you and proud of you, you lived so hard and so well and so beautifully, so joyously and so magnificently. I know you smiled, and I know you laughed, and I know, even though you were scared, you went away satisfied with the way you lived your life.

I'll miss you.

I wish I had seen you more.

I wish I had told you I loved you.

I wish we could have raised a glass one more time.

I wish.

I wish.

I look at my friend and I cry. When they close the box and everyone stands I stand with them and we follow the hearse to the cemetery. I watch the box that holds my friend get lowered into a hole in the ground and just before it vanishes I hold up my hand and say good-bye, I'll miss you, good-bye.

I go to the airport.

Get on a plane.

Fly home.

My wife is asleep when I walk into our house. I kiss her on the cheek and get into bed next to her.

Every moment.

Every precious moment.

As I fall asleep I wonder how much time I have left and how it will happen and what I'll see and how I'll feel and what I'll say when the lights go out.

Will my accounts be balanced.

Will they.

When the lights go out.

Paris, 1992

Sitting on a bench in front of *The Gates of Hell*. Sun is hot, high
and shining the museum just opened it's the middle of summer
if I want any peace here, any time alone with *The Gates*, I have
to come before the crowds arrive. I have a bottle of water a pack
of cigarettes one of my notebooks a pocketful of black pens. I'm
writing. Not journal nonsense. Not the musings of my day. Not my
quaint observations from the café or what I had for breakfast, but
the beginnings of a book. And despite what the cheesy journalers
and writers of how-to books and the professors at writing schools
say, writing for publication is vastly more difficult than journaling.
Nobody is going to read your journal. If they do, or if you ask
them to read it, they're not going to say anything honest about it.
It could be the biggest piece-of-shit journal in the history of the
world, and whoever reads it will smile and tell you how talented
you are and how much they enjoyed it. When you write for real,
for publication, with the intention of putting your work into the
world, every word matters. Every sentence matters. Every comma,
punctuation mark, grammatical choice. How the words read and
sound and what they look like on the page. They are all a decision
and they all matter. And every decision made should have a reason
behind it. There's pressure. Pressure to make the right decisions, and
make them again and again, again and again. If you do it correctly,
and you do it well, people outside of you, people you don't and will
never know, will read what you write. And they'll have an opinion
on it. And whether you like their opinion or not, their opinion is
valid. And so when I sit down to write, I take it seriously. I know
what I want to do and what I want to say and I can hear it and see
it in my mind, and I can feel it in my beating heart. It's ambition
and rage and radicality. It's sex and love and the smell of cum. It's

sadness and pain. It's the joy and freedom of not giving a fuck, and
it's the burden of caring too much. It's the blunt force of my soul
laid bare. It's direct and economical. Nothing wasted. Nothing
flowery. Nothing to impress you with my virtuosity or my skill. I
want to make you feel, as I do, deeply and powerfully. I want to
shake you and move you and make you look away from the page
because I've overwhelmed you, I want to force you to come back
because you want to be overwhelmed again. I want to sear myself
into you in a way that you will never forget. And though I know
this, and I can see it and hear it and feel it, as I sit on a bench,
The Gates of Hell in front of me, a twenty-one-year-old American in
Paris, lost and wandering, found and focused, I can't do it. I can't
do it yet. Yet. And so I work. Write. Think. Feel. Try to get what
I want and what I know and what I feel on the page. I stare at the
black ink on brown paper. I listen to the sound the pen makes as
I move, see the marks appear. And I believe, in a way that could
never be taught, that at some point I'll be able to do what I want
to do, to write what I see and feel and hear. If I sit and work and
believe long enough, maybe a year, maybe five, maybe ten, maybe
twenty-five, what's in my head will match what is on paper.
As I stare at the notebook, and think about the next word, and feel
the morning sun on my face and arms, and listen to the birds in the
trees above me, and smell the bread of some local boulangerie, and
taste the remains of the black coffee I drank on my way here, I feel
someone moving toward me, I hear footsteps on the gravel path, a
shadow passes over. I don't look up. I know there's an empty bench
a few feet away but the person sits next to me. There are two feet of
space between us. I glance down, I see a pair of black Converse All
Stars, short black socks, long thin pale legs. I think about moving, or
turning away, figure the person will take whatever picture they want
to take, move on. And so I stare at the black ink on brown paper, at

the empty space on the page that I am going to fill. And as I think, I hear a voice.

What are you writing?

A woman, though I knew that already. Slight accent on the English that I can't specifically place, though I'd guess somewhere in Scandinavia. Voice is sweet and low, like coffee with a little cream and ten spoonfuls of sugar. I don't look up, or respond. I hear some rustling in a bag, a lighter ignite, and the intake of breath, I smell tobacco, the harsh and delightful odor of relief and addiction. I hear the voice again, don't look up.

You're playing hard to get. That's kind of cute.

Chuckle, but don't look.

You can look at me. I'm not Medusa. You won't turn to stone.

Another chuckle.

You're a stubborn one. At least answer my question, I'm curious.

What am I writing?

Yes.

None of your goddamn business.

She laughs. I stare at the black ink, brown paper. She does not leave, and I hear more rustling. I try to find my train of thought, find my way back to what I was doing, but it doesn't happen. I sit up, look over, tall and thin, pale, long deep thick wavy dark-red hair, freckles on her cheeks and across the bridge of her nose, brown eyes the color of cocoa, thick pouty lips like cherry pie, no lipstick. She's wearing a white short-sleeved sundress with little skulls all over it, red skulls, black skulls, yellow skulls, blue and pink and green skulls, her black Converses and little black socks. She's crushingly beautiful, and doesn't appear to be trying to be at all, and the dress, the black humor of it, the mocking cuteness of it, make her more so.

Nice dress.

She smiles, straight white perfect teeth.

Thank you.

Dig the shoes too.

They're comfy. Good for walking around.

Where you from?

The Northlands.

I laugh.

Which one of them?

One of the ones in the North.

I laugh again. She motions to my notebook.

What are you writing?

A book.

A book. Wow. Fancy.

I laugh again.

What is your book about?

You know *Le Misanthrope*?

The play by Molière?

Yes.

Yes, I know *Le Misanthrope*.

She says *Le Misanthrope* with an almost perfect French accent.

I'm writing a book based on *Le Misanthrope*, but set today, in New York.

She laughs.

Is that funny?

She nods.

It is.

Why?

Nobody will read that.

Why?

Le Misanthrope is about the biggest dickhead in the world.

He's a man of integrity.

All he does is bitch and moan and complain.

He's in love, he's tormented.

He's in love with the meanest, most miserable wench on the planet.

I laugh.

I guess you don't like *Le Misanthrope*.

I'm sure it was wonderful three hundred years ago, but now? Don't write that book. It will be awful, and no one will read it.

You a literary critic?

Nope.

Writer?

God, no.

Just like sitting down next to writers and harassing them?

You're almost cute. Almost.

She smiles and holds her index finger close to her thumb, almost.

I figured I'd sit with you and see what you were doing.

Now you know.

I don't fuck writers, though. They're drama queens. I did it once and the poor boy cried and wanted to snuggle after we were done.

What makes you think I want to fuck you?

You don't?

I shake my head, lie.

Nope.

She smiles, motions toward my hand.

May I?

I nod, she takes my hand lifts it slowly toward her mouth. She opens her lips slightly, thick and pouty like cherry pie, no lipstick, looks me straight in the eye, puts my index and ring fingers into her mouth, and she sucks them. Her mouth is warm, soft and wet, and her eyes are staring into mine, light brown the color of cocoa. She pulls my fingers slowly out, her tongue running along the bottom of them, her lips surrounding. I'm breathless, my cock is immediately and instantly hard, and I want to fuck her more than anything in my life. When my fingers are out, she sets my hand in my lap, never looks away.

Now?

Yes.

Yes?

Yes.

She smiles. My fingers are still warm, wet, my cock hard.

And I'm not much of a snuggler, so you don't have to worry about that.

She laughs.

And a writer? Are you much of one of those?

Yes.

What have you written?

I hold up my notebook.

That's it?

I have a few more of these.

Published?

Not yet.

So you're a pretend writer.

No.

You're not a real one until you're published.

If that's how you think of it, cool. It's not how I do.

How do you?

That it's just time. That when I do publish I won't be any more of a writer than I am now, I'll just have done more work.

What kind of books do you want to write, besides *Le Misanthrope*, which you definitely should not waste your time doing.

I want to burn the fucking world down.

She smiles.

I like that.

It's a beautiful perfect smile.

Thank you.

Maybe I will fuck another writer.

I smile.

What do you do?

What do you think?

No idea.

I'm tall and thin and I wear cool clothes.

Sounds like a good gig.

It is.

How do you get a gig like that?

Genetics and luck.

Pay well?

Ridiculous.

What do you do in your free time?

Play.

What's that mean?

She smiles.

It means I play.

We stare at each other for a moment, pale green and light brown like cocoa. My heart is beating, nerves tingling, I'm dizzy and I'm high. Something about her. Eyes or hair or lips, smile, attitude, her long thin pale legs, the slight accent from the Northlands, the skulls on her dress, the way my fingers felt in her mouth, that she knows *Le Misanthrope*, that she hates my book idea that she likes the idea of burning the world down that my cock is still hard. Something about her. The way her skin felt when she touched my hand. Something about her. Her deep thick heavy red hair. Something about her. The shampoo she used or the soap, pheromones, I don't know, something. My heart is beating, nerves tingling, I'm dizzy and I'm high. I want to kiss her, taste her lips, suck her tongue. I want my hands on the insides of her thighs, the arc of her ass. I want to kiss her neck, chest, I want her nipples hard between my teeth. I want to lick her ass, her pussy, her clit, move inside her, stay inside her, deep hard and wet, eyes locked, hands, the tips of our fingers.

I want to hear her moan.

We stare at each other for a moment, pale green and light brown like cocoa. She leans forward and she softly and slowly blows on my cheek, her breath is sweet I close my eyes she blows on my cheek sweet breath and warm. When she stops I open my eyes, she's smiling.

Time for me to go.

Why?

I have things to do.

What?

Things.

I laugh.

What's your name?

I'll tell you next time we see each other.

When will that be?

I don't know.

You have a number?

Let's leave it for the Gods to decide.

I laugh.

The Gods?

I am from the Northlands, we still believe.

She stands.

Until.

I nod, smile.

Until.

She turns and walks away and though I want to stare I want to follow her I want to go wherever she goes I don't. I look down at my notebook black ink on brown paper. I look up at *The Gates of*

Hell at the lust and pain and ecstasy and horror towering over me
immovable and permanent. I look into the blue of the sky endless
and beautiful.
I can still smell her, feel her breath on my cheek sweet and warm.
My cock is still hard.
Until.

*   *   *

My new best pal is a garbageman named Philippe. He's from a
fancy French family that owns hotels and vineyards, but decided to
spend his compulsory military service on the back of a garbage truck
instead of running around in the woods pretending to be a soldier.
We met through an American girl he dates, to whom I used to sell
cocaine in America. She came here to work for her father's very large
global real estate company and she heard I was in Paris and tracked
me down and I went out with her and Philippe we met at a fancy bar
off avenue George Cinq filled with young French professionals. We
ended up at Polly Maggoo yelling at tourists, pissing in the gutter,
eating sandwiches from Maison de Gyros, and vomiting into the
Seine from Pont Neuf I woke up on the ground beneath Fontaine
des Innocents. It was a wonderful evening, though I remember
very little of it. We went out the next night I woke up in square du
Temple. We went out the night after that I woke under a tree on
boulevard de Clichy. Philippe has the type of hours and the type of
job that are conducive to bad behavior. He starts work 4:30 a.m.,
finishes at 10:30 a.m. It doesn't matter if he smells because he
handles trash all day. It doesn't matter if he's sick he just blames the
garbage. When he's done he sleeps until 5:00 or 6:00 p.m. If he has
a date with his girl he goes out with her. If he doesn't he comes and
finds me, sometimes at my apartment, sometimes at Polly Maggoo,
sometimes at Shakespeare and Company, sometimes at Stolly's. He

loves to drink, smoke, laugh, eat, yell, wander, he's always down
for trouble, for an adventure, for doing something most people
would regret but that makes us holler with joy. And he is my one
friend who does not live in my world. Who is part of and can
move easily within the higher echelons of French society. He has
a large apartment in the 8th arrondissement, the fanciest and most
upscale part of Paris. He can go to popular clubs and most likely
knows the people who own them. He summers in the South, on the
Mediterranean, where his family has a house in Beaulieu-sur-Mer,
halfway between Nice and Monaco. Most of the time we go out,
he is dressed in nice clothing, pressed pants and tucked-in button-
down shirts, a sport coat with a nice label and suede shoes. His
wallet is always full, he's going to business school when he finishes
his service, he'll doubtless be successful doing whatever he wants to
do. For now, though, he's a garbageman, and a drunk, and a maniac.
And my new best pal. Encouraging me to have another drink, talk
to a girl I might otherwise ignore, showing me places in Paris I
wouldn't know or know to look for. He takes me to a joint in the
11th that sells absinthe if you know the secret password (*Rimbaud*),
and not the fake shit that most people drink, but the real juice that
makes you smile and buzz and hallucinate and dream. He shows me
where to buy cocaine in Saint-Denis train station, and which dealers
will rip me off and which won't. He gives me the addresses of two
bordellos, one in the Marais and one in Montmartre, where the girls
flirt and you can smoke hash from a hookah and they have steam
rooms and hot tubs and massages between sessions. He takes me to
Les Bains Douches to laugh at and make fun of celebrities and gawk
at the models we see on the covers of magazines. He often pays for
everything, despite my protests, says every penny is worth it, that
his French friends are more concerned with politics and business
and the vintage of the wines they drink than having any real fun and

raising any real hell. Sometimes he brings a briefcase with him, in
which he keeps his green garbageman uniform, sometimes he puts it
on while we're out, sometimes he vanishes in the middle of whatever
we're doing, I know he's going to do his job and I'll see him soon
enough. And though he has never seen or read a word of anything
I've written, he is the first person I know who believes in what I'm
doing and doesn't think I'm insane for doing it. If you want to be a
great writer, Jay, he says, you need to live and see and feel and dream
and love and fuck and cry and fail and scream in the streets and get
kicked right square in your fucking nuts, all the great writers did
those things, and you're doing them and you're wonderful at them,
especially the getting kicked right square in your fucking nuts part,
so of course someday you'll write a great book, and everyone will
hate you and you'll get in a shitload of trouble and you'll sit at home
and laugh your head off about it, of course! And though it's not the
type of endorsement that will get a book on the shelves or into the
canon, it means something to me, that maybe I'm not crazy, that
maybe I will pull this off, that maybe my way will be the right way
for me, it means fucking something. And so I take his advice. Live
and see and feel and dream and love and fuck and cry and fail and
scream in the streets and get kicked right square in my fucking nuts.

*   *   *

My relationship with the couple who own and run the boulangerie
below my apartment continues to deteriorate. Though I still go
there daily, and oftentimes twice daily, they seem to be growing
increasingly hostile toward me. My order has been refined so that I
always get one of two things, either a baguette or a sandwich *poulet*,
which is a ten-inch piece of baguette with chicken and lettuce and
tomato and mayonnaise in it. Despite still trying to speak French
and be friendly, when the Old Lady sees me she stops smiling and

asks in her sternest voice: *Sandwich ou baguette?* When I answer she
hands me the product and takes my money and glares at me until
I leave. Good times, man, good times with my neighbors, good
fucking times.

*   *   *

I meet a girl named Suzie at Café de Flore. We're both sitting
outside, facing boulevard Saint-Germain, squashed into the small
chairs at the small tables drinking the small coffees mine is black hers
is a café crème. We're next to each other she's reading a magazine I'm
reading *Justine* by Lawrence Durrell. Our legs keep brushing against
each other, accidentally or not, at one point we both put down our
reading material to watch the crowds walk by there is no greater city
than Paris and maybe no greater café than Flore to watch the crowds
walk by. It's late afternoon I offer to buy her a drink she orders
champagne and though I don't normally drink it, I order one as well.
She has long black hair, blue eyes, she's wearing a Chanel dress and
heels, works in fashion PR, sending out invitations for fashion shows
and deciding where people get to sit, an endeavor she compares to
being a referee at a knife fight, people will kill each other for the
right seat, and kill her if she doesn't give them what they want. She's
from England was raised in Knightsbridge, educated in Switzerland,
spent her summers at her father's estate in Gloucestershire, she has
thin arms, beautiful hands, French manicure. Her accent is a delight,
each word delicate and sophisticated and somehow more intelligent
and considered and wonderful than any of the words I speak in
my slow, base American drawl. We talk about people walking by
imagine who they are and where they're going we talk about the
current American president who she thinks is a jackass we debate
whether Michelangelo or Raphael is greater, whether we prefer the
Rodin Museum or the Picasso, whether le Centre Pompidou is a

beautiful building or absurd. We switch from champagne to whiskey we play footsie under the table we move closer together our hands start to play in the same way as our feet. I pay our bill and we leave walk through Saint-Germain it's a clear hot summer night and it feels like the world is shimmering. We walk along the boulevard past the lights from glittering cafés through the crowds drinking and eating. We walk down rue de Buci no cars no vehicles, chairs and tables in the street all of them full there's laughter and words and the eyes of a thousand people seeking love and sex and conversation and ideas. It's hot and dark and Suzie and I are holding hands walking flirting playfully bumping each other, we stop for ice cream, we get one cone to share, I watch her tongue sliding along the strawberry crème and I want them both in my mouth. We cut up rue de Seine it's darker less crowded she takes me into her building a beautiful perfect charming Paris house three or four hundred years old converted into apartments, there's one per floor, she's on the second floor, I'm walking up the stairs behind her watching staring wanting imagining knowing what's going to happen.

She opens the door.

We step inside.

She hangs her keys, turns around, smiles, asks me if I want a tour.

I say no, I don't want a tour.

I step forward.

Kiss her.

Lips and tongues and breath.

I press her against the wall.

Hands held above her head with one of mine.

Lips and tongues and breath.

I smell alcohol and cigarettes and the summer, I smell the fading remnants of her perfume. I smell the anticipation of sex.

Lips and tongues and breath.

Hands.

Up her dress in my pants.

Wet and hard.

Lips and tongues and breath and hands wet and hard.

We're both drunk, drunk enough for inhibitions to be gone, but
sober enough to know what we're doing, sober enough to know how
we want to do it. She moves off the wall leads me into the apartment
a sofa in the living room light is streaming through a tall French
door it is otherwise dark. She pushes me onto the couch, takes out
my cock and lifts her dress, climbs into my lap. I pull the dress off
her shoulders the straps of her brassiere with it, she sits on my cock
and I start kissing licking and sucking her tits.

She moves slowly.

My mouth is alternating between her tongue, neck, and nipples. My
hands in her hair the small of her back cupping her ass.

She moves slowly.

I can feel her dripping on my thighs she can feel me throbbing
inside her.

She moves faster.

We're both moaning.

She moves faster, harder.

Faster.

Harder.

Faster harder.

Whispers into my ear says tell me when you're going to cum.

I say

Soon

Almost

Now

She moves off of me, gets on her knees in front of me, puts my
cock in her mouth, her lips surrounding her tongue along her hand

moving, I'm hard and it's wet and the world goes white white white God.

Lips tongue and hand moving.

White white white.

God.

I don't ever want to move or think or feel anything other than this now forever I don't want this to end.

White white white.

God.

She stays on her knees until. When she moves I'm soft she comes up next to me kisses me rests against me in my arms. We don't move or speak there is light streaming into the room through the tall thin French windows. Thirty minutes later maybe longer maybe less she stands and leads me into her bedroom it's clean white and simple, bright Matisse cutout prints on the walls it's like something out of a magazine. We fuck on top of her covers white white white God we fuck again under her covers white white white God we fall asleep when I wake up the next morning she's gone.

I look for a note or some indication she wants to see me again but there's nothing.

I'm gone.

*   *   *

As much as I drink or smoke and as much as I walk and wander and as much as I dream and as many paintings or sculptures I see I never forget why I'm here, to read and discover and become. I am here to put words on paper one word after another after another, I am here to figure out how to make them more than what they are simple words. I am here to learn how to play with fire. I want to fucking burn burn burn, I am here to learn how to play with fire.

*   *   *

Originally a train station. Tracks went bad and it fell into ruin.
Became a center for Nazi mail in World War II. After the war
an empty building occasionally used as a film set. Scheduled for
demolition in 1970, saved by the Directorate of the Museums of
France in 1974. Renovations begin in 1981, and are finished in 1986.
Holds the greatest collection of Pre-Impressionist, Impressionist, and
Post-Impressionist art in the world. Three million visitors yearly.
I go to Musée d'Orsay once a week or so. It's not far from Saint-
Placide, an easy walk. I go to look at the sculptures, look at the
paintings, to sit amongst them, be humbled by them. I love art,
looking at art, feeling art, and reading about and talking about art,
but the main reason I go to Musée d'Orsay, and all of the museums
and galleries in Paris that I frequent, is because I want to learn how
to think, how artists think, how specific artists think, and why they
made what they made. I want to know what was in their hearts and
minds, in their blood, what drove them, and what it cost them.
As I think about books and how I want to write them, I think
more about art than I do other books. There are rules with books.
What something is called, how it is read, rules of grammar and
punctuation, rules about how words should be laid out visually on a
page, about how they should be used and with which other words.
There are rules about publication and classification, how books
can be sold, where they have to be shelved. The rules are stupid.
Meaningless. And they are there to be broken, disregarded, and
defiled. And though I still read and love books, despite the dumbass
rules that govern them, I go to art when I think about how I want
to write books. There are no rules in art. No governance. There is a
canvas, or a block of marble, or a piece of paper, or a hunk of wood,
and there is whatever the artist wants to make with them. The artist

is not limited in the colors they can use, or the types of paint, or the brushes, they are not limited by the strokes they can make and how and where, or by what tools and what size tools or how many chisel marks they can leave and where they have to be. An artist has materials, and they make something out of those materials. When they are finished they have a work of art, and it is what it is, and it either works or not, it is either effective or not, beautiful or not, moving or not. It either makes history and becomes history, or it is discarded and forgotten by history. It is what it is and you have to react to it on its terms. When I look at art I don't have to consider whether the work of art is fiction or nonfiction, whether it is a genre painting or literary painting, whether it is serious or commercial, where the artist went to school or whether the publisher has prestige or not. It is what it is. Something someone made because it was inside them, because they were compelled to make it. The art dictates the terms. I want to write books in the same manner. I have words inside me, and I am compelled to make something with them. They will be what they will be, on their own terms, books. Fuck all the rest of it.

The art at Musée d'Orsay is magnificent, an embarrassment of riches, a symbol of the cultural and artistic dominance France enjoyed through the eighteenth, nineteenth, and first half of the twentieth centuries. The work starts in the 1840s with Ingres, Delacroix, Courbet. Moves into Corot, Cabanel, Moreau, Pissarro, Carrière. To the great Manet. To the famous Degas and Cezanne and Monet, Sisley and Cassatt, Renoir and van Gogh. To bad Paul Gauguin and crazy Toulouse-Lautrec. To the cursed Camille Claudel and her tormentor Rodin. To Seurat and Derain and Munch and Klimt. To Mondrian. In any museum, I am always drawn to the most radical work, the work that caused the most problems, created the most controversy. The work that did what nothing had done before it, that confused, divided, and enraged, the work that marks the viewer, changes them, forces them to have an opinion on it. If I can walk past a work of art, dismiss it, see it without wanting to understand it, without it forcing me to engage with it, than I have no need for it, and I'm not interested in it. It may be beautiful, but it's boring. I want to see, and feel, and understand, and experience, the most difficult and most troublesome art.

Today I'm on my way to see *Olympia,* by Édouard Manet. It's all I want to see. Painted in 1863, after his last painting *Le déjeuner sur l'herbe* had been rejected by the state salon for obscenity. *Olympia* is a large portrait of a nude woman on a bed, one elbow up, leaning against a pillow, an orchid in her hair, a black silk ribbon around her neck, a servant delivering her flowers. She's looking directly out of the canvas, directly at the viewer. It's a defiant, confrontational look, as if she's just told you to go fuck yourself. It's based on Titian's *Venus of Urbino,* which was painted for Cardinal Ippolito de' Medici around 1534, and portrays an elegant and magnificent Venus reclining in an environment of great luxury, filled with symbols of piety and virtue. Olympia's pose is identical to the pose of Venus, but where Venus represented a feminine ideal, Olympia represents feminine power. She is clearly in control. The environment is not one of piety and virtue, but rather the residence of a courtesan, and her look, and indifference to the flowers being delivered to her, show that she is in control of who comes to see her. Instead of the girlfriend of a Cardinal, she's a woman of her own means, using her body to direct her own life. Aside from the philosophical underpinnings of it, it's a beautifully rendered work, clearly painted by someone with virtuosic skills. When it was first exhibited in the Paris Salon of 1865 it caused a scandal, was described by critics as *vulgar* and *immoral* and *an affront to civilization*, and survived multiple attempts to destroy it. A barrier was built to keep viewers away from it, the first time a painting in a Salon had required protection. Manet was amused, and delighted, and is reported to have said, while he laughed, *They wanted a new Venus, and I gave them one, a real one, a true Venus, the type you might see on a sidewalk or in a dance hall, and she is beauty to me.* The painting set the tone for the rest of his career, during which he regularly painted subjects considered obscene, or reset historical paintings in ways that shocked modern audiences. He is considered the Father of Modernism, and easily the most influential painter of his time.

I laugh whenever I see *Olympia.* Imagine what Manet was thinking about when he conceived of it, how he felt as he painted it, I wonder if he knew what it was going to do, how the critics and the public would react to it. I wonder if, in an age where he could be anonymous, he ever went to the room where it was exhibited, and watched people melt down in front of it, saw them cringe, saw them reel, heard them discuss it, condemn it, damn it. I hope he did, and I hoped he loved it, and I hope he fell asleep with a smile. To me *Olympia* is a monument to how art should be made, and what it should do. And it's everything I want to do. And so I go stand before it. Look at it. Think about it. Study it. Laugh with it. Learn from it. Acknowledge its greatness.

Up the stairs to the second floor past tourists with cameras no flashes allowed, I walk into the room where *Olympia* hangs. For the past two weeks, since the moment I met her, I've often thought of the girl in the skull dress, her words, her smile, the way she said good-bye, her deep-red hair. And as I have thought of her, I've looked for her. In cafés and in the streets, in bookstores and bars, as I've walked past restaurants, in galleries and parks. At the Musée Rodin and in front of *The Gates.* Whenever I saw red, even when I knew it wasn't her, my heart jumped, and I hoped, and I wanted, and I pursued until I knew it wasn't her. Like so many other girls

I've met in my life, whether I was with them for a minute or five, for an hour, a day or a week or two, I assumed I would never see her again, that Paris was too big a city, that the minutes we had together would be our first and our last, that her life would go on without me in it.

Until.

Until.

Until.

I walk into the room where *Olympia* hangs, and she is standing in front of it, wearing jeans and heels, a white sheer blouse, a light-blue Hermès bag in her hand, her red hair flowing down her back. She's with a man in a gray suit, fancy shoes, hair slicked back. I can see him gesturing as he speaks, though I can't hear what he's saying. I walk toward them, step beside him, listen. She's staring at the painting, doesn't notice me.

The original, the Titian, is in Rome, and I've seen it a number of times, and I actually prefer it. It has a regality to it that this picture doesn't, as great as it might be.

I interrupt.

You've never seen the original.

He turns toward me. As does she. He speaks.

Excuse me?

You're full of shit. You've never seen the original.

She smiles, he scowls.

Who are you?

Just a dude.

He imitates my American accent.

Just a dude?

I nod.

Yeah.

He's still scowling, she's still smiling.

And what do you know about me?

That you've never seen the *Venus* by Titian, that you wear too much cologne, and that you're trying too hard to impress your lady.

Fuck off.

Cool.

What do you know?

That the Titian painting is in Florence, not Rome.

You're wrong.

No, I'm not.

Have you seen it?

Nope.

How do you know?

Because I can read.

You're wrong.

I laugh.

I'm not.

Fuck off.

Heard you the first time.

Go back to America, you pig.

Someday, my friend. Someday.

He stares at me. She's smiling. I look at *Olympia*, motion toward it. And this one is better. This one burned the world down. And you're a fucking idiot if you think otherwise.

She laughs, he shakes his head, takes her hand, leads her away. I smile at her as they leave, she reaches out and runs the tips of her fingers against the back of my hand as she passes. My heart jumps and my smiles grows and I turn and watch her walk away and as they move into the next room, she turns and smiles at me and my heart jumps and no matter what happens for the rest of the day, it will be a good fucking day. When they're gone, I turn back to the

painting, and I stare at it, I wonder at it, spend more time than I
normally do in front of it.

A real Venus.

A true Venus.

The type you might see on a sidewalk or in a dance hall.

And she is beauty to me.

*   *   *

I try to stop drinking. I'm tired and my body hurts and I'm
throwing up constantly, sometimes with blood, I know I need a
break. After eighteen hours I'm sweating and shaking and seeing
shit I know isn't there and hearing shit I know isn't there and my
heart feels like it's exploding. Louis finds me on the floor of our
bathroom and wants to take me to the hospital I tell him I need
a bottle of wine, just get me some fucking alcohol. He gets me a
bottle and I drink half of it in a single pull, the other half right
after. I immediately vomit but enough of the wine stays in me to
end the sweating and make the shakes go away, I stop seeing shit
and hearing shit that I know isn't there, my heart slows and my
thoughts become more clear, I drink another bottle of wine and
I go for a walk and I end up sitting on a bench near La Fête des
Tuileries. La Fête is a happy place, maybe the happiest in Paris,
there's a Ferris wheel and a small roller coaster and flying swings
and bumper cars and a haunted house and games and prizes. It's
bright and loud and I can hear children yelling and playing and
having fun I can feel their happiness in the dark of night, I can
smell cotton candy and caramel apples and popcorn. I sit on the
bench and drink and stare at the lights of the Ferris wheel going
around and around, I smoke and listen to kids being happy being
kids without the bullshit of life bearing down on them, without
the anticipation of death in front of them. Nobody sits with me,

or acknowledges me, when people see me they hurry past, I'm just another lonely drunk on a park bench, another lonely drunk wasting his life away. I wonder where and when and how I went wrong, or if I even did, if this is just who and what I am and if I should just accept it. I know I don't want to die. I know it's possible that I will. I know I should stop but I don't know if I can or if I even want to stop. I'm twenty-one years old and I've been drinking and using for almost a decade. Aside from books and love, drugs and alcohol are the only things that ever made me feel like I was okay. I want answers but none come. I have a bottle of wine and a pack of cigarettes and a bench to myself and I have the lights and sounds and smells of La Fête and I have Paris and the night and a dream and a beating heart, for now I have a beating heart.
I take a draw from the bottle.
I want answers but none come to me.

*   *   *

I go to an AA meeting.
I go to a church.
I go through the self-help section of an English-language bookstore.
I taper down from four bottles to three bottles to two bottles to one.
I have trouble sleeping, but I also don't want to move or get out of bed.
Books I read bring me no joy, I'm too tired to leave the apartment I'm too tired to walk I'm too tired to look at art. I'm as rude to the couple in the bakery as they are to me I eat one baguette a day it tastes like wood. Coffee is no solace cigarettes are no friend. I smoke some hash with Louis it makes me hate the world and hate myself even more.
Three days four days five days six they run into each other.
The other way may kill me but this is no life either. And I know nothing in between, don't want anything in between.

Work save vote obey teach your children to do the same, die and rot
in a fucking hole in the ground.
Fuck this shit.
Fuck that shit.

*　　*　　*

Banging on my door I ignore it.
Banging on my door.
Doesn't stop.
Someone yelling my name.
I'm half-drunk working my way through a bottle of Jack Daniel's.
Started a new book. Girl was right. A book based on *Le Misanthrope*
is stupid. This one is called *Vandal*. About a kid who wants to
destroy his high school. The school deserves it.
Still banging on my door, still yelling.
Jay.
Jay.
Jay.
I walk over, open it, Philippe standing in front of me. I'm wearing
boxers and black tube socks, no shirt. Philippe laughs.
What the fuck happened to you?
I shrug.
I don't know.
You look like you've lost twenty pounds. And you were already
fucking skinny.
I was sick.
Now?
I'm back.
Put on some clothes, we're going out.
Where?
Dinner, drinking, carousing.

I could use a bit of all of them.

He laughs, I walk over to pull on some pants, a T-shirt.

You got any nice clothes?

Why?

We're going to eat some good food.

Not really.

He turns walks into Louis's room. I put on my shoes. He comes back with a purple polo.

Put this on.

Really?

We're going somewhere good.

I don't have any money for anything good.

Don't worry about it.

I put on the polo, we leave the apartment walk through the 6th arrondissement rue Saint-Placide to rue de Sèvres to rue des Saints-Pères to Saint-Germain. It's busy, crowded, de Flore and Deux Magots are both full, we go across the street to Brasserie Lipp, an old-school brasserie with a giant orange awning and an enormous neon sign above. There's a line but Philippe walks around it, I follow him. As we work our way inside he waves to the maître d', who smiles and waves us forward. He and Philippe hug each other, speak, and though I can now speak functional French, and don't need to use English anywhere in Paris, I have trouble when the French speak quickly, and don't understand a word they say to each other. We are immediately led past any number of annoyed people who have clearly been waiting, to a table along one of the walls.

The room is beautiful. Oak-paneled ceiling with murals painted into large squares. Tall mirrors on the walls with paintings of bamboo and palm trees between them. Brown leather banquettes with a blue-and-yellow checkerboard floor, white tablecloths and napkins, stainless silverware. It's as classic a restaurant as exists in

Paris, imitated and revered. Philippe thanks the maître d', discreetly
passes him a tip. A waiter arrives and Philippe orders, two bottles
of Bordeaux one for each of us, foie gras de canard, toasts, escargots
de Bourgogne, deux filet de boeuf, sauce béarnaise, frites. When the
wine arrives, he raises his glass, smiles.
To not looking like a POW.
I laugh, raise my glass, drink.
For the next ninety minutes we eat drink laugh. There is a parade of
people who come to our table to say hello to Philippe, some are his
friends some are his father's friends, he introduces me to all of them
as Jay Bush, nephew of President George Bush, tells them I'm in
Paris to learn French and spread the gospel of big wars and cheap oil.
I speak with a fake Texas accent, tell everyone big wars and cheap
oil are both underrated, they all leave befuddled and confused. The
food is magnificent, and easily the best meal I've had since I arrived,
and probably the first true French meal. The foie gras melts in my
mouth, the snails are marvelous little bits of rubbery magnificence,
the steak rare and bloody, the béarnaise sweet and heavy, the frites
crispy and hot. Philippe orders one of every dessert on the menu and
we take a few bites of each profiteroles glacées, mille-feuille, crème
caramel, mousse au chocolat, tarte Tatin, le Mont-Blanc Angelina.
When we're done I'm half-drunk and my stomach feels like it's going
to explode. When the check comes, Philippe waves me off and pays
it. I thank him and when he says don't worry about it I thank him
again.
We leave and decide to cross the river. Philippe wants to go to Les
Bains Douches, says it is the first and potentially last time I have
ever been dressed well enough to get past the doorman and he isn't
going to let the opportunity pass. We take rue Danton to place
Saint-Michel, walk across Île de la Cité and Pont au Change to
place du Châtelet. It's ten o'clock and it's not late enough to go to

Les Bains so we cut over to place Edmond-Michelet and look for a
place to drink for an hour or so. On the first floor of an old corner
building, there's a small bar called La Comédie. There's a large green
awning, a sign, tables outside a few of them taken but most not.
We walk inside sit at the bar the place is a simple old-fashioned
French drinking establishment, my favorite kind of place. A tall thin
bartender with jet-black hair and eyes matching walks over smiles
and asks us what we'd like, we order drinks start looking around.
The patrons are mostly young and, like us, appear to be having a
few drinks before going elsewhere. Philippe asks me if I see anything
interesting I say no the bartender brings us our drinks straight
double bourbon for me, scotch on ice for Philippe. He smiles pays
asks the bartender her name she says Petra, he asks where she's from
she says Oslo. As we drink we talk to her in between her serving
other customers, she came here a year ago, her best friend is a model,
she lives in the neighborhood, she was a ballet dancer but got hurt,
she'll go home at some point but for now she's happy. We order a
second round, a third. As Petra delivers the drinks the bell at the
door rings she looks toward the bell, smiles, waves. Philippe and I
turn to see who she's waving at and I laugh and my heart jumps and
my head spins and I'm high.
Tall and thin and pale.
Long deep dark-red hair.
Freckles on her cheeks across the bridge of her nose, light-brown
eyes the color of cocoa, thick pouty lips like cherry pie, no lipstick.
She smiles and walks toward us she's wearing a little black dress and
a pair of Air Jordans. Petra pours a glass of vodka when she arrives
she playfully punches my arm, speaks.
Nice shirt.
I laugh.
Thanks.

What the fuck are you doing here?

No idea.

Just ended up in my local?

Yep.

Petra hands her the vodka, speaks.

You know him?

Kind of.

How?

He tried to fuck me at the Musée Rodin, and again at Musée d'Orsay.

Philippe laughs.

Good work, Jay.

I laugh.

I didn't try to fuck you.

She smiles.

Absolutely you did.

I didn't.

You thought about it.

Maybe.

And you would have if given the chance.

Maybe.

Philippe laughs.

Maybe my ass.

She looks back at Petra.

Remember the almost-cute American writer I told you about, the one who ruined Jean-Luc's day?

Yeah.

That's him.

He's cute.

Almost.

Yeah, you're right, almost.

He's tried to fuck me twice.

Petra laughs.

I believe you.

Philippe motions to an empty stool.

Join us for a drink.

She smiles.

Yes.

And so we drink, talk, laugh. She's also from Oslo, is a model, not a supermodel but a real model, does editorial and runway shows, lives in a loft in the Marais, makes money, when she's not working she wanders around France, Italy, Spain. She likes books, art, clothes, alcohol, cocaine. She laughs quickly and easily, gives better than she gets, and is charming as fuck. If she didn't scare the shit out of me, I'd be desperately in love with her, and every moment I'm near her, I want to know her more, talk with her more, laugh with her more, I want to touch her heart, know it, feel it. I get up to go to the bathroom, piss, look in the mirror as I wash my hands, tell myself to calm down, to walk back, get her name, get her number, calm down, as I open the door to step out she steps in and closes the door, flips the lock, and drops her bag on the floor. She smiles.

Alone at last.

We're inches apart.

Yes, alone at last.

I have to leave in a few minutes, I'm going to meet some friends.

She takes my hands.

But I want to play before I leave.

She leans forward softly kisses my neck.

Play?

Kisses my ear.

Yes, I want to play.

I'm hard, I want, she knows I want.

You're a cute boy, Jay.

Softly kisses my lips.

Thank you.

You still writing that dumb book?

I put my hands up her skirt.

No.

Run the tips of my fingers along the insides of her thighs.

No?

You were right.

Around her ass.

Yes, I was.

We both move toward each other kissing deeply slowly heavily, lips and tongues, her hands are immediately in my pants, I lift her off the ground set her on the sink tear off her thong. She says now I ask her if she has a condom she says now, Jay, now.

I step between her legs.

Move inside her.

She's tight and wet, leans back against the mirror.

Forward.

Deeper inside her.

Forward.

Tight and wet.

She moans pulls my face to hers kisses me. I start moving inside her, slow hard and deep, her hands gripping the sides of the sink, my hands on her shoulders, we're looking into each other's eyes pale green and light brown like cocoa.

Do you like my pussy, Jay?

Deeper.

Yes.

Harder.

Does your cock feel good in my pussy?

Faster.

Yes.

Pale green.

Do you love my pussy?

Cocoa.

Yes.

Deeper.

Tell me.

Harder.

Tell me you love my pussy.

Faster.

I love your pussy.

Hands gripping.

Tell me how good your cock feels inside me.

Gripping.

Feels so good inside you.

Deeper harder faster.

Fuck me, Jay, fuck me.

Deeper harder faster.

Eyes locked.

Fuck me.

And hearts and souls and bodies.

Fuck me.

Locked.

Fuck me.

I'm hard and deep inside her fucking her on the bathroom sink her tight little black dress still on her thong on the floor my pants at my knees our eyes locked, our hearts and souls and bodies locked.

Cum inside me.

Cum inside me.

Cum inside me.

Blinding breathless shaking overwhelming exploding white God I cum inside her my cock throbbing we're both moaning eyes hearts souls bodies one.

One.

White.

God.

Cum.

Cum.

Cum.

I close my eyes let out my breath.

Cum.

I lean against her both breathing hard I'm still inside her smiling. She takes my hands lifts them and places them around her body, she puts her arms around me, we stay still and breathe, hard inside her, tight and warm and wet around me, we breathe. She gently pushes me away, we look into each other's eyes, she smiles.

That was fun.

I smile.

It was.

I like how you feel.

Me too.

She moves me away, moves off the sink.

I've gotta go.

I pull up my pants.

I want you to stay.

She picks up her bag.

We'll see each other again.

She puts her arms around me, pulls tight.

How do I find you?

Come here. Tell Petra you're looking for me. Or tell me if you have a local, and I'll come there for you.

Polly Maggoo.

She laughs.

That place is a dump.

She lets me go.

Give me your number.

She shakes her head.

We don't need numbers. We'll find each other when we want to find each other.

At least tell me your name.

She smiles, kisses me.

Katerina.

She turns, opens the door.

My name is Katerina.

She leaves, and I watch her walk away, through the bar, out the door, into the night.

Tall and thin and pale.

Long deep dark-red hair.

Freckles on her cheeks and across the bridge of her nose, light-brown eyes the color of cocoa, thick pouty lips like cherry pie, no lipstick.

Katerina.

Her name is Katerina.

Los Angeles, 2017

Hi
Hi
Hi
Hi
Hi
I think that's enough.
Hi
Come on.
Hi Hi Hi Hi Hi Hi
Really?
Hi
Should I just give up?
Yes.
Hi
Hi :)
Hello
What are you doing?
Watching TV.
What are you watching?
Dumb political bullshit. People yelling at each other.
Why do you watch it?
It passes the time.
Not writing?
Not really.
You have enough money to be retired?
Definitely not.
Why aren't you writing?
Just finished a job, trying to figure out what to do next.
What job?

I wrote a pilot for a TV series.

Was it good?

No idea.

Will it get made?

Probably not.

Why?

The network hired me to write a show about the apocalypse. I turned it in and they said it was too violent and too dark. I told them it's the apocalypse, that means the end of the world, most of the population dies and civilization ends. They asked for a *blue sky* version of the apocalypse.

What does that mean?

A happier, gentler version.

That's stupid.

Yes, it is.

So what are you going to do?

I don't know.

Why don't you write another book?

I don't know.

You should.

Maybe.

Not maybe, yes.

Maybe.

Why did you stop?

I didn't.

I don't count those books under a fake name, or the books about aliens, or any of that Hollywood nonsense.

That made me laugh.

Do you count those?

I didn't actually write them.

Then they shouldn't have your name on them.

It's more complicated than that.

Because your name means more money?

More or less.

I never imagined you'd sell out.

Neither did I.

I loved the first books you wrote, before you sold out.

You read them?

Yes.

Thank you.

I remember when I saw the first one. In the window of a bookstore next to a sign with your picture. I almost started crying. And then I read it, and I did cry. Many times.

I'm sorry.

Don't be sorry.

I made you cry enough.

We both did terrible things.

Still sorry.

And mostly I was so happy for you, Jay. You did it, it was amazing, you said you were going to burn the world down and you did.

You're gonna make me cry.

It had been so many years.

It took a while.

Ten years?

From the time I arrived in Paris to the day the first one was published it was twelve.

I thought about you in those years and wondered what happened.

Now you know.

Did you ever think about me?

I did.

You know who this is now?

I do.

How?

I looked up your name, the name you use on here.

Like it?

Made me smile.

I thought you'd do it the first day.

It was fun not knowing.

And now?

I'm happy I know.

It's been so long.

It has.

We got old.

Never thought it would happen.

I'm glad you know now.

So am I, Model Girl.

That made me smile.

Good.

Hi.

Hi.

Hi.

Hi.

Hi.

Enough

Hi. Hi. Hi. Hi. Hi.

Paris, 1992

It's the third week of August. Paris is empty. Or rather, Paris is empty of French. Except for those who work in restaurants, bars, cafés, and stores, everyone else is gone. I don't know where they all went, maybe the South, maybe Spain or Italy, maybe America, but they aren't here. There are no disdainful looks on the Métro. No judgment oozing from the cafés. No scowls when they hear my accent. No laughing when I use improper grammar or the wrong tense. The old French have closed the boulangerie and are away somewhere, and can't be rude to or ignore me. The general air of superiority that hangs over Paris is gone. I hope wherever it went, and wherever all the French went and the bakery couple went, someone is scowling at them and making them feel dumb. They all fucking deserve it.

Yes, Paris is empty, except for the tourists. I have been here long enough, and speak French well enough, and know my way around the city easily enough, that I don't consider myself a tourist anymore. I'm not a French, and I could live here for fifty years and would never be one of them. I won't call myself an ex-pat, which is a term that whenever I hear it makes me think of an ass-pimple, and makes me think the person using it is an ass-pimple. I'm not a resident, and have overstayed my legal term of visitation, would probably get kicked out of the country if I somehow got caught, but I'm not a tourist anymore. I'm just a motherfucker in Paris. A nobody in Paris. A young man lost and wandering in Paris. A dreamer in Paris. And because I'm not one of them anymore, I hate the fucking tourists. I hate their dumb guidebooks. I hate the way they ask for menus in English. I hate it when they stop in the middle of the sidewalk because they're lost. I hate it when they stand in front of paintings like idiots who spend all their time in front of the TV, just staring but having

no idea why they are looking at it or what they are seeing. I hate
their cameras, and the constant posing that goes on everywhere, fuck
those fucking cameras I wish I could throw them all into the Seine.
There are English, Canadians, Australians, hordes of Japanese, armies
of Scandinavians that I can't tell apart, and masses, endless invading
masses of Americans. I hate the Americans the most. Goddamn,
if they aren't the worst. And though I am still American, and love
American liquor and American drugs, American cars and American
food, American cigarettes and American music, American girls and
American swearwords, American tourists are just awful. They wear
bright ugly clothing. Most of them are fat. They wear baseball hats
backward. They're loud. They act like they're naïve, but they aren't,
and they're actually just trying to garner sympathy, which they are not
going to get in France. They get upset because everyone hates them
and they don't understand why, but they do understand why, and it's
because they act like idiots. And the yapping, it never stops. Yes, the
French are rude. Yes, Paris is beautiful. Yes, the food is amazing. And
yes, we won that war and we kicked Nazi ass and saved civilization,
but it was fifty fucking years ago, stop fucking bringing it up. Stop
bringing it all up. And please, please please please, stay the fuck home
in August. Just stay home and go fishing. Or go to the Monster Truck
Bash. Or shoot some guns into trees. Or jump in your RV and drive
somewhere filled with other Americans, where you can have a giant
BBQ and drink warm beer and throw up in your cooler and stay the
fuck out of Paris.

When I decide I can't take it anymore, can't hear one more fat
dude in a camo T-shirt talk about how the Big Macs in France taste
different, I decide I'm going to leave Paris. Go on my own vacation.
Be like the French, except for the ones who are stuck working and
serving the scourge of tourists. I'm going to run as far and as fast as I
can until the calendar reads September. I meet Philippe for a drink.

I ask him where I should go and he says to Hell. I laugh and tell him
I have that trip planned for later in life. He says avoid the South,
which is packed and miserable in the summer, and avoid the coast
which is cold and packed and miserable in the summer, he says go
somewhere no one else wants to go. Both of my grandfathers were
French immigrants to America. Both came from Alsace after WW1.
One was from Strasbourg, the other from Nancy. One died when I
was two, and the other spent most of my childhood in prison after
he got caught embezzling money from his clients (he was a lawyer
before getting sent away). I can't say I have any real connection to
them, but I think it would be cool to see where they came from,
where I come from. I ask Philippe about going to Alsace, riding
trains and hitchhiking my way there, tell him I like the idea of going
back to the homeland, to the place where my people come from. He
scowls at me, asks me if I'm dumb. I tell him yes, I may very well
be dumb, though I'm not sure why it has taken suggesting a trip to
Alsace for him to realize it. He asks me how dumb I think I am, I
tell him I'm probably a 6 on a Dumb Scale of 1 to 10. He tells me
I'm higher than that, probably an 8, maybe a 9, I tell him I'll go to
a 7, but no higher. He says I'm an 8.5 minimum, but probably a 9.
I ask him what has brought on this sudden analysis of how dumb I
am, he tells me anyone who wants to spend their summer vacation
in Alsace is incredibly dumb, and he wants me to acknowledge it. I
laugh, ask him why going to Alsace is so dumb, he tells me that all
the French leave Alsace in the summer and go south, that the only
people in Alsace right now are Germans, and they're even worse than
Americans. I tell him I want to see where my grandfathers came
from, he laughs.
Do you think there's a fucking sign outside the door, Jay?
I shake my head.
No.

At whatever little shithouse dump where they lived, do you think
there's a fucking sign?

I laugh.

No.

Do you think they're going to have a parade for you?

Probably not.

There's a reason they fucking left and went to America.

Yeah, though I don't really know what it is.

It's because Alsace sucks. It's cold and rainy and miserable. And it's
boring. And in the summer it's full of Germans, who drink gallons of
beer and sing songs about fresh air and war and soccer and Christmas
festivals, and who are the only people on earth worse than Americans.
I don't mind Germans. And I love Americans, as long as they're in
America. Once they're in France they're awful.

I have a much better idea than some dumb pilgrimage to Alsace,
which will only result in you throwing up on yourself after getting
drunk on beer with a bunch of Germans.

What's that, Philippe?

I'll take a couple days off.

I thought you said garbagemen don't get days off.

If I spill some garbage on my head I can call in sick for a few days.

Great plan.

Right?

What kind of garbage are you going to spill on your head?

Something nasty. Like rotten food. Probably seafood. Rotten
shellfish can make you really sick. Especially if you dump a big bin
of it on your head.

Great.

I know just the place.

Do it.

I will. Tonight.

And what should we do with your days off?

Amsterdam?

I don't really like weed, and I just spent a couple nights on rue Saint-Denis.

Fun?

I don't really know.

So fun.

Yeah.

Berlin?

You just said you hated Germans.

They aren't really German in Berlin. They're Berliners.

Too far.

We could see the wall, take a piss on it.

Too far.

It's a shame you don't have a girlfriend.

Why?

I'd get Laura and we could go away somewhere.

Where?

My parents own hotels. We just pick one and go.

And have a romantic couples vacation?

Or you and I get drunk and do dumb shit and the women casually sip fancy wine and complain about what idiots we are.

That sounds pretty fun.

Super fucking fun.

Sorry to let you down.

You don't know anyone?

I know one girl, maybe.

Call her.

Don't know her number.

Go to her place.

Don't know where she lives.

Sounds serious.

I laugh.

Who is she?

It's the girl from the bar.

The model?

Yeah.

She's really cool and funny and beautiful.

She is all of those things.

If I was her I wouldn't go away with you.

Can't argue with that.

She'd probably get along with Laura.

I would think.

But you don't have her number or know where she lives.

Nope.

Good luck with that.

I'll go by the bar where we saw her, ask her friend.

That's a long shot, Jay.

It's the only one I've got.

Philippe finishes his drink. Tells me to call him in the morning and let him know my plan, tells me that whatever I do, he's dumping the seafood on his head and taking a few days off and heading out with his lady. He leaves, I order another drink, another, another, build up my courage another. I finish start walking through Saint-Germain across Pont des Arts past the back of the Louvre past all the little pet shops on Quai de la Mégisserie into the 4th past Les Halles filled with break-dancers North Africans selling shit from North Africa past buskers singing love songs in French and English past men selling flowers. I stop and buy a rose from an old man with a bucket full of them. A simple red rose. Just one. If I see her. Whether she says yes or no. A simple beautiful deep-red rose. If I see her.

I walk into La Comédie. It's half-full. No Americans, except for me.
I see Petra behind the bar walk over sit down on a stool they have
good tall broken-in bar stools here soft cushion but not too soft.
Petra sees me smiles walks over says

Hi.

Hi.

Drinking?

Double Jack and coke.

She laughs.

So American.

Starts making the drink.

Looking for Katerina?

Maybe.

She laughs.

You're not a regular, and this place isn't much of an attraction.

It's not bad.

It's fine. Easy. A place where people come for a drink before they go
somewhere else, or for a nightcap on their way home.

She hands me my drink. It's strong, good. The whiskey burns, the
sugar soothes it. She watches me taste it, smiles.

It's more than a double.

I smile.

Just the way I like it.

I take another sip. Petra holds up a finger, indicates she'll be back,
moves down the bar to help another customer. I set the rose on the
bar, stare at it, wonder where she is, Katerina, Katerina, Katerina,
I stare at the rose it's simple and deep red beautiful for Katerina I
wonder where she is I wonder. Petra comes back.

That's cute.

I laugh.

Thanks.

She's used to guys sending her fifty of those, or taking her shopping in the Triangle d'Or, or zooming off to Monaco or Capri or Ibiza for the weekend.

I could only afford one.

Maybe that's why she likes you.

I smile.

She tell you that?

She smiles.

She's a bit crazy, but she doesn't normally fuck guys in the bathroom.

I smile again.

Good to know.

I take another sip, burns, soothes.

Any idea where she is?

She shakes her head.

Nope.

Think she'll be around at all?

No idea.

I finish the drink.

If she does...

What should I tell her?

You know Polly Maggoo?

She laughs.

That place is a dump.

Sure is.

Doesn't even have toilets.

Something charming about a hole in the floor.

That's your spot?

Yeah.

It's not Ibiza.

Maybe that's why she likes me.

She laughs, I leave some money on the bar, enough for a solid tip,
pick up my rose, stand.

Thanks for the drink. You make them well.

No problem.

See you around.

Yeah.

I leave walk back through the edge of the Marais across Pont au
Change, Île de la Cité, Pont Saint-Michel. The sun is down it's dark
the streetlights are glowing sidewalks crowded tourists everywhere
the cafés bars and restaurants full I hear music voices laughter the
whine of motor scooters an occasional horn I smell food everywhere
deep heavy magnificent food I had a small piece of a baguette in the
morning I almost threw it up and nothing since I'm hungry as fuck
everywhere I go I smell food drifting through the dark through the
glow through the noise the smell of food drifting hungry.

I carry the rose with me. Guard it. Make sure no one bumps into it,
hits it. It's her rose. Red and solitary. For her. Only her. Sometimes
I keep it near my chest, near my heart, sometimes I let it fall to my
side. It's been a week since I saw her. Since she kissed me good bye
and went into the night. Left me in the bathroom with my pants at
my ankles and my heart pounding, hands shaking, dizzy and happy
and dreaming, closed the door behind her and walked away. I've
been to *The Gates of Hell,* didn't see her, the d'Orsay didn't see her,
through Montmartre and Le Marais didn't see her, Saint-Germain
didn't see her, walked avenue Montaigne and les Champs-Élysées
didn't see her, tried to get into Les Bains Douches they wouldn't let
me in didn't see her. As I walk now with a rose in my hand half-
drunk and hungry I look for her in every café down every alley in
every shadow in the ring of light from every lamp at every table in
every door at every chair I carry the rose, protect it, keep it safe, red

and solitary, for her, her, her, I walk and I see and I smell and I look
for her, for her.

Turn down rue de la Huchette no cars just people and Greek
restaurants the smell of roast lamb I walk past Maison de Gyros
in all of its glory the smell makes me insane the idea of a giant
greasy pile of fake lamb and French fries and hot sauce makes me
drool. I have enough money to eat or drink it's an easy decision. I
cross rue du Petit Pont the large doors of Polly Maggoo are open I
can hear Led Zeppelin playing chairs have been moved out of the
dark dingy interior onto the sidewalk a couple are filled a couple
knocked over a couple empty. I walk into the bar order an absinthe
they only serve it to regulars look around. A bunch of old drunk
Algerians, a couple very drunk old French, a couple large thugs of
unknown origin huddled against the wall, a single woman, looks
like she's in her sixties but probably much younger, sitting at the bar
drunk and mumbling. No tourists. Not a one. With all of the sweet
French fancy bars and cafés nobody wants to come to Polly and
get stared at by a bunch of crazy, often hostile idiot drunks, myself
included. I pick up my drink walk outside sit down in one of the
chairs watch the world go by, couples hand-in-hand groups of girls
laughing groups of young men shouting an old couple silent and
content, families looking around half-lost half-awed, it's summer
in Paris hot and dark and alive, hot dark alive. After three glasses of
absinthe, the edges of lights start to blur my thoughts start to blur
my body starts to blur sounds echo *boom boom* I can feel the world
spinning literally feel see hear it spinning *boom boom* hot and dark
and alive *boom*. The rose is sitting on my lap safe and intact, red of
petals deeper, heavier, sweeter, I stare and wish I could fall, swim,
lose myself, drown in it deep heavy sweet red take me drown. I'm at
the point of the night where I can go home or go to the unknown,
to oblivion. Every drink I take will move me closer to blackout, to

loss, to the hell of walking unconsciousness, to the bliss of it. Every drink will further blur the edges until everything blurs, will make the world spin more and more and more, make every sound explode, every drink I take will hasten the darkness, the loss of memory and control, the loss of humanity, every drink will further reduce me to a grunting screaming madman, every drink I take will hasten hasten hasten the loss. I reach this point every night, have this choice every night, I am aware that I make this choice every night, I am aware and I know and every single fucking night I go there. Oblivion desolation loss rage violence idiocy the unknown darkness, the darkest darkness black. I know and I'm aware and I choose and I go. Oblivion and desolation and blackness I go.

I stand go back to the bar I'm going to order a double I am going to fucking go dark black desolate it is time for me to check the fuck out of the world for a while check the fuck out. Polly is more crowded now, more tourists, Germans Americans Canadians a few English a few Irish most drawn by the rumor of available absinthe though some drawn by a place that doesn't shine the way everything else in Saint-Michel shines. The regulars are all sitting in the corners in the shadows on the edges, isolated and scowling, lost in their drunkenness, dreaming through the blur of inebriation that September arrives soon, that all these motherfuckers go home. I move through the crowd slowly, each step an effort my legs heavy feet heavy body heavy, I'm unsteady and off-balance each step, each step. I hear some yelling, turn toward two large Irish and two large Germans facing off, somebody spilled a drink and somebody refused to apologize and somebody said something dumb, the pushing has started the punches are coming soon. Polly is a small place, it's going to erupt and it is going to be magnificent. Chairs tables glasses bottles fists and feet blood and damage, the whole bit, it is going to be magnificent.

I love fights. Love watching them develop, watching them happen, watching how people engage in them, whether they run or throw punches, love watching shit get wrecked, watching how people act in victory and in defeat. Most fights are dumb and disappointing. Men yelling at each other, throwing a couple wild haymakers that miss, grabbing each other and rolling around on the ground before they run out of breath and get separated and yell some more. Every now and then, though, you get a good one. Dudes are sober enough or brave enough or skilled enough or smart or sneaky enough to land a punch, to do some damage, to provide some entertainment. And as much as I love watching a fight, I love being in them. Not because I'm very good at fighting, because I'm not, and not because I win, because most of the time I don't, but I love them for the simple thrill, for the excitement, for the danger, for the unknown. A fight makes your fucking heart beat, beat, beat faster. That moment, however long or however brief, when you know it's going to happen, but you don't know how or exactly when or how it is going to end. It's humanity at its most base, it's man five thousand years ago, when we fought for food, for water, for shelter, for survival, grunting idiots throwing each other around until one of us submitted, until one of us won.

I arrive at the bar. The bartender, a Turk in his fifties named Omer who always wears black heavy-metal concert T-shirts and smokes cigarillos that smell like dogshit, motions toward the four about to fight, speaks.

Do me a favor?

What?

Get that outside.

There are fights in here all the time.

Usually between people too drunk to do any damage. Those idiots are going to fuck this place up.

You want me to fight all four of them?

Just get them out of here.

I'm too fucking drunk.

You won't feel the pain.

Probably right about that.

Help me out.

What do I get out of it?

A night of free booze.

For just me or friends?

Just you.

Absinthe included?

No.

Two nights, absinthe included.

No.

The yelling is louder, they're pushing each other, four big dumb meathead tourists. One of them bumps into a table, glasses fall, shatter. Omer pushes me away.

Fine. Two nights, absinthe, go.

I smile, hand him my rose.

Hold this, protect it.

Protect my bar and this will be just fine.

I laugh, turn toward the four, take a few steps toward them, yell

You dumb fucks.

They keep pushing each other.

HEY. YOU. BIG DUMB UGLY MOTHERFUCKERS.

They stop pushing each other, look at me.

**We don't like dumb pieces of shit like you fucks coming in here
and causing trouble. You understand me?**

I'm fifty pounds lighter than the smallest of them. I have no chance
and I know it. But I'm still thrilled, heart beating, ready. I smile.

You understand me you fat ugly tourist shitbags?

The largest of them steps forward. He's a German in a tank top, short blond Nazi hair.

Are you talking to us?

I am.

Seriously?

Nice tank top, fuckboy.

He looks down at it, it's bright green and has some German writing on it, it's ridiculous.

What's wrong with my tank top?

You think people wanna see your fat arms and your back hair? They don't, you dumb fuck. You look like a fucking idiot.

Fuck you.

Let's take it outside, TankTop.

You want to fight me?

We kicked your ass in France in '44 and '45, I'm gonna kick your ass in France right now, you sausage-eating mouth-breathing lager-drinking motherfucker.

I turn and walk out of the bar onto the sidewalk. Everyone in Polly is watching, laughing. Some of the regulars have gotten out of their seats to see what happens. TankTop and his friend and the Irish are coming out after me. I know I'm doomed, that I'm about to get crushed, that I have absolutely no chance. All I want, aside from the two nights of free drinking, is to get in one shot, to make one of them hurt as much as they are going to hurt me. My only chance at that is to be devious and sneaky and quick and get it in first. I take a deep breath. The four are stepping out. I hold up my hands like a boxer, I know that TankTop will watch my hands. I'm wearing combat boots, which have steel toes. I smile, wave my hands around, try to distract.

You ready, TankTop?

Shut up.

I pretend to throw a punch, he flinches.

You ready, SausageBoy?

Shut the fuck up.

After I kick your ass, I'm going to find your local Christmas Festival and take a shit on your mama's apple strudel.

He charges, throws a punch at me, as he does I kick him in the shin with the steel toe of my boot. We both land. A kick to the shin is a brutally effective and entirely unexpected fighting technique, and the waving of my hands and the blabber from my mouth was to distract him from its imminent arrival. He starts screaming, falls to the ground. A punch to the eye, and in this case, specifically to my eye, is also an effective fighting technique, and I stumble backward, my balance gone, most of what remains of my consciousness gone. His friend and the two Irish are immediately on me, throwing punches, kicking. I do the only thing I can, which is fall down and curl up in a ball and hope it ends soon. They punch me, kick me, punch me some more, kick me some more. Head face ribs arms shoulders stomach thighs back of the thighs, one of them kicks me on the side of my ass, which hurts immensely. I don't know how long it lasts, maybe fifteen or twenty seconds, but it feels like a decade or two. I hear some yelling, the word *stop* in both French and English, hear TankTop screaming about his leg, Omer telling them to leave or he'll call the police, hear them telling Omer to go fuck himself. I lie on the ground, curled up, in pain, everything hurts, my ears are ringing, I can feel blood running down the side of my face. I feel a presence looming over me, hear Omer asking me if I'm okay, feel his hand on my back, asking me again if I'm okay. And despite every part of my body hurting like a motherfucker, especially the side of my ass, which feels like someone drove a rusty iron spike into it, and despite the fact that I'm bleeding and can feel my eye swelling, I am okay. Physical pain passes. With enough drink, and enough drugs, I won't feel anything. And the physical pain is nothing compared to the pain I inflict on myself. Hit me kick me beat me I don't care. You can't hurt me as much as I've already hurt myself.

I uncurl, sit up. I blink my eyes about fifty times, everything is blurry. I look around see the street the streetlights cars people walking past people staring I see Omer smiling at me, I see people standing along the edge of the large French doors that lead into the bar. Everything fucking hurts I wipe my hand along the edge of my eye it comes back red I can feel the eye swelling. I laugh. What a fight. Got my ass kicked, but it was fun. And the look on TankTop's face when I told him I was gonna shit on his mama's strudel, openmouthed big-eyed surprise, followed by rage, it was worth it just for that. And no real damage, nothing that will be visible in a week.

Omer offers me his hand and I take it he helps me stand fuck it all hurts everything hurts. He smiles, speaks.

You're a good boy.

I need a fucking drink.

He laughs.

Whatever you want.

Triple Jack and Coke.

I'll bring you two.

We step toward the bar.

How bad is my face?

Small cut, you'll probably have a black eye.

Where did they go?

He points toward place Saint-Michel.

That way.

Another step, two.

You got my rose?

Yeah.

Can you bring it with the drinks?

He laughs.

Of course.

I sit in the first available chair I see. Take out my cigarettes. Omer pats my back, which hurts, says he'll be right back. I light a cigarette, take a deep drag, lean back in the chair, pick up a napkin, press it against the cut at the corner of my eye. My heart is still pounding, it will take a while to slow down, a couple of the other regulars come over to shake my hand and laugh and see if I'm okay, they compliment me on my shin-kick move, as soon as Omer comes back with the drink I take half of it in a single swallow the whiskey burns and the sugar soothes and I'm slightly better. I sit with the regulars for a while, we keep laughing, wonder where TankTop is now, eventually they drift back to their own tables their own shadows their own loneliness and pain, they drift back to their own alcoholism and misery. I finish my drink have another, everything hurts less, I don't get out of my chair except to piss, I smoke and watch people walk past and slowly make my way toward oblivion, toward the darkest darkness.

I don't know what time it is but the crowds are thinning. It's deep night, when the only people out are looking for something. Looking for drink, looking for drugs, looking for sex or love, looking for a friend, looking for a fight, looking for trouble or adventure, looking for enlightenment or damnation, looking for sin, looking to find something everything whatever they can find, looking. I love the night, love the darkness, the simplicity, the menace, the possibility, the emptiness, the heaviness, the stillness, the quiet, the echoes, streets with no cars and parks with no people, buildings with no lights and vacant trains still running, my mind is clear my heart pure I feel everything more deeper truer in the deep hours of the darkest night I love.

I look down at the cracked broken scarred sidewalk laugh about my dumb fight reach for my glass it's cold and sweating almost empty I move the glass toward my lips and I look up and I see her.

Long red hair heavy and flowing.

Light-brown eyes like cocoa.

Pouty lips like cherry pie.

Smiling.

Walking toward me.

Smiling.

Some kind of little white designer dress.

Smiling.

Adidas sneakers.

Smiling.

I smile and raise a hand smile wider I'm happy to see her so happy I kept the rose safe I smile wider and stand everything hurts I smile and stand she speaks.

Writer Boy.

I smile.

Model Girl.

What the fuck happened to you?

I laugh.

Got in a fight.

Ten feet away both smiling.

I guess you lost?

Laugh again.

Yeah.

Five feet away.

How'd the other guy look?

There were four of them.

She laughs.

You fucking idiot.

She steps into me, kisses me, softly no tongue her lips on the edges
of mine moving slightly I can feel her breath and smell fading
perfume, I reach for her hand and take it she kisses me softly
whispers

I heard you were looking for me.

I was.

What do you need?

This.

So I can go?

No.

Please?

No.

Pretty please?

Whatever you want.

She smiles so close her breath on my lips and cheek the smell of
fading perfume her hand in mine our eyes open pale green and light
brown cocoa into each other our eyes. I move the rose into her hand,
she takes it.

I got you a rose.

I saw it in your hand, I was wondering.

Now you know.

Why do I get such a sweet and wonderful gift?

Because you make my heart beat faster.

She puts her free hand on my chest, above my heart.

I can feel it.

Good.

She takes my hand, puts it on her chest.

Can you feel mine?

Yes.

Also beating faster.

Yes.

You like that, Writer Boy?

I do, Model Girl.

She kisses me, softly, the tip of her tongue on my lips, on my tongue, slowly, dancing, slowly dancing. It's a long kiss fifteen seconds, thirty, we keep our eyes open stare lock hands both of our hands we kiss our lips and tongue and breath slowly, softly dancing, our hearts beating faster, a kiss for a minute she smiles and pulls away.

Can I stay awhile?

I'd dig that.

Get a chair for me?

Take mine.

I step away from her, from my chair, motion for her to sit in it.

You want a drink?

Champagne?

Doubt they have it, but I'll ask.

If not, one of whatever you're having.

I walk into the bar, almost everyone in it is in oblivion, I ask Omer if he has champagne he tells me he has one bottle. I ask him if I can trade the bottle for one of my free nights he sees Katerina sitting outside, smiles.

For her?

Yeah.

You know her?

Yeah.

Girlfriend?

No.

Potential girlfriend?

Maybe.

And this will help you?

Probably.

Have you fucked her?

Fuck off, man.

I want to know.

Fuck off.

He laughs.

Just wanted to see if you actually liked her.

Now you know.

He turns around opens a small refrigerator, pulls out a bottle of
Freixenet, which isn't real champagne and is something slightly
tastier than carbonated horse piss. He sets it on the counter in front
of me.

You know how to open it?

Yeah.

He sets two glasses next to the bottle.

I'll expect details.

I laugh.

Fuck off.

I pick up the bottle and the glasses walk back set them down on the
table pull a chair from another table sit down next to Katerina, next
to Katerina, she smiles.

Got me the good stuff.

I laugh.

All they had.

She grabs the bottle, tears off the foil, looks around, speaks.

Pick a target.

What do you mean?

I'm an expert corkswoman. Could blast a fly off a horse's ass from
fifty feet. Pick a target.

I smile look around. Polly's is half-empty, no tourists, streets almost
entirely empty. A man passed out in the corner, a few solitary
drinkers, a couple men with drinks and books, a couple arguing over

something I can't hear them, two middle-aged businessmen sitting inside playing chess, one of them who's wearing a hat is nodding off his head falling until he wakes up startled, awake until his head starts falling again. I know them by face, though not by name, they come in once a week and play chess and drink, they don't talk to anyone but each other, by the time they're done neither can walk or talk, I have no idea where they go or how. Katerina sees me looking at them and smiles.

I won't hurt him.

She holds the bottle, expertly weighs it in her hands, gives it a slight shake. She points the neck of the bottle toward the man as he's nodding off again she gradually eases the cork out of it until

Pop.

The cork flies across the entrance of Polly and into the bar, and just as the man's head falls, the cork hits the brim of his hat, knocking the hat off his head and onto the chess set, the pieces all fall. The man jumps, shocked, knocks the table over, sending his drink and his friend's drink and the chess set onto the other man's lap. That man jumps, his lap covered with beer, and starts yelling. The other man is on his knees looking for his hat. I look at Katerina, who is watching them, and smiling and giggling, and I speak.

That was fucking amazing.

She turns to me, smiles.

I wish we had another bottle.

I laugh.

Me too.

She stands, the man has his hat back on his head, his friend is still yelling at him, he's looking around trying to figure out what happened, she picks up the bottle.

Let's get out of here.

Already been in one fight tonight.

Would you defend me?
I would.
Such a sweet boy.
She kisses my cheek, I laugh, she takes my hand, we start walking
away.
Into the night
The darkness
The possibility
Hands held
Smiling
A bottle of champagne
The night
And the darkness
Empty streets and a clear black sky.
Possibilities.

Don't Tell

When you're young
They don't tell you
That life
No matter how it works out
For good or bad
Rich or poor
Happy or not
Life
Never really changes
You will always feel
Lost
Confused
Insecure
And alone
Like a failure
Like you could do more
Be better
Smarter
Work harder
Like everyone knows something
You
Don't
Know
As if redemption or joy or security
Is right around the corner
As if
Someday
Everything will be okay
When you're young

They don't tell you
That no matter
Whether
You find
What you're looking for
Get
What you want
Earn
What you need
That no matter
Whether
You make your dreams
Big or small
Reasonable or outlandish
Private or public
Come true
That you will never feel
Safe
Loved
Accepted
Comfortable
Strong
Sure
Serene
Satisfied
Whole
Complete
That whatever happiness you know
Will be
Fleeting
Vanishing

Like mist
A mirage
Streams of the warm summer sun
Like a song
You hear it
Feel it
Lose yourself in it
You're delighted
Inspired
Rapturous
You stop thinking
Or knowing
You just feel
Until it ends
Until it ends
And
It
Always
Ends
When you're young
They don't tell you
That your heart will break
And
It
Will
Never
Heal
That
Your heart
Will break
Again and again

Again and again
Your heart will break
Again
And
Again
And it will
Never heal
Never
Never
When you're young
They don't tell you
So you believe
You believe
You believe
When you're young

Paris, 1992

Lying in bed my arms around her we're face-to-face her arms
around me our heads on the same pillow our eyes open staring
into each other open. Louis isn't home. It's late morning the heat is
already up neither of us is wearing anything, there's a simple white
sheet covering our bodies. She leans forward, kisses me softly, licks
my lips with the tip of her tongue, playfully bites my lower lip. I
smile as she moves away, I speak.
Good morning, Katerina.
Good morning, Jay.
Kind of a wonderful way to wake up.
You like it?
I do.
Want more of it?
Yes.
Yes?
Yes.
She smiles.
Yes.
I smile she moves forward, lips, tongues, breath, hands moving, legs
wrapping around each other the white sheet goes away she rolls me
over she's on top of me holds my arms down kisses my neck licks my
ear her nipples rubbing against my chest hard she whispers
Do you like this, Jay?
Yes.
Want more of it?
Yes.
Holding my arms down licking my ear kissing my neck she moves
down whispers
Don't move.

She kisses my neck chest nipples her tongue circling around I
shudder a wave of ecstasy moves through me her lips and tongue on
my stomach lower her hands on my chest I shudder the insides of
my thighs shudder takes me into her hand speaks.

You ready, Jay?

Yes.

Tell me.

I'm ready, Katerina.

Her hand is moving slowly up and down slowly our eyes are locked.

Ready for what?

You.

Me.

Yes.

Runs her tongue slowly from base to tip shudder.

Ready for this?

Yes.

Say please.

Please.

Tongue around the tip eyes locked hands down she takes me into
her mouth I shudder she moves slowly up and down our eyes locked
slowly

Up.

Slowly.

Down.

Shudder.

She never looks away I want to close my eyes lose myself in sensation
and joy lose myself in her lips and tongue but we stay locked I
shudder again and again she moves slowly up and down I shudder.
She lifts her head smiles.

Like that, Jay?

Love.

What else do you want?

Everything.

She moves up, her hands running up my arms, her body up my body.

Everything?

Yes.

Yes.

Yes.

Yes.

She kisses me lifts her hips reaches down moves me toward her, lower her hips I'm at the edges almost in her and I can feel her wet almost inside, almost, she speaks.

Is this what you want?

You know.

Tell me.

Yes.

Tell what me you want.

To be inside you.

Me.

Yes.

She smiles she's over me and on top of me holding my arms down at the wrists our eyes are locked she lowers her hips I raise mine I move inside her inside warm and wet and tight and calm and peaceful and ecstatic and joyous I softly moan she moans our eyes are locked she whispers

How's that feel, Jay?

Mmmmmm.

She lowers her hips deeper deeper deeper she smiles.

No words?

I smile, shake my head.

Lower, deeper.

I love how you feel inside me.

I smile.

Lower.

Deeper.

Be a good boy for me.

Smile wider.

Don't cum too fast.

Lower and deeper until she can't go any farther she starts slowly moving her hips we're both softly moaning she's holding down my arms I could move but I don't want to move, I don't ever want to move. And it's not just deep and hard inside her, it's not the smell of sex or the sweat or the heat, it's not her deep heavy red hair hanging, it's not her beautiful small nipples hard and covered with my spit, it's not her soft moans like some song from paradise, it's not her pussy the sweetest tightest wettest I have ever had the absolute pleasure to experience, it's not that being inside her makes me feel safe and warm and happy and eternal it almost makes me believe in God it's so wonderful, it's none of those things no matter how magnificent, I don't ever want to move because of her eyes. Light brown like cocoa they're open slightly a deep sparkle inside them like a light into me, into my heart and mind and soul, a light that goes forever and ever and ever her eyes are smiling and laughing and singing and dancing and they're the most beautiful things I have ever seen and they make me believe that life isn't the steaming pile of shit I know it is they are so beautiful, they are so beautiful, they are so beautiful I don't ever want to move.

She keeps moving gradually faster but never too fast I almost cum once twice three times four I stop myself I don't ever want to move or stop looking into her eyes and I want to be in her forever. She leans down starts kissing me her tongue dancing along my lips dancing with my tongue she bites my lips moves her hips faster faster faster whispers

I want to cum, Jay.

Reaches down with one of her hands starts rubbing her clit.

I want to cum and I want you to cum.

Faster

Lips tongue

Inside her

I want to cum.

Her hand on her clit

Faster

Faster

Faster

I want you to cum.

Faster faster faster faster

Short breaths stifled moans with each movement of her hips another lips and tongues holding me down I start to cum she can feel she arches her back red hair falling over her chest I start to cum my cock throbbing inside her I can feel her stomach tightening she stops breathing still moving faster faster I'm cumming inside her white God safe secure ecstatic white God exploding God joyous God she leans down her eyes open light brown like cocoa beautiful sparkling dancing singing I don't ever want to move short of breath smiling moaning ever.

Ever.

Ever.

She lies on top of me I'm still hard still inside of her, she kisses me puts her head on my chest lets go of my hands I put my arms around her. She's sweating, breathing heavy so am I, sweating and breathing heavy, hands quivering heart beating body tingling so am I.

We lie there don't speak. The sun is up and streaming through the white sheer drapes in front of the French windows. The world is awake outside voices and cars, footsteps. I smell her hair falling over

my chest like faded flowers I smell the remnants of her perfume
I smell sex and cum. I close my eyes, our breathing slows we lie
together for five minutes, ten, thirty, I don't know how long we lie
there in each other's arms, she lifts her head and looks up at me and
smiles.

I have some rules, Jay.

Don't cum inside you again?

No, I love that.

Really?

So much.

I don't want to have a kid.

I haven't had my period in two years. Occupational hazard. No need
to worry.

Cool.

Back to the rules.

Okay.

My rules.

What kind of rules?

Rules for whatever we are.

What are we?

Friends.

Cool.

Friends who fuck.

Even better.

I don't want a boyfriend.

I'm not really boyfriend material.

Don't ask where I live, don't try to find me, don't be upset or mad or
have temper tantrums if I'm not around or we don't see each other.

Cool.

Don't ever say I love you.

What if I do?

What?

Love you.

You don't.

How do you know?

We barely know each other.

That doesn't matter.

It does to me.

No, it doesn't.

How do you know?

I just do.

You're wrong.

I'm right.

No.

We love each other. I know it, you know it. We don't have to say it.

And I won't. Ever. But it's true, and we both know it.

She laughs.

Fuck off, Jay.

I laugh.

Okay. Cool.

I'm serious.

I got it. You have rules. You're serious. Cool.

She laughs.

Making fun of me?

Yes.

I'll kick your ass.

You think?

You looked in the mirror yet today?

I've been busy.

She laughs again.

You're pretty fucked-up.

Yeah, I can feel it.

I'll go easy on you for the next few days.

Next few days?

Didn't you ask me to go away with you last night?

I did.

So the next few days.

You're saying yes?

She smiles.

I can call Philippe and we go away together?

She nods.

Yes.

I smile.

Wonderful.

But I have to stop at home first.

Cool.

Alone.

I got it.

We can meet at the train station.

Great.

But we're just friends, Jay, not boyfriend and girlfriend

I'm not boyfriend material, Katerina.

In an odd, very fucked-up way, you kind of are.

If you actually think that, you're even more fucked-up than I am.

I might be.

I hope not.

You never know.

Let me believe what I want to believe, which is that you're some kind
of smart, funny wiseass who likes the right kinds of art and reads the
right kinds of books and has badass opinions about them, who is
the best kisser in the world, who fucks like an angel, and who is the
coolest, most beautiful girl I have ever met or seen, and definitely
ever been in bed with.

She smiles, a wide smile, a true smile.

Thank you, Jay. That's the nicest thing anyone has ever said to me.

I have a black heart, but sometimes it sings, and sometimes there are stars in it.

She laughs, punches me.

You might actually become a famous writer with lines like that.

I'm gonna burn the fucking world down.

You might.

I will.

She smiles, wide and true.

Yes, you will.

She kisses me a quick sweet peck on the lips, stands, gets dressed.

I light a cigarette, watch her get dressed, which I know is kind of creepy, but I am kind of fucked-up, and I do have a black heart, which only sometimes sings and only sometimes has stars in it, and because as I told her, she is the most beautiful girl I have ever seen. When she's finished she kisses me again, another sweet quick peck.

Which station?

Gare de Lyon.

Twelve thirty?

Yes.

See you there, Writer Boy.

See you there, Model Girl.

She smiles.

Leaves.

I sit in bed and smoke a cigarette.

My black, black heart.

Sings.

Shines.

Los Angeles, 2017

You believe in love at first sight?

Yeah.

Ever happened to you?

Yeah.

More than once?

What do you think?

Yes.

Yes.

Yes.

Yes.

How many times?

Couple million.

Hahaha.

I'm serious. And it might be more than a couple, might be like eight million.

You're still funny.

Yeah, Mr. FunnyMan, the King of Comedy.

How many times?

Why?

I'm curious.

Why?

You know why.

You want to know.

Yes.

Yes.

Tell me.

Literally first sight?

Yes.

Can't be second sight, or third or fourth?

Now you're just fucking with me.

I am.

Mr. FunnyMan, the King of Comedy.

That's me.

Literally first.

Four.

Who?

A girl in eighth grade. I had started a new school and she was sitting in front of me in English class. Fuck, I was crazy for her. The first time and all. Just fucking crazy.

And was she for you?

Eventually.

What happened?

She was a ballet dancer and went away to school when we were sixteen. Even then, I was drunk and crazy and addicted and it just collapsed.

Where is she now?

In the town where we grew up. Teaching dance, raising a kid. I think she's happy, hope she is.

Next.

A girl in college.

San Francisco?

Yeah.

I know that story. You had to choose, Paris and the dream, or her.

Yeah.

You made the right decision.

One of the few good ones I have made in my life.

You're too hard on yourself.

No, I'm not.

You are.

I've left a trail of wreckage behind me, don't think I don't know it.

Next.

You know.

Tell me.

You already know.

I want you to tell me.

You.

Me.

Yes.

Say it.

I fell in love with you the first time I saw you, immediately, the first second, the first ten seconds, the first thirty, it was over, I was done, in love, with you.

At *The Gates*.

With my dumb little notebook.

It was cute.

I was 21.

So young.

Young and lost and desperately in love sitting in front of *The Gates of Hell*.

I remember it so well.

Me too.

Your dirty white T-shirt and combat boots.

Your crazy beautiful skull dress.

I don't want to cry.

I don't either.

Do you need me to say it?

No.

I did.

I know.

Immediately.

I know.

Lost and found and head-over-heels and scared shitless.

I don't want to cry.

I don't either.

I fucked it all up.

You didn't.

I'm sorry. So sorry.

We both fucked up. We were both monsters. Let's move on.

I've wanted to say I'm sorry for 25 years.

Now you have, move along.

Next.

Yes, next.

My last one.

Four of four.

My wife.

When?

I was 28. In Los Angeles. Venice. I had just moved there. Gotten a little house. She lived next door. As I was moving shit in, walking through the little front gate, she came out of her house with her roommate. She was wearing running shorts and a T-shirt, hair in a ponytail. I looked over, and I was just stunned, and speechless, and my arms were full of boxes, and I set them down, and I said hi, and she smiled and waved and said hi, and I knew, however we know this kind of thing, that I was going to marry her, spend my life with her, I knew as much as I've ever known anything.

How long did it take?

We were close friends for a couple years. And I loved her the entire time, more and more the longer I knew her. I wasn't ready to be married, was still struggling to write a book, had done a bunch of shit in Hollywood but it was all garbage, and I was scared, scared of being married, scared of that commitment, scared that I wasn't worthy of her. She started dating someone and moved to San Francisco and I missed her. I just missed being around her every day. Talking to her, hearing her opinions on shit, hearing her laugh, watching her think, I just fucking missed her. So I called and told her to come home, that I knew she didn't love the dude she was with more than she loved me, and that I wanted her to come home and we'd get married.

And?

She told me to fuck off.

I like her.

You would.

She still tell you to fuck off?

All the time.

I really, really like her.

Like I said...

And?

And what?

And what happened?

I told her to go look in the mirror, to look herself in the eye, to try to tell herself she didn't love me more than the dude she lived with, and if she could, we didn't ever need to see each other again, and if she couldn't, she should come back to Los Angeles so we could get married. She came back a couple months later, we dated for six months, got engaged, got married.

And?

And I still love her. In a lifetime full of terrible decisions, it's the best one I ever made. She's smarter and funnier and cooler than me, a better person than me. And she makes me a better person than I actually am.

That makes me happy.

Thank you.

☺☺☺

Please, no.

Not an emoji dude?

I like words.

☹

Please!

I'll stop.

It's your turn now.

What?

I went through my life, or at least this part of it. Your turn now.

Not today.

That ain't fair.

I would like to tell you to fuck off. Like the old days.

I think I can handle it.

Fuck off.

☺

That felt good.

☺☺

Fuck off.

☺☺☺

Paris, 1992

As I walk to Gare de Lyon, I imagine some scene out of a corny romance movie, where I'm standing on the platform, and the train is about to leave, and Katerina hasn't shown up yet, and I'm holding a bouquet of roses, and I'm scanning the station for her, and the whistle blows, and my heart starts to break because she hasn't shown up, and as I scan through the crowd for the final time I see her and my heart is suddenly whole and full and brimming with excitement and joy my heart is literally skipping and I wave to her and she smiles and we lock eyes and I gesture toward the train and motion for her to hurry and she starts to run and as she comes onto the platform the train starts pulling out and we're still smiling and our eyes are locked and I'm gesturing for her to hurry and as she approaches I start moving along the platform so when she's next to me we can move together and when she is I smile and say hi and she smiles and says hi and I say I'm happy you made it and she says I wouldn't miss it for the world and we rush along the platform hand-in-hand trying to catch up to the last open door on the train and we're running and smiling and laughing and we catch it and she jumps in as the doors start to close and I follow jumping in just as the door shuts and we laugh and hug we made it we made it we made it and we give each other a kiss and I say we're going to have a great weekend and she smiles and says yes, the best, absolutely the best weekend ever, the best.

But no such thing happens. I walk into the *gare*, which is a very nice gare as far as French gares go, and I look for the track number for the 12:45 train from Paris to Beaune, which is a small village in Burgundy. I find the track number and walk to the track, and standing there, together, chatting like they've been best friends forever, are Philippe, his girlfriend Laura, and Katerina. Philippe sees me, laughs.

What the fuck happened to your face?

I got in a fight.

Who'd you get in a fight with?

Four dudes. At Polly. Omer was worried they were gonna fight each
other and wreck the place.

Place is already wrecked.

I guess he likes it wrecked as is. He offered me two free nights
drinking if I took them outside. So I did.

You do any damage to them?

Kicked one of them in the shin.

That's it?

Yeah.

They laugh, Philippe looks at Katerina.

You really want to be seen with him like that?

There is a cut over my left eye, which is also black. A bruise on the
right side of my jaw. My arms chest back legs and ass are covered
with bruises, though no one can see any of them. Katerina gives me
a hug.

I like my baby a little beat-up. Makes him cuter.

They laugh, she gives me a sweet little hug and a peck on the
cheek, we walk down the platform and get on the train, no rush,
no running, no triumphant moment as we step across the void. We
walk through the aisles, Philippe bought the tickets and we have
four seats facing each other, a little table between us. I bought four
bottles of cheap wine on my way, a baguette. Laura packed a little
picnic, sandwiches poulets, some fancy stinky cheese, some pâté. We
set it all on the table, Philippe looks at me.

No glasses?

I loaned my crystal to the Louvre for an exhibition, couldn't bring it.

They make paper cups, you know, plastic too.

I reach for one of the bottles.

More fun drinking out of the bottle.

Laura hands me a corkscrew, I smile, hold up the bottle.

It's a screw-off.

They groan, laugh. I unscrew one of the caps, hold up the bottle. Who first?

Katerina points at me.

You first, so we see if it kills you.

I smile, take a long pull, it's strong, cheap wine. A bit bitter, and it burns going down, but it has alcohol in it, so it's good with me. I smile.

It's poison, but you'll need to drink a few gallons of it to die.

They laugh, we open the other bottles, start on the food, though Katerina doesn't touch it. She and Laura talk about clothes, designers, Katerina has all sorts of gossip about them, has walked in shows for many of the designers Laura likes, is already booked for the fall shows, which are at the end of September. She does one or two a day, doesn't really eat in the weeks leading up to them so she's thin, wears the fancy clothes and has her hair and makeup done, does the walking, which she calls prancing, collects her checks. Says the shows don't pay that well, but they help her get the editorial jobs, which pay very well, and help get her campaigns with B-list designers, which pay extremely well. Says she has a couple model friends, but that the business in general can be vicious and competitive, and that the other models can be vicious and competitive, and that she is friendly with everyone, but generally avoids complications. She wants to work, make money, save money, wear beautiful clothes, beautiful jewelry, go on crazy ridiculous spontaneous trips, drink champagne, snort cocaine, dance, fuck, do everything she shouldn't, have magnificent times, the best times, times that she will remember when she's old and can't walk and her grandchildren are tired of her talking about all her amazing times, she wants to be free, unencumbered, liberated, her own woman, to live and feel and work as she pleases, as free as she should be and can be as a twenty-one-year-old in Paris who makes good money, she wants to do as well as she can for as long as she can, see where life takes her, maybe go home, maybe go somewhere else, maybe stay in Paris, who knows. Philippe, who has been reading a business plan, temporarily dropping his gig as garbageman and taking up his role as the heir to his family's business, looks up.

You don't want to marry Jay?

She laughs.

I don't want to marry anyone.

Laura wants to marry me.

Katerina looks at Laura.

Really?

Laura smiles.

He won't be a garbageman forever.

Philippe holds up the business plan.

Eleven more months.

Katerina smiles.

Wedding, kids, the whole bit?

Philippe nods.

If she'll agree to it.

Katerina looks at Laura, who is still smiling.

All in good time.

Philippe sets down the plan.

And I need to sow my wild oats for a while.

Katerina laughs.

With Jay.

Phillipe nods.

Yes, with Jay. Fucking professional oats sower.

I laugh.

I'm not a professional anything. Never have been, never will be.

Katerina punches my arm.

Isn't he cute. The rebel without a cause.

I laugh.

I have a cause.

At the same time, Philippe and Katerina say

Burn the world down.

I laugh.

Write books that burn the world down.

Laura speaks.

What do you mean by that? Burn the world down?

Write books that change people. How they think and feel and live.
How they view the world, how they view themselves. Books that
confront them. Books that scare them. That make them either love
the book or hate it. Books that force people to take a position, that
inspire people to either burn them and ban them, or love them
and defend them. Books that divide. Books that make the world
irrevocably different than it was before they were written. Books that
make history because they changed the world.

Philippe laughs.

I've never heard you say so many sentences in a row before.

Katerina laughs.

I wish he'd do it more often.

Laura looks at me.

Really think you can do that?

Somebody in every generation does. Why not me?

What if you don't?

I will.

But what if you don't.

I have faith in myself. I don't know why, but I do. And I'm going to
do it, I have no doubt.

But what if you don't.

Then I'll die trying, and I'll die without regret.

Laura smiles.

I like that.

Thanks.

You might actually do it.

I smile.

I actually fucking will.

Katerina lifts her bottle.

To burning the fucking world down

We all raise our bottles, say

To burning the fucking world down

And we drink

Drink

Drink.

To burning the fucking world down.

The ride is a little over three hours. Laura and Katerina keep talking, Philippe goes back to his business plan, I read *Les Miserables*, which is a lame and corny Broadway play, but is an amazing and epic fucking book. We arrive in a small cute French town it has a boulangerie, a boucherie, a pâtisserie, a wine shop, a bookstore, a couple restaurants. We take a taxi to a smaller town that has more or less the same shit. We pull up to a series of small limestone buildings, like a mini-château complex, on the edge of the town. They look a couple hundred years old, slightly beat-up, as if they were once beautiful and could be again. As we get out of the cab, Philippe holds up the business plan.

My family is thinking of buying this place. We're supposed to be undercover guests. See if the hotel is any good, if the restaurant is good, if the wine is any good. Don't use my last name while we're here.

I laugh.

Some spy shit.

He nods.

Some super hotel spy shit.

Katerina speaks.

Can I kill someone? Like a real spy.

Philippe points at me.

Him. If he blows my cover. Take him the fuck out.

We laugh, walk through the gates into the hotel, check in. Philippe uses a fake last name, which makes me want to laugh, but I don't. The inside of the hotel is the same as the outside, probably nice once, could be again, a bit run-down and in need of some love. We go to our rooms, agree to meet in the restaurant for dinner in a few hours. As soon as the door to our room is closed, Katerina and I are on each other, lips tongues hands bodies clothing off we fuck against the wall, on the desk, on the floor, in the bed, after we cum I stay hard inside her keep kissing her slowly my hands on her body our eyes open lidded after a few minutes we start fucking again in the bed, slow and deep I move as far inside her as I can I stay there slowly thrust my hips against her we cum again, I stay hard inside her, I stay hard inside her.

We fuck four times before dinner.

Shower together.

Hold hands as we walk to the restaurant.

Dinner is fun. Food is mediocre. Wine is delicious. I drink too much of it. So does Katerina. So does Philippe. Laura is the only one of us who isn't insane. She almost drinks too much, but also knows she'll need to help Philippe back to their room, so she stops long before we do. We eat dessert. Crème brûlée. I love crème brûlée, though this isn't any better than the crème brûlée I can get in America. And it's too burned on top, the crème isn't crèmey

enough. I eat three of them anyway. I'm tired and hungry after
traveling and fucking all day, my body still hurts from getting my
ass kicked, Philippe pays the bill we go back to our rooms. As I
stand at the sink brushing my teeth Katerina comes behind me,
puts her arms around me.

Ready to fuck some more?

I'm tired.

That's a first.

What?

A man who doesn't want to fuck me.

I laugh.

I want to, but I'm tired and drunk and I hurt everywhere.

She kisses my neck.

I have a solution.

Yeah?

Yes.

She steps away, takes my hand, leads me out of the bathroom, sitting
on the glass table at the foot of the bed are two long lines of cocaine.
I smile and my heart immediately starts beating faster, if I were a
dog I'd start drooling.

Where did you get that?

I'm a model in Paris.

Is it good?

Magnificent.

Not the Saint-Denis train station bullshit?

I'm a model in Paris, Jay. You think I do that garbage?

No.

No, I don't.

Get wired and fuck all night?

That's the idea.

I find my pants, take out a roll of francs, pull one off and roll it into a tight tube. I get on my knees in front of the table, Katerina next to me, I offer her the bill.

Ladies first?

I want to watch you go.

My pleasure.

I put the bill in one nostril press the other closed lean over put the bill at the base of the line inhale. Powder moves quickly and easily through the tube and into my nose, it stings burns very slightly chemical very slightly bitter. My heart starts pounding. I close my eyes take a deep breath. Heart pounding. Every bit of insecurity inside of me disappears, every bit of doubt. Heart pounding. I open my eyes everything is brighter, clearer, crisper. Heart pounding. I look at Katerina who is somehow more beautiful, no makeup and deep-red hair everywhere light-brown eyes and freckles and lips somehow more beautiful. Heart pounding. She smiles.

Good?

Yes.

As advertised?

Better.

Happy.

So.

She smiles takes the bill does half her line and we fuck on the floor do more fuck in the bed do more fuck in the shower do more take a bath and play with each other do more go for a walk through the grounds of the hotel into a vineyard find a ridge and sit and watch the sun rise we walk back to the hotel and fuck again in the bed we fuck again. We fall asleep in each other's arms, the sun is high and the birds are singing, we fall asleep in each other's arms and the sun is high and the birds are singing.

*   *   *

Philippe and Laura leave Puligny-Montrachet after two days. Laura has work, and Philippe has garbage to collect. And his mission is complete, he has seen the hotel, can report back to his family, he thinks they should buy it and fix it and make it fancy.

Katerina and I stay for a week.

We sleep late.

Drink coffee at the local café every afternoon.

Read.

Go for walks in town through vineyards along roads long simple walks in the countryside sometimes we hold hands it's warm and simple and calming and right, sometimes we bump hips and shoulders it's playful and flirty and cute and right, sometimes we talk we have long conversations about books or art or how to live or why to live they're intense and passionate and thought-provoking and right every minute every hour every day we spend together is right, right, right.

Sometimes we eat at the hotel restaurant, sometimes we go to one of the places in town, sometimes we don't eat, we just stay in the room and get wired and fuck, again and again, again and again, we stay in the room and get wired and we fuck again and again.

I try to write, but I can't. Whenever Katerina is near me I want to talk to her, listen to her, touch her, kiss her, hold her, allow myself to be held by her, look into her eyes, see her smile and hear her laugh, be inside her, feel her heart beating and feel my heart beating, whenever she's near me I can't think or feel or experience anything but her and I don't want to think or feel or experience anything but her maybe this is because it's new maybe it will fade right now it's real and it's wonderful and it's overwhelming and it's right.

August becomes September I have nothing waiting for me in Paris, or anywhere else, but Katerina does. I tell her we should never go back just find a little hut somewhere nearby a little hut for the two of us she laughs and says it's time I have nothing waiting for me in Paris but she does.

Final night we go out for dinner drink champagne toast smile flirt play footsie hold hands and bump hips as we walk when we get to the hotel we do two final lines split a last bottle of champagne and fuck all night our lips and our tongues and our hands and our eyes all manner of things hard and wet and deep again and again and again. I fall asleep inside her I don't want to ever leave I fall asleep my arms around her I don't want to ever leave I fall asleep my heart beating I don't want to ever leave. She said we can never say I love you and I won't say it but I know.

I know.

I know.

I love you.

*   *   *

We wake up and check out. Katerina wants to pay the bill, I pay it even though I can't really afford it. The hotel gives us a ride to the train station we both fall asleep as soon as the train pulls out. I wake up just before Paris there's a coffee waiting for me, Katerina smiles, speaks.

Hi.

Hi.

Almost home.

How long?

Soon.

Soon like an hour or soon like now?

Maybe fifteen minutes.

Fuck.

She laughs.

Don't like Paris anymore?

Nothing to do with Paris.

Don't want to leave me?

No, I don't.

She smiles.

That's cute of you, Jay.

I'm a cute dude, Katerina.

A cute monster.

Won't disagree with that.

Seems like we were gone a long time.

We were.

More like six years than six days.

A fun, sweet, amazing trip.

Yes.

Yes.

She smiles, I smile.

Thanks for the invite.

Thanks for accepting it.

I'm happy I did.

We should do it again.

Maybe.

Maybe?

Maybe.

Definitely.

For now we say good-bye.

What do you mean?

Exactly what I said. For now we say good-bye.

Good-bye can mean an hour or a day or a month or forever.

Probably not forever, though you never really know. But it's going to be for a while.

What do you mean?

She laughs.

Exactly what I said.

I thought we had a great time.

We did.

So?

Great times end.

I don't understand.

I told you before we left there were rules, and I told you I didn't want to fall in love.

You told me to never say I love you.

One thing leads to another.

I'm not saying it.

And I'm not letting myself go there.

Too late.

Maybe for you, not for me.

Too late.

No, it's not.

It is.

You have books to write, the world to burn down, I have clothes to wear and shows to be in and pictures to smile for and money to make.

I'm not gonna stop you from doing any of that, or from doing anything you want to do.

No, you're not.

What's that mean?

You know what it means.

It's too late, Katerina.

Maybe for you, Jay.

I've looked into your eyes, and I've felt your heart beating, and I've seen your hands shaking, don't fucking pretend this is just me.

Where am I from, Jay?

Norway.

Where?

Oslo.

Where?

Don't know.

What do my parents do?

Don't know.

Are they still married?

Don't know.

How many siblings do I have?

Don't know.

When I was a little girl, what did I dream of growing up to be?

I don't know, Katerina.

A doctor, Jay. I wanted to be a doctor.

Cool. Go do it now. Go back to school.

I'm from East Oslo, a place called Grünerløkka. My father worked on an oil rig in the North Sea and was lost in an accident when I was fourteen. My mother never recovered from it, and spends all her time staring at the ocean and praying for my father's return. My brother, who is two years older than me, wanted to be a lawyer. When I was fifteen and in school, I got scouted and signed and brought to Paris to be a model and guaranteed fifty grand a year. Now I make considerably more than that, and half goes home to my brother for school and for my mother, and half goes into an account so when I can't do this anymore I won't have to marry some dumb, old, rich, perverted fuck.

I'm sorry.

For what?

That I didn't know.

I didn't tell you.

And I'm sorry for your pain.

We've all got our pain.

Doesn't mean I'm not sorry for yours, and doesn't mean I wish you didn't have it.

Thank you.

I won't ever be a burden to you, or fuck up your plans, or stand in your way.

You already have.

Bullshit.

And you will continue to.

How?

A boyfriend is bad for business. Maybe not if you're a supermodel and the big jobs come easy, but that's not me, and that's not my life. The shows are coming up and this is one of the two busiest times of the year. I should be meeting designers, and photographers, and editors, and the owners of companies, most of whom are men. I should be out hustling and booking jobs, not fucking you in some run-down château in the country.

Five minutes ago you said you loved it.

I did.

So?

So I probably lost a couple gigs because of meetings I canceled.

Sorry.

Don't say it again, don't be fucking sorry for me.

I stare at her, don't say a word, just stare. And pain, the kind that hurts worse than anything physical, starts to envelop me. Comes from somewhere deep, as deep as anything inside me, maybe my heart, maybe my soul, maybe my spirit, maybe my brain, probably all of them, heavy and crushing and overwhelming pain, the kind that makes people drink, stay in bed for weeks at a time, reach for the motherfucking revolver and pull the trigger. She can see it, feel it, knows it, looks away and looks out the window, we're in Paris now, entering the station, the same station we left a week ago. I clench my jaw, shake my head slightly, try not to cry. As the train slows, she looks back at me, eyes light brown like cocoa into pale green, speaks.

Spend your time on your books. Read and look at art. Live your crazy life and chase your crazy dream. And as much as I might want to be part of it, it's not going to happen, Jay. I'm not going to be part of it.

I got it.

I'm sorry.

Don't be fucking sorry for me, Katerina.

She smiles.

That's my line.

If you say it to me, I can use it.

She laughs, stands, leans over, kisses me on each cheek, lingering on each for a moment, steps away.

Burn down the world, Writer Boy.

She picks up her bag and walks away. I watch her go and clench my jaw and shake my head slightly, try not to cry.

Pain.

Rising.

Enveloping.

Overwhelming.

As deep as anything inside me.

I try not to cry.

Los Angeles, 2017

In Paris it was pen on paper.

London pen on paper.

South Carolina pen on paper.

Minnesota pen on paper.

Six months in Chicago pen on paper, six months in Chicago laptop computer.

A year in Los Angeles laptop computer, two years in Laurel Canyon desktop computer, three more in Venice desktop computer.

Five years going back and forth between SoHo and Amagansett with a laptop computer.

A year in Beaulieu-sur-Mer with a laptop.

Five more years going back and forth between SoHo and Amagansett with a laptop computer.

Five years Malibu laptop.

Wherever I was, whatever I used, pen and paper or a machine and a screen, every session started the same way.

The void.

An empty space.

A blank page.

Every session started the same way, restlessness and confusion and insecurity and need and fear desire ambition faith doubt hope and despair, words and images rolling and spinning and dancing twisting flying, appearing and disappearing, words and images speaking to me, calling to me, screaming at me, taunting me and whispering to me and waiting for me, words and images inside my mind, inside my heart.

There would be days with nothing, days where the translation from my mind and heart failed, days where I read what I wrote and I was embarrassed and ashamed, day after day after day of words without meaning, sense, or direction, words without weight, words without movement, words that couldn't dance or sing, week after week, month after month, year after year, words that embarrassed me and ashamed me.

Every day was the same. And despite the result, I still believed. I don't know how or why or what kept me going, but I believed if I sat long enough and worked hard enough and put word after word after word after word after word I would learn, learn to translate, learn to decipher, learn to decode, learn how to get the words and images inside me rolling and spinning and dancing and twisting and flying, appearing and disappearing, onto paper, or onto the screen.

I'd write read edit ashamed and embarrassed throw it away or delete it. I never finished anything 10 pages 20 pages 35 pages 110 pages 235 pages throw it away or delete it but I still believed yes I still believed I still yes I still.

Believed. Because sometimes. A sentence or a paragraph or a page or two. Sang or danced or demolished or delighted. Sometimes what was in my head and my heart appeared on the page or the screen. Like fucking magic. Some kind of sorcery. As if someone else held the pen or typed the keys. It sang or danced or demolished or delighted.

So I kept.

Kept.

Kept.

Reading.

Looking at art.

Living my crazy life.

Chasing my crazy dream.

I worked shitty jobs at night and wrote when I got home at dawn I fell asleep at noon I woke up at six went back to work.

Simple.

Focused.

Monastic.

Happy.

I wrote a movie because I believed it was easier than writing a book fewer words a set structure it was commerce not art. I sold the movie and I didn't have to work shitty jobs anymore.

I wrote more and took jobs writing movies.

I read.

I looked at art.

Why is a toilet on a wall art? Why did Pollock paint the way he did and why did it matter? Why is a soup can on a wall important? What are Fauvism Cubism Futurism Surrealism Dada. How did Abstract Expressionism change the world. What are Existentialism Pop Art Superrealism Photorealism Neo-Expressionism Postmodernism and why should I give a fuck because I did. I learned art is about doing what had never been done before, challenging paradigms, moving them, defying them, destroying them. If there is a rule break it, if you are taught to do one thing do something else, if someone tells you something is wrong it is probably right.

And so instead of trying to write the right way, I started writing the wrong way. Grammar how I felt like using it punctuation how I felt like using it words in whatever way I pleased putting them on the page

However

I

Fucking

Pleased.

I had never lived my life according to rules or expectations. Why should I write according to them.

Fuck

Them

All.

An obvious lesson. One I should have known. One I followed absolutely as soon as I learned it. Fuck them all. And as soon as I did, the words and images rolling spinning dancing twisting flying, appearing and disappearing, the words and images speaking to me calling to me screaming at me taunting me whispering to me waiting for me the words started appearing on the screen appearing.

It took a decade. Ten years alone in a room with my heart and mind, my insecurity and my confidence, my doubt and my faith. Ten years dreaming ten years with a pen and my two fingers typing because I never learned to do it properly ten years of words sentences paragraphs pages chapters books entire fucking books inside of me.

I wrote the first forty pages of my first book in two days. I smoked four packs of cigarettes and drank a couple gallons of coffee. I listened to old metal, punk, early rap, love songs from the eighties, disco. I sang as I worked I got up and danced as I worked I allowed myself to be demolished as I worked I was delighted as I worked. And when I read the pages, for the first time I wasn't embarrassed or ashamed. I wasn't throwing them out, I wasn't pushing delete.

It was right.

For me.

From my heart and from my head.

Right.

Fuck them all, fuck them all, fuck them all.

For me.

And so I went, computer, two fingers, cigarettes and coffee, music and myself. I stopped doing everything else and ten twelve fourteen sixteen hours a day, day after day after day, I sang and danced and demolished and delighted, day after day after day I stared myself down and dared myself to keep going, day after day after day after day I bared my motherfucking soul laid it down raw and unfiltered and without compromise or apology, day after day after day after day. I didn't give a fuck about anything except the next word the next sentence did it look right sound right read right feel right, I didn't give a fuck about genre or classification, I didn't give a fuck about fact or fiction, I didn't give a fuck how it would be read or received it was words on a page it was a story being told it was the clearest purest most direct statement of expression I could make all that mattered was the next word, the next sentence, was it right, was it fucking right.

I was never happier. More serene and content. More satisfied and complete. Alone at the machine. Hour after hour day after day week after week month after month. I had words and music, coffee and cigarettes. My heart and my mind and my soul laid bare. Every morning as I fell asleep I imagined burning the motherfucking world down. Lighting some punk kid up the way books lit me up. Turning on the bulb in their soul that had been turned on in mine. Dividing confronting forcing people to have an opinion, to take a position, to love or hate, to cherish or burn, to revere or to ban. Every afternoon I woke up and went back at it.

Word after

Word

After

Word

After

Word.

The void.

The empty space.

The blank page.

Filled.

Singing dancing demolished delighted.

Filled.

One book two books three books four. Over ten years. One two
three four. I went to the desk and I sat down with the machine and I
confronted the void I confronted the empty I confronted the blank
I confronted myself and my fear and my insecurity and my doubt I
confronted them all and I fucking vanquished them. It wasn't easy
and often not fun, it was always work and labor and time and focus
and intensity, but day after day month after month year after year
I sat down and stared at the void blank page empty screen and I
turned on some music and I drank some coffee and I smoked some
cigarettes and I fucking went at it as hard and as true and as right
as I could without a care for anything but the next word, sentence,
paragraph. I didn't give a fuck who published or when or what critics
would say or how many copies I'd sell all that mattered was the void
blank page empty screen and words with power and love and pain
and loss and beauty and horror and sex and drugs and truth as I
saw it and I felt it and I knew it, all that mattered was at the end
of the day the void blank empty screen was filled with words, my
words, words from my heart and mind, my words singing dancing
demolishing delighting vanquishing.
And
The
World
Burned.
It fucking burned.
One book two books three books four. Hatred and love, bannings
and burnings and lawsuits, headlines and talk shows and readings
with thousands of people, book tours around the globe enraged
journalists and devoted fans terrified editors and canceled contracts
best-seller lists and movie deals the world it fucking burned. It was
magnificent and terrifying and surreal and thrilling and terrible and
heartbreaking and inspiring and exhausting. I gave it everything and

it took everything, all of my dreams came true, and at the end I was
in a hotel alone in the middle of the night somewhere in Europe
when you're in a different city every day you forget where you are,
I was lying in bed staring at the ceiling and streams of moonlight
were dancing across the bed and I started to cry, I started to cry and
I couldn't stop, an hour, two, three I cried and I felt lost and scared
and full of doubt and insecurity and whatever I had, whatever had
driven me and carried me and forced me to do what I did, whatever
was in my heart and my mind that allowed me and granted me the
gift to do what I did and fill that motherfucking void was gone, it
was gone, it was fucking gone. I cried all night. I finished my tour
and I came home and I hugged my wife and I kissed my children
and I went to bed for a day or two wondering if I would wake up
the same empty and gone and I did, I woke up and I was empty and
gone.

Empty and gone.

Empty and gone.

So I did other things.

Took meetings.

Smiled.

Shook hands.

Wrote for money.

Things that didn't require what I had lost.

Empty and gone.

Things that didn't require my heart and mind.

Empty and gone.

I engaged in the most American of activities, capitalism and
commerce.

Someone asked me if I had sold my soul, I laughed and told them I
didn't have a fucking soul to sell.

One job two jobs three jobs forty.

Capitalism and commerce.

Empty and gone.

My dreams had all come true.

And I had given them everything I was and everything I had and everything I could be, everything.

And I was empty.

Gone.

And what I didn't realize.

Was that when your dreams come true.

You have to dream new.

You have to dream new dreams new.

You have to dream new dreams new and you have to wake up every morning and make them come true you have to dream new dreams new.

Burn the fucking world down, Writer Boy.

Do it.

Let's see if you still can.

You have to dream new dreams new.

Or you die.

You have to dream new dreams or you fucking die.

So here I sit.

In my little barn, or cottage, or studio, whatever you want to call it, on the back of our property, away from the house, away from the noise, away from people, away from the world.

The void

A blank page

An empty screen

In front of me.

Burn it down.

Again.

Motherfucker.

Burn it down again.

Because you can.

Because you want to burn it.

Because you have to burn it.

You fucking have to or you will put a bullet in your fucking brain.

Burn it down.

Again.

Writer Boy.

Find whatever you lost your heart and mind, your passion and desire, your ambition and drive find the part of you that doesn't give a fuck about anything but words one after another after another words find it you motherfucker.

Void

Blank

Empty

Burn.

Paris, 1992

Because the old French hate me, I have taken to going to the boulangerie every morning, or every afternoon, depending on when I wake up, in my boxer shorts, a T-shirt, and a pair of Louis's slippers, which are bright pink and covered in some kind of bright pink fur. When I order, I speak in an idiotic and very exaggerated French accent *Je voudrais une baguette, s'il vous plait*. And because the French, or at least these French, believe in their *Liberté, Equalité, Fraternité* bullshit, they continue to serve me, but aside from passing me my goods and taking my money, they do not acknowledge me in any other way. I have decided that these particular French can go fuck themselves, even though I like, and will continue to eat, their bread and other yeasty, wheaty, floury delights.

*   *   *

I try to instill some discipline into my life, make some rules.
No drinking before 3 p.m., unless the shakes are so bad I can't hold my pen, which is often.
Write for at least four hours a day.
Read for two hours a day.
Eat something more substantial than bread, or Maison de Gyros sandwiches, maybe even some vegetables, just make sure whatever it is doesn't cost too much.
Come home before blackout starts, sleep in my own bed, unless someone I like invites me to sleep in their bed, but try to be aware of falling asleep.
No cocaine.
Try to stay in at least two nights a week.
Speak French all the time, even when I feel like a fool and am not completely sure what I'm saying or I don't know proper words,

tense, or grammar. Only use English if I'm with people who don't
speak French.

Get a beret.

Wear the beret.

Don't be afraid of the beret.

Do some laundry, dirty clothes that smell bad aren't cool.

Smoke fewer cigarettes.

Push-ups and sit-ups three days a week.

Write some letters to friends back home.

Call Mom and Dad.

*   *   *

Paris is Paris again still some tourists but not many. Americans are
mostly gone, back home planning new wars, shooting each other,
and working on their trucks. I start to wander again. It's still warm
in September the French sky an endless blue, the Seine heavy and
serene and eternal, the nights long and bright with a high moon, the
streets full, cafés crowded, museums empty, I wander.

*

Sèvres–Babylone 10 to Odéon 4 to Réaumur–Sébastopol 3 to
Père Lachaise the Métro is old and cute and quaint and slow and
loud and crowded. The French always claim it's the best public
transportation system in the world, it might be the oldest and the
original but it's like your grandpa's old car that he loves and will
never give up that old shitty broken-down noisy smelly car that
desperately needs to be either fixed or taken to the motherfucking
junkyard. Seeing sculptures in underground alcoves is cool and fancy
mosaics are cool and weird witchy old-school entrance signs are
cool, but I really just want to get from one place to the next without
motherfuckers going on strike. I have a book with me *Our Lady of*

the Flowers by Genet and a notebook and a pen with me I don't look
up while the trains move I read and get lost in the words I read and
get lost until.

I arrive get out walk toward a massive stone wall and a massive
stone gate both gray and worn pocked with weather and age and
the weight of history and sorrow, these are not the smooth shining
polished surfaces of a palace or an opera house they are the barrier
between the living and the dead. Behind them lie a million bodies
in the ground and two to three million sets of bones in marble and
limestone ossuaries, there are as many dead as there are alive in Paris,
as many dead as alive. I walk under the gate say a prayer for all of
them even though I don't believe in God or prayer I pay my respects
to the rich and the poor and the famous and the unknown, those
who died surrounded and those who died alone, I pay my respects to
all of them respect to the dead. I buy a map from a man selling them
his eyes are shifty and scared he may be worried about police may be
worried about something or someone else there a million under the
ground and two to three more interred, the map shows me where all
of the notable and notorious are spending their eternities.

I walk and look and breathe carefully there may be spirits in
the air, I have more than enough torment and distress inside of
me already. I find Molière first my old friend the writer of *Le
Misanthrope* and *Tartuffe* I thank him for his words and apologize
for mine. I find Edith Piaf whose songs I hear in every French
bar café restaurant and taxi I hear them played by buskers on the
streets and I hear them in fucking elevators the first 700 times they
were amazing now they make me want to tear out my toenails, I
don't tell her that when I look at her tomb I smile and sing a few
lines from *La Vie en Rose, Quand il me prend dans ses bras, Il me
parle tout bas, Je vois la vie en rose* (look it up if you don't speak
French motherfuckers, because now I do!). I see Chopin I don't

know his tunes but I know he's fancy and made happy cheery
delightful tunes I go to Proust I tell him his books are lyrical and
beautiful but boring as fuck and way way way too long. I say hi
to Balzac his bones are here his soul is at Musée Rodin, I kiss the
wall of Oscar Wilde's Egyptian tomb thank him for paving the way
for all of the insane drunk sex-addicted fuck-ups of the world to
dream of being writers. I find Géricault who made one magnificent
painting and has one magnificent tomb a corny bronze version of
the painting on the front of it. I find Abelard and Heloise and I
wonder, I find Victor Noir kiss his lips I wonder. I find Richard
Wright and kneel in front of him and I apologize for the nation
that drove him out and I thank him for being a better writer than
I will ever be, I start looking for Jim Morrison and I find him long
before I find him. Yeah, Jim Morrison. Famous for his long sultry
black locks and his sultry belly button and his sultry voice and his
insatiable appetites for booze drugs women and his mediocre songs
and terrible poetry and his infantile temper tantrums. Yeah, Jim
Morrison, died in a bathtub and buried here. As you approach his
grave there is graffiti everywhere, marker scrawled on surrounding
tombs, lyrics from his mediocre songs, excerpts from his terrible
poetry. As I see and walk toward I also hear a kid playing guitar
and singing, he's a young American (go the fuck home) with
long hair in a black T-shirt his voice is not sultry though he is
trying really fucking hard. When I see the grave I see flowers and
beer cans and whiskey and wine bottles, needles empty packs of
cigarettes records cassette tapes more flowers piled on top of the
stone spread everywhere surrounding. There are seven or eight
people all young longhairs, male and female, drinking smoking
staring at the grave one of the girls has tears on her cheeks the
others all look sad I can still hear the dude singing he still sucks.
I look at one of the dudes, speak.

Why you so sad?

He nods toward the grave.

Jim, man.

Yeah, he's in there somewhere.

He's everywhere, man.

Everywhere?

Yeah.

Where you from?

Nova Scotia.

Canadian?

Yeah.

And they like the Doors in Canada?

Live for them, man. Live for them.

I stare at him for a moment. Look at the girl and her tears, look at all the shit spread everywhere, written everywhere, hear the shit still being played, look back.

You really like the Doors?

Yeah, man. Live for them. You don't?

No, man, I don't.

Why you here then, man?

Was just wandering around, looking at the graves.

This is the one, man. Jim is here.

I laugh. He seems offended.

Why you laughing, man?

The Doors kind of sucked.

He shakes his head.

No.

I nod.

They did. That corny fucking organ. Those awful lyrics. That Light My Fire nonsense, it all kind of sucked.

The girl looks up at me, horrified. The dude looks like I've just spit in his face.

You should respect the dead, man.

I laugh.

You think all this shit everywhere is respecting the dead?

It's what Jim would have wanted, man. It's all for him.

Another reason he sucks.

The girl starts crying. I laugh. The dude recoils. He puts his arm around her, comforts her. I feel a little bad for being an asshole, but not really. He looks up at me.

You should leave, man. You're upsetting my lady.

I'll leave if you agree to pick up whatever shit you've left here.

Why, man?

Because this is a beautiful place.

Yeah.

And all this shit makes it ugly.

It's for Jim, though.

He's fucking dead. Has been since you were a baby. It doesn't make a bit of difference to him.

Yeah, you're probably right.

So pick up whatever shit you put down, maybe a bit more, and I'll walk away. If not, I'm just going to sit here and make fun of you.

I'll make that deal.

Cool.

Cool.

Tell your lady I'm sorry.

She looks up.

And if she ever wants me to light her fire, I promise to take her higher. I laugh, he shakes his head, the girl looks down at the grave and looks like she's going to cry again. I walk away, past all the garbage,

past all the dumb mementos, I stuff my pockets full of crap to throw
into the first garbage can I see, I pass three more young men on their
way to see the tomb, they're smoking weed, which normally I would
be in favor of, but not here.

One million under the ground, two to three more interred.

Their peace.

Their rest.

Their eternity.

Fuck Jim Morrison and his stupid grave.

*

Place des Vosges is my new favorite place to read. I bring a blanket
and wear my beret sometimes I borrow a turtleneck from Louis
usually black but occasionally red. Vosges is a sweet little park, a
perfect square divided into four perfect squares, fountains and grass
in each square, some fancy old trees in the middle, all surrounded
by luxurious red-brick apartment buildings filled with rich guys and
their beautiful wives and their perfect children. Something is different
about the grass. It's thicker, more comfortable, like a tickly mattress,
like a field filled with feathers stuck upright into the ground, it's green
like a summer leaf not a speck of brown anywhere, I imagine some
grass expert created it for some royal motherfucker to enjoy, after
which the expert was killed by the royal motherfucker, probably by
guillotine, so no one else would ever have the secret extra-green fluffy
grass formula. It's a comfortable park. Mellow. Not heavily trafficked
like Luxembourg or the Tuileries. I can read in peace. I can think
deep thoughts all day, the deepest motherfucking thoughts I've ever
thought, enhanced by the turtleneck and the beret, and I can think
them without being interrupted. I can watch the young couples walk
by and imagine what my life might have been like with my girlfriend
from home, so nice and sweet and stable, so domestic, so promising,

or I can watch young couples and imagine life with Katerina if I were
a billionaire who could buy her mom a big house and pay for her
brother's school and allow her to stop modeling, except when she
fucking felt like it. I find peace in place des Vosges. Peace and calm in
the fancy green grass amongst the beautiful buildings and the happy
people, peace and calm are things I do not know, have not known, in
some ways they make me uncomfortable, I know rage and madness
and mayhem, peace and calm make me want more, more, more. It's
still warm but not hot, sometimes cool but not cold, the leaves on the
trees are starting to turn, a blanket a book a bottle of water a cigarette
or two deep thoughts and dreams that will never come true. Peace and
calm I like it. Solitude I like it. Alone in the world as it lives around
me I like it. Use whatever dumb analogy there shelter from the storm
or the eye of the hurricane or an island in the stream I find it here in
place des Vosges. Sometimes I stay past the sun setting I lie and stare
up at the sky no stars the lights of Paris drown them out, but I can
imagine and I place them where I want to see them the stars of mind
the stars of my heart the stars of my soul stars that I create the stars of
my life in the night sky above me. I can dream on them. Wish upon
them. Sometimes cry because of them. Miss them and yearn for them
and hope they will fall for me or into me or upon me the stars of my
life real and imagined in the night sky above me place des Vosges.

*

Even though you see it everywhere, even though it looms day and
night over the entirety of the city, even though it is unavoidable
and inescapable, I have thus far successfully dodged stepping on
the grounds of or going to the viewing vistas of La Tour Eiffel.
One morning I say fuck it and have a strong coffee and put on
my sneakers and walk over and work my way through all the
motherfuckers selling dumb souvenirs and get in line and ride the

elevator up and stand on both viewing vistas. Whatever tourists are still in Paris all seem to be there, I look around it's a nice view but it doesn't make my heart sing. I leave. I'll never go back. Fuck La Tour Eiffel. Paris is the Seine. Paris is the smell of coffee on a sidewalk. Paris is the crumbling limestone of a million buildings that would be palaces anywhere else. Paris is a bottle of wine as the sun sets, a beautiful woman smoking a cigarette under an umbrella as it starts to rain, a book you've never heard of left on a bench. Paris is sex in an alley. Paris is a forgotten painting in an empty wing of a museum that takes your breath away. Paris is a cathedral where God is no longer worshipped. Paris is not some big dumb piece of metal with a bunch of assholes selling T-shirts and scarves and bad drawings of the big dumb piece of metal. Paris is your broken heart after it has healed, the dawn sky red yellow orange and blue just before the sun appears, the party you've always dreamed but have never found. It is not some big dumb piece of metal. I'll never go back there and I'll see the city without it, despite its presence. I'll never go back. Fuck you, La Tour Eiffel.

*

I can't stop drinking.
I try but I can't.
I go to AA meetings and I go to churches and pray.
I get down on my knees next to my bed and I ask for help.
But my hands start shaking and my mind starts spinning and my heart starts racing and the only way to stop them is to start again.
So I do.
It makes me hate myself, it makes me ashamed of myself, it makes me want to die.
But I can't stop.
So I forget about my dumbass rules.

Or at least the ones regarding alcohol.
I take.
I drink.
I consume.
What I need.
I can't stop.

*

At the Banana with Louis and a group of his friends, four or five men
and a couple of women. They call me *the token straight* and I am most
likely the only heterosexual man in the joint. It's loud and bright there
are men wearing dresses and men in thongs dancing on pedestals,
waitresses with deep voices some stunningly beautiful some fully
transformed, others as they are. I dig the disco music it's bright and
happy and makes you smile even when you don't want to smile. One
of Louis's friends thinks I'm gay, and they are debating the subject,
trying to decide if I am in a deep closet or if I am just a straight
man who can live with and hang out with gay men. I stay out of the
debate, watch the crowd and listen to the disco and drink my gigantic
fruity delicious drink, and whenever they ask me my opinion, I just
say *hétéro*. After an hour or so, Louis taps me on the shoulder, speaks.
We have decided how to settle this debate.
Thank God, it's been stressing me out.
Really?
No, not at all.
Well, we have decided.
Excellent.
One of Louis's friends, a tall blue-eyed blond man from Rotterdam
named Stijn, who is crushingly handsome, and who if I were gay I
would definitely want to fuck, leans forward.
Have you ever been with a man?

You mean fucked one?

Yes.

No, I've never fucked a dude.

Stijn looks at Louis.

You see?

I laugh.

He doesn't know.

Laugh again.

What don't I know.

Louis speaks.

Whether you like fucking a man or not.

Maybe the fact that I don't want to is indicative of the fact that I probably wouldn't enjoy it.

One of Louis's other friends, a dark Frenchman named Guillaume, who is also crushingly handsome, chimes in.

You don't know until you try.

I don't want to try.

Stijn speaks.

Because of your closet.

I don't have a closet, just keep my shit in piles on the floor.

They laugh, Louis speaks.

I can confirm that, I have the only closet in our apartment.

Stijn speaks.

I can see it, I know it, you're gay.

I laugh again.

I'm not.

One of the women, a beautiful young blond French named Melanie, who is an actress, speaks.

He's not gay.

Guillaume speaks.

Why do you think that?

Because I can tell when he looks at me that he wants to fuck me.

I laugh again, speak.

True, I do.

A third friend of Louis's, a swarthy Italian photographer named
Lorenzo, speaks.

Maybe he's bi, and he'll fuck all of us.

We all laugh, Louis speaks.

There's one way to settle this.

He looks at me.

Pick one of us, make out with him for one minute, see if your cock
gets hard.

Can I pick Melanie?

You make out with her after one of us. See which makes your cock
harder.

It'll be her for sure.

Stijn speaks.

No way. Once you taste one of us, you will never go back.

I look at Melanie.

You down with this plan?

She smiles.

I am.

You got some gum so my breath will be fresh when we start? I want
to make sure you enjoy this.

She smiles again.

No gum required, Jay, I'll enjoy it.

I smile, turn back to Louis and friends.

If I do this, you gotta agree that I'm just a hetero who hangs out
with gay dudes and stop giving me shit all the time.

Lorenzo speaks.

Unless your cock gets hard.

Unless my cock gets harder than when I make out with Melanie.

Louis speaks.

I accept that deal on behalf of all of us.

I speak.

Cool.

Guillaume speaks.

Now you choose. Who do you want?

I look at them. All handsome motherfuckers, all in great shape, if I were gay I'd want to fuck them all. Before I can choose, Stijn moves forward, puts his hands on my cheeks, pulls me toward him, starts kissing me. I do not resist, I kiss him back, lips and tongues, his hands are strong, his lips and tongue strong, aggressive, we both stand, kiss, heavily, deeply, I can feel his scruff on my face, his breath heavier than a woman's breath, his tongue bigger and thicker. Fifteen seconds, twenty-five, forty, he runs one of his hands down my neck, my chest, my stomach, he reaches for my cock

Which

Is

Not

Hard.

He kisses me deeper, heavier, more aggressively, tries to reach into my pants, unzip them, I let his hand wander, he goes in, puts my cock, which is still not hard, in his hand, keeps kissing me. Louis yells *une minute*, I step away, smile, look at Louis, speak.

Not hard.

Stijn looks hurt, turns to Louis.

I can't believe it.

Louis laughs.

Not hard.

I look at Lorenzo and Guillaume.

Satisfied?

Lorenzo speaks.

Maybe you try with one of us?

I laugh.

No, now I get to try with Melanie.

I turn to Melanie, smile.

Ready?

She smiles, stands.

Yes.

I step toward her, lean in, my hands on her hips, start to kiss her, slowly, softly, our lips barely touching, tongues dancing, her breath sweet and light, I take one of her hands in mine, the other around to the small of her back pull her into me, lips heavier and deeper, tongues heavier and deeper, I'm immediately hard, completely lost, lost in her kiss, her body against mine, our hands entwined, the faded smell of her perfume, lost. When Louis calls *une minute* we keep going lips and tongues and hands I can hear him and his friends laughing below the music we keep going. After a few moments I step away, though I don't want to, and I look to them, smile, speak.

Anyone need to check.

Melanie bumps me playfully.

I will.

I smile, she reaches for my cock, which is as hard as it gets, gives me a little squeeze, looks at them.

C'est comme une barre de fer.

They all laugh. I lean toward her, whisper

Get the fuck out of here?

She leans forward, whispers so I can feel her breath on my ear

Oui.

I turn back to Louis and friends, smile.

Been a wonderful night. Happy we resolved our debate. Louis, the scarf will be on the door so don't bother coming home.

They laugh.

Melanie and I leave we get a taxi sit in the back lips tongues hands she takes my cock out I cum in her mouth before we're halfway home. We go back to the apartment I tie the red scarf on the door and return the favor she cums in my mouth and it's magnificent. We spend the night saying *oui, oui, oui.*
Oui.

*

At Polly drinking off one of my free nights Omer tells me Katerina came by looking for me the night before and she asked Omer where I was she wanted to see me. I thank him for the information, and I do not go looking for her.

*

Fashion Week approaching you can feel it when it happens Flore and Deux Magots are busier than normal the crowd elegant and sophisticated and beautiful. I avoid going near them I don't want to see her, I don't want her to see me. I avoid the 1st avoid the 8th avoid the 4th. I don't go out with Louis many of his friends work in fashion as assistant designers, stylists, makeup artists, bookers, photographers their world becomes smaller when the shows approach. I stay home read and write go to bars in Montparnasse to sex clubs in Pigalle places I won't see Katerina or anyone who reminds me of Katerina, on most nights I get blind stinking drunk usually alone. Two friends from school in America leave a message with Louis they're spending the fall riding trains around Europe a last bash before they go home to become cogs to save vote obey and fucking die they're coming to Paris I go out to the Saint-Denis train station and buy three grams of shitty blow figure we'll get wired get drunk go fucking crazy. They arrive tan and happy they've been in Portugal, Spain, Italy, Greece, the South of France staying in the sun before the weather turns,

coming north as it does. As I come home from Café du Bac, where
I often spend my afternoons drinking coffee and whiskey, I find
them sitting on the ground outside the door to my building. I smile,
speak.

Boys.

Kevin, a rail-thin skinny motherfucker with long black hair, who
actually looks like Jim Morrison, which makes me laugh, and who
was my roommate for two years at school, stands, gives me a hug, a
strong hug for a strong friendship, speaks.

My man. Been too long.

I hug him back, strong for strong.

Missed you.

You too.

My other friend, another skinny longhair motherfucker, though
Greg's hair is thick and brown and he looks more like Paul Bunyan
than a rock star, stands, speaks.

You look awful.

I laugh.

No healthy living for me.

He laughs, another strong hug another strong friend. We separate,
they pick up their backpacks, which are the size of small houses,
we walk past the mailroom through the courtyard upstairs to the
apartment. I have a couple bottles of cheap red wine and the cocaine
they want to see some of Paris so we walk bring our treats with us
through the 6th to boulevard Saint-Germain to rue des Écoles to rue
Saint-Jacques to le Jardin sit in the grass the royal motherfucking
grass. We drink the wine, dip filterless cigarettes into the cocaine and
smoke it a poor man's freebase, they tell me about the end of school
my disappearing act created a little drama and slight disbelief, they
both spent the summer working in bars in Aspen before coming to
Europe. Kevin hands me a piece of paper I ask what it is, he tells me

that my ex called him this summer and asked him to give me her
number if and when he saw me, I thank him and put it in my pocket.
They ask me about life in Paris I ask them about their travels, my life
and their travels aren't that different from each other girls and booze
and drugs and adventure and stupidity, though my life also has art and
books and writing and self-inflicted misery and self-inflicted ambition.
We sit in the park until the sun goes down and we're driven out we're
drunk and wired Kevin and Greg both have pockets full of money and
want a night. I take them to all my spots, dinner at Maison de Gyros,
beer at Texas Star, whiskey at Stolly's, sangria at Bar Dix, absinthe at
Polly, we smoke cocaine all night Kevin finds a girl and disappears
Greg and I walk home at dawn sleep.

We're woken by someone banging on the door. Sun streaming
through the windows, Greg is in my bed and I'm on the floor. I
walk to the door my head is pounding and my lungs hurt I open the
door. Kevin is smiling, not wearing a shirt, he steps inside, speaks.

Hey dude.

Where's your shirt?

No idea.

Where'd you spend the night?

Girl's apartment.

Where?

No idea.

How did you get home?

Walked.

Just walked around until you found my street?

A sympathetic German who felt sorry for me gave me directions. It
wasn't that far.

Not that many Germans in Paris. A Frenchman wouldn't have
helped you, or would have sent you the wrong way.

We walk into the living room. Greg is sitting up, he speaks.

Fuck.

Kevin and I laugh.

I feel like I died.

If we had kept going we might have.

Kevin sits on our little sofa, I sit on the floor. Kevin speaks.

This German dude that helped me get back here had a good idea for us.

Greg shakes his head.

No ideas right now. Please, no ideas.

I laugh, speak.

What was it?

Kevin speaks.

He saw me looking at one of those street maps, asked me if I was lost and I said yes. We started chatting and he said if I liked getting drunk and lost I should be in Munich right now, not Paris.

I speak.

I like being drunk and lost. Why Munich?

Kevin smiles.

Oktoberfest.

Greg groans.

No fucking way.

Kevin nods.

The biggest drinking festival in the world. Right now. A train ride away.

Greg shakes his head.

No fucking way.

I smile.

Let's do it.

Kevin stands, smiles.

I'm taking a quick shower, packing a little bag, going. I'd like you both to join me.

I smile.

I'm in.

Greg groans.

Fuck you both.

We take showers, pack small bags. Kevin looks at his Eurorail schedule there are trains between Paris and Munich every hour we go to Gare de l'Est, another beautiful old French gare in a city full of beautiful old gares. We buy our tickets each get some canned beers to make some of the pain go away and prepare ourselves for the pain to come, we find our way to a little cabin. We play cards and talk about old times and old friends I read for a while *Narcissus and Goldmund* by Hermann Hesse appropriate for a trip to Germany it's a beautiful and brilliant book, intimidating as fuck, I could spend a million hours working and I know I will never write as well as Hesse. Six maybe seven hours and six maybe seven beers later we arrive at Munich Hauptbahnhof a giant train station in central Munich it's not as beautiful as a Paris gare but it is practical and efficient as fuck. The train was relatively crowded, clearly others coming for Oktoberfest, Kevin and Greg and I follow the crowd through the station, no dirt anywhere, no garbage, nothing out of place, nothing other than exactly what is needed and required. As we pass a few shops, all selling practical and necessary products, such as deodorant and toothpaste and potato chips and soda, I notice one selling lederhosen. I stop and stare and smile, getting to say the word *lederhosen* is worth whatever they cost lederhosen. I turn to my friends, speak.

Boys.

They stop, see what I see, lederhosen.

If we're going to do this, we should do it right.

We walk inside the shopkeeper is getting ready to close but he is German and thus always prepared to do some business, especially with dumb, drunk Americans. I tell him we need some affordable and durable lederhosen, that we are in Munich to show people how dumb, drunk Americans come correct to Oktoberfest. He doesn't really understand what I'm saying, which is cool, but he understands enough to know what we want and to guess our sizes within a reasonable margin and sell us what he says are three sets of affordable and durable lederhosen. Mine are a little big, a little loose, I wear them with black socks and my battered combat boots, a white long-underwear shirt. I debate whether to buy an alpine hat with a little white feather, or rock my beret and give a nod to my current place of residence. The beret almost always makes me look like an idiot, and even more so with the lederhosen, so I put it in my bag and add the alpine hat, which is a lovely shade of faded pine-tree green. Kevin and Greg go the same route, and after fifteen minutes we are ready to go to Oktoberfest in proper beer-drinking attire.

There is a flow out of the train station we enter it and move with it to a taxi line we get into a cab the driver is an old German he laughs at our clothes and welcomes us to Munich. We ask him where we should go he tells us the tents at Theresienwiese, the ancient fairgrounds of Theresa, that the entire city is there drinking great steins of lager. We ask him what we should do while we're in town he says drink beer, eat pretzels, dance and sing and have long friendly kisses with beautiful German girls. We laugh we are absolutely fucking down for that plan he asks us if we know anything about Oktoberfest we say no and he becomes a jolly encyclopedia of facts. Oktoberfest, he says, is the biggest funfair in the world, with more than six million people attending every year. It was started in 1810, when, on October 12, King Ludwig married Princess Therese of Saxe-Hildburghausen and invited the entire city to the wedding festival. The citizens of Munich had so much fun, they just kept doing it, and today there are Oktoberfests all over Germany, though Munich's is the original, the biggest, and the best. There are rides, games, concerts, contests, and beer, millions and

millions of liters of delicious German beer. As we near the site, the
traffic gets bad, he tells us to get out and walk, just follow the crowd.
We thank him for the ride and pay him and follow his advice. The
closer we get the larger the crowd. We can see the lights from the
rides Ferris wheels and twisty-turny vomit-inducing spin machines
and bumper cars, we can hear the intermingling of music mostly
polka, we can smell food roasting chicken and pork, popcorn and
baked pretzels. We decide on some rules: if we get separated the
entrance of whichever tent we enter first will be our meeting place
every night at six o'clock, if two or more of us like the same girl we
all walk away from her, we take turns buying rounds.

We enter the fairgrounds there are people everywhere, tens of
thousands of people, they are drinking beer from huge steins,
eating roasted pork legs, pretzels, and chicken, walking and talking,
standing in lines for rides and games and entrances to tents, yelling
and cheering and being filled with some jolly old alcohol-induced
happiness. We work our way to the tents there are ten or twelve of
them lined up in two long rows with a central thoroughfare. To call
them tents is an understatement, the understatement of the fucking
century. They are massive, the size of enormous warehouses, the size
of Walmarts in America, the size of gigantic airplane hangars, they
hold thousands of people. Some appear to have more than one story,
and all of them look like they are permanent structures, built of wood
and steel with tiled roofs, enormous temples devoted to the joys of
beer in Germany in the middle of autumn. I laugh at the spectacle of
it all, at the scale of it all. I am an alcoholic, and it is simultaneously
an alcoholic's most magnificent dream and greatest nightmare. There
is an endless supply of alcohol here, more than I could ever drink in
a thousand lifetimes, and I plan on drinking absolutely as much as I
can. At the same time, I know I am going to fuck myself up, fuck my
body up and my mind up, and even though I know what I am doing

is fucked, there is nothing I can do to stop it. So be it. It's been this way for a long time, since I was fifteen or sixteen years old, and it will continue until I either figure out how to stop it or it kills me. I see one as a far more realistic possibility, and it is not the one that involves stopping. I just hope it doesn't happen here, while I'm wearing cheap lederhosen and a green felt alpine hat with a fake white feather in it. We look at a map the only tents we've heard of are Hofbräuhaus and Löwenbräu-Festhalle. Hofbräu is where Hitler liked to have a beer, and we are not fans of Hitler, so we take that off the list and decide to go to Löwenbräu, which we have heard of because they make cool TV commercials that run during football games in America and because, whether it is true or not, we perceive it to be fancy, way fucking fancier than Budweiser or Miller Lite or Busch or Pabst Blue Ribbon or Milwaukee's Best. We walk toward the Löwenbräu-Festhalle. It is a mammoth fake A-frame ski chalet painted blue and white with a couple flags out front, a logo above the door, a giant wooden statue of a lion holding a stein of brew on a platform below the logo. We walk inside the Festhalle our hosen in full glory there's a polished hardwood floor, a giant arched ceiling at least fifty feet high, enormous ribboned chandeliers hanging from the ceiling, row after row after row of polished hardwood picnic tables and benches. There are probably five thousand people inside the Festhalle, every bench full, there is a polka band, a dance floor, waitresses in dirndls, which are magnificent beer-drinking Oktoberfest dresses, the yin to the lederhosen's yang, they are rushing around with six eight ten steins of beer in their hands, I have no idea how they hold all of them and move at the same time. We stroll through the aisles until we find an open spot on one of the benches. The table is all Germans, a couple in their twenties, another couple in their thirties, a group of men in their fifties laughing smiling talking drinking. We sit down say hello to them they ask where we're from we tell

them America, they are all from Munich. We order some steins
and a waitress brings them we raise a toast with our new friends to
Oktoberfest!!! We drink the steins quickly and efficiently in the spirit
of the host's traditions we order another round do it again. We sing
traditional beer-drinking songs we get up and try to dance the polka
we learn how to order in broken German it's fun and cheerful, an
evening of joy and comradery and raised glasses and high-fives we
drink stein after stein after stein of delicious golden foaming lager
stein after stein. At a certain point my mind goes black and my
memory disappears I wake up the next afternoon in some bushes
in a park near Theresienwiese. I still have my money, a pack of
cigarettes, and a lighter, my lederhosen have what appears to be a
giant ketchup stain on them and there is a half-eaten bratwurst in
my pocket. I'm hungry, so I blow the lint off of it and I eat it and I
don't know how I thought it tasted last night, but at the moment it
is delicious. I walk back to the tents look for Kevin and Greg there
are people everywhere it's a fool's errand to try to find them so I walk
into a tent order a stein and start drinking. I meet two couples from
Cologne who invite me to visit and see their magnificent cathedral
and the Shrine of the Magi maybe some of the Magi's wisdom would
rub off on me, I meet four girls from Athens who love to dance they
stand in a circle around me and laugh at my pathetic and terribly
awkward polka moves. I meet a group of Canadian backpackers
they are only willing to hang out with me because I live in Paris
we have two steins together and raise a toast to the Great White
North, I meet some Dutch who say their beer is better and offer to
show me where the best weed in the world is sold if I ever come to
Amsterdam. I go to the entrance of the Löwenbräu-Festhalle at six
o'clock Greg and Kevin aren't there I wait for an hour they don't
show up. I go inside find a table I sit with some American sorority
girls on a semester abroad in Florence we talk about art and drink

until I'm so drunk I can barely speak I think I make out with one
of them maybe two I black out and wake up the next afternoon
facedown on the floor of a hotel room there are two girls and a guy
asleep in the bed I see Swedish passports sitting on the nightstand.
I go back to the fairgrounds my lederhosen are covered with beer
and food stains and I smell like a run-down brewery, I think about
getting a shower somewhere or getting a hotel room and sleeping,
even though I just woke up I want to go back to sleep. I feel like
death. My heart is pounding my stomach burning my head feels
like there are spikes being driven into it, my hands are shaking and
I know there is only one way to get right and though I hate myself
for it, I do it. I walk into the closest tent and order a beer, drink it
as fast as I can. I immediately vomit, and there appears to be some
blood in my vomit, but enough of the beer stays in me to slow down
my heart and ease the shaking and quell the pain in my head. I
order another beer I drink it as fast as I can. Heart slows, hands still.
Another, and I'm better. I eat a pretzel to absorb some of the alcohol
I don't remember the last time I ate, maybe yesterday the bratwurst
from my pocket. I drink another stein, wait for six o'clock, walk to
the entrance of Löwenbräu-Festhalle, Greg is waiting for me. His
lederhosen are covered with mud, on the front and back, and his
long hair is tangled and there are flecks of dirt in it. I laugh, speak.
What the fuck happened to you?
I hooked up with some girl.
Was she wearing a dress made of mud?
We went out behind the tents and rolled around in the grass. I was
pretty fucked-up.
I laugh again.
Where is she now?
Inside with a few of her friends.
We joining them?

Yes.

Seen Kevin?

No.

When did you get separated?

Yesterday afternoon.

Where did he go?

We were with some older German ladies. I went to the bathroom,
when I came back, he was gone.

That sounds promising.

They were in their early forties, really gorgeous.

Dirndls?

No, but they might have had them in their closets at home.

I laugh, he speaks.

Where you been?

Not sure really. Blacked out both nights.

We hear Kevin before we see him, his voice cutting through the
crowd.

Motherfuckers!

We turn, he's walking toward us. His lederhosen are clean, he looks
showered and rested, a big smile on his face. I speak.

What's up, where you been?

Met a beautiful German woman. Maybe the most beautiful woman
I have ever met. We drank some beers, she took me back to her
place, rocked my fucking world all night, cleaned my clothes and
took me out for lunch. I think I'm in love.

I speak.

Why you here with us?

Her husband was coming home today from Berlin.

Greg and I laugh, Greg speaks.

That's kind of amazing.

Kevin nods.

She kissed me good-bye, told me to have a wonderful life, and to
never forget her. And I won't. Ever.

I speak.

You getting fucked-up with us tonight?

That's what we're here to do, right?

Let's go.

We walk into the Festhalle, as always it's bright and loud and
festive and joyous and crowded, people drinking talking singing
dancing new friendships being made, new love affairs being started,
even though I'm half-drunk and feel like a piece of shit and I'm
exhausted, it is hard not to be happy and feel good. We find a spot
on a bench there are three old couples on the other end of the
bench. They are all wearing wedding rings, two of the three are
holding hands, the other sitting side-by-side their bodies touching
each other. While Kevin and Greg order steins and look around
the surrounding benches for girls to flirt with or friends to make
I watch the couples. They seem happy, content, serene, there is a
conversation among all of them, they're laughing, smiling, animated,
at one point they all stand and lift their steins and raise a toast and
click glasses and drink and sit back down. I can hear them, but don't
understand a word they're saying, and don't need to understand
their words to see and know that they're blessed. They have lived a
large part of their lives. They are married and still in love. They have
friends. From the clothes and jewelry and watches they are wearing I
can see they have achieved a certain level of security. I'm jealous. For
whatever dreams I might have, that's the real dream. A long happy
life with someone who loves you, a long happy life with friends who
make you laugh, a long happy life where you're not shitting your
pants over money every day, a long happy life where you can raise
a glass and give a toast and laugh and have some idea what you're
saying and maybe even remember it the next day. I'm happy for the

couples at the end of the table. Bless them all. I hope someday to have something remotely close to what they have. If I'm lucky. If I even live that long. If I figure out how to do what I want to do. If I find someone who can love me, if I can learn to love myself.

Kevin nudges me I turn toward him he motions toward some American girls a few tables over, speaks.

Cute.

Yeah.

Go over?

I look at Greg, speak.

What do you think?

Better than sitting here by ourselves.

I motion toward the couples.

We got them.

Kevin and Greg both laugh, I speak.

They're cool, man. Way cooler than us. We could probably learn something from them.

Kevin laughs again.

I'm not here to learn.

I laugh.

Fair enough.

Greg stands, with his full stein of foamy lager.

It's our last night, let's go.

We walk over. Spend the night drinking and laughing and drinking with the four American girls, who are studying in London and came to Munich for the same reason we did. We move from tent to tent at a certain point we start drinking Jägermeister with our beer, blackness and oblivion soon follow, blackness and oblivion. My next memory is waking up on the train as it pulls into Paris Gare de l'Est. I smell awful, my lederhosen smell like beer and vomit, my head is pounding, I'm sick and shaking. Greg and Kevin aren't much better. Three dumb

crazy drunks. Though for them it is only an occasional gig, and for me
it is my only gig. We make it back to my apartment Louis isn't home.
I get into bed drink half a bottle of wine so I can sleep, I close my
eyes, I wake up twenty-four hours later shaking I run to the bathroom
and vomit. Bile and blood. Over and over and over. My kidneys hurt,
they literally hurt, my head hurts, my mouth is dry, my vision is
blurred, my thoughts spin spun spinning spunt. I drink some water
as much as I can straight from the bathroom faucet, I splash it on my
face, I rub cold water on my arms let it drip off the tips of my fingers.
I drink some more. I walk back to my room Kevin and Greg are gone.
There is a note on the floor next to my bed. It says

Epic Visit. Sleep it off and get back at it. And call if and when you come
back to America. Later. Kevin and Greg.

I get back into bed and though I don't want to do it, and doing it will
make me fucking hate myself and want to die, I know the only way
to go back to sleep is to drink. I take the remaining half bottle of wine
in a couple long draws. A chill runs down my spine, my stomach is
immediately on fire. But the rest of me calms and says thank you,
thank you, thank you, for giving us what we need, thank you
I close my eyes.
Pull the covers over my head.
Curl up into fetal position.
Breathe.
Breathe.
Breathe.
I wait for my heart to slow down my hands to stop shaking thoughts
to slow.
Eyes closed covers over fetal calm.
I hate myself.
I'm sick.
I hate myself.

Los Angeles, 2017

I started going to Church in Paris.

Whenever I felt lost or depressed or like I wanted to die, I went to Church.

I'd sit alone.

Read the Bible.

Look through the Book of Common Prayer.

Watch light move through stained-glass windows.

Imagine all the weddings at the altar, all the baptisms, all of the funerals.

Imagine how many services had taken place.

How many people had worshipped.

What they thought.

What they felt.

What they believed.

How they prayed.

What they prayed for.

If their prayers were answered.

Sometimes I'd kneel.

Sometimes I'd stand.

Sometimes in the front of the Church, sometimes in the back.

I'd stare at the floor.

Stare at the Cross.

Wait.

And stare.

Wait.

And stare.

Wait.

I always wanted to believe. To find comfort or relief. To discover some connection between me and God, or me and Christ, or me and the Holy Spirit.

Or me and all of Them.

I wanted a sign.

Something.

Anything.

A sign.

That they knew I was there.

Sometimes I read prayers from the Book. I'd read them quietly but with my voice at a level so that if someone was listening they would hear me.

Sometimes I read verses from the Bible.

Sometimes I looked at the Cross and spoke.

Asked for help.

Or shared my thoughts.

Sought advice and counsel.

Vented.

Cried.

Begged.

Begged.

Begged.

Paris, London, back in America before I went away.

While I was away, not locked up, but sick, sick as fuck near death with others who were the same.

I didn't want to die.

I was scared.

So scared.

So fucking scared I wet my bed every night for the first week.

They had a Chapel so I went.

Read the Bible.

Got on my knees.

Prayed.

Begged.

Cried.

I wanted a sign.

Something.

Anything.

Please.

A sign.

I got over my sickness.

I'm supposed to say I recovered.

But I didn't.

I defied it.

Mocked it.

Taunted it.

Fought it.

I beat it.

And if there was a sign, I missed it.

Or I wasn't aware enough to see it.

I kept going to Church.

Sometimes for the silence.

The deep heavy cavernous silence.

Sometimes for the peace.

Sometimes to read books, not the Books of God, but just books, novels, the *Tao Te Ching*, Rimbaud and Baudelaire, and for some reason when you read in a Church, everything you read is heavier, more insightful, more impactful, more powerful.

I'd talk to God.

Say

What's up, Dude? How are things in Heaven?

Ask God for advice.

I really dig this girl but she doesn't dig me, thoughts?

Curse Him.

I'm in fucking pain and I'm asking for your fucking help.

Good times.

Bad times.

Once a month, or once every couple months.

Church.

When I could write well enough to write books, I wrote books about God.

People thought they were about other things, about drugs or sex or a city or a friend, but they weren't.

They were about God.

My struggle with, my lack of, my yearning for, my faith and my doubt, my rage directed toward.

Cover of my first book had the hand of Adam reaching to touch God the hand was covered with little sprinkles alluring and devastating a hand reaching for God covered with temptation.

Another was my own Bible, a Bible about a God I could believe in.

Every day.

I thought about God.

Now and then, sometimes for no reason but often because

I went to Church.

Sat stood kneeled talked laughed prayed complained cursed sang read looked every time I went I looked.

For a sign.

I wanted to believe.

I wanted.

Wanted.

Life moved, good times bad times, triumph and disaster, joy and devastation, life moved.

One day.

One day.

One random day.

I got a note.

It was sent to my publisher.

Who sent it to my office.

Which is what they do when people send me notes.

The note was in a nice envelope on nice paper.

And it said

I read all of your books. And an interview where you said you wished you believed in God, but that you didn't. You're wrong, absolutely wrong. You do believe in God, you just don't understand your belief, and you don't understand how to believe. Someday you will, someday God will touch you. Until then, hold on....

I thought about the note long after I read it.

Usually I put such things in a box, under my desk, and when the box is full, it goes into storage, with a couple hundred other boxes, filled with similar things.

But I kept this one.

And still it sits, three years after it arrived.

On my desk.

In the corner.

It sits.

My black desk.

Plywood painted black sitting on two black file cabinets.

And I see it.

I think about it.

And I know the person who wrote it

Is right.

I'm old now.

Not in years yet, but in experience and pain, sorrow and regret, in good intentions gone horribly wrong and bad intentions yoked with guilt, I'm ancient now.

And I hope.

I learn.

Or see.

Or know at some point know.

How to believe.

How to look at myself in the mirror.

How to fix what I have broken.

How to smile and feel it.

How to love without pain.

How to settle the accounts I've defaulted on so many, so many.

How to wake up and pray.

How to look up and believe.

I wonder if I deserve it, any of it, am I worthy or am I worthless.

Do I get another chance or have I used them up.

I still go to Church.

Show me a sign.

A sign.

A sign.

Show me.

Paris, 1992

Though it takes a week to recover, I never stop drinking. I vomit two or three times a day, but I'd rather be sick than deal with delirium, and I'd rather be sick than deal with trying not to be sick. I wake up drink. Work until I start shaking drink until I stop shaking. Work until I start shaking again drink until I sleep. Do it again. Day after day and October passes. Louis tells me I need to get out that I'm killing myself I tell him if I die I will be dying for my art and there is no more noble way to die. He tells me I'm an idiot and he's right. I'm a fucking idiot. But I don't know anything else except being an idiot, and I don't want to do anything else, so I keep on with it. Drink and work and sleep. Drink work sleep.

*

I finish two hundred pages of my book I am convinced it is a masterpiece. I read it and I realize it's garbage and I should never show it to anyone. I get a box out of the Baker's garbage bin put the two hundred pages of the book in the box. I walk to square Boucicaut and find some rocks and I put the rocks in the box with the pages. I walk to Pont Royal and throw the box, and the rocks and pages in the box, into the Seine. As I watch the box and the rocks and the pages sink below the surface of the water I decide to spit on them. I lean over the rail and hawk the biggest, greeniest, nastiest, most disgusting loogie I can and I spit down into the water where all my bullshit nonsense writing just sank. And for whatever reason it makes me smile. Months of work. Gone. With a box and some rocks and some spit. Good fucking riddance.

*

November it gets cold rains every day. People love Paris in the summer but I love it now. Fuck the sun. The gray looming and drifting and enveloping. Over Paris. In Paris. On every street, around every building, in every alley. Paris with sun is like a beautiful woman in a designer dress easy to fall in love with and easy to walk away from because you know she's too beautiful to be yours. Paris in the gray is a femme fatale who draws you in and makes you fall in love and makes you believe she loves you and once you're all the way in, she knifes you. I keep writing every day but I go out more, I choose life more, back to wandering and watching and getting lost, back to hours standing in front of paintings, back to nights at Stolly's and Sacré-Cœur and Bar Dix and Polly Maggoo. It is said that a happy and stable life is about balance I can't ever find it. Whatever I see I want to see more, whatever I taste I want to taste more, however long I walk I wish I could keep going, whatever I take or drink or touch more more more. And the gray and the beauty below it and within it, the beauty consumed and enhanced by it invites you toward more, it sings to you and it caresses you more more more the true Paris, the Paris of drifting, enveloping Gray wants to give more. And so I go out and in and around and I dance to the song and I shudder at the touch and I marvel at the beauty and I follow the direction more more more, and I wait for the knife in my back, I wait and I look forward to that fucking knife, more.

*

A relatively sober afternoon cleaning the apartment. I find the number Kevin gave me, the number in San Francisco. I walk over to the phone it's nine hours behind Paris but I know she wakes up early. I dial a few times and hang up before it rings. Part of me wants to talk to her to hear her voice to smile at the words she chooses to

know how she is and what she's doing to smile and feel my heart
beating faster, to allow a flood of love and joy and memory to come
into me even if I just heard her say one word hello it would all come
back, all of the hope and the need and the inspiration, everything
that made me okay when I was with her. If I heard one word hello.
And part of me knows better. Knows that if I start down that road
there is no good place for it to end. That I couldn't do it before and
even if I wanted to do it now, if every cell in my body in my heart
mind soul and spirit wanted to be with her and follow that path,
I couldn't do it. I wish I could but I couldn't. And that part of me
that knows better is countered by part of me that doesn't care, that
wants the pain from the sound of her voice, wants the heartbreak it
will cause, wants the chaos and self-destruction that will follow it, I
want it that pain more more more I want it. The two sides. Love and
pain. I dial half the number hang up. Dial most of the number hang
up. Pick up the phone, stare at it, don't dial at all hang up. I dial the
number it starts to ring I hang up. I take a drink, a long drink from
a bottle of cheap red wine it burns I dial and let it ring. One ring
two and three she answers.

Hello?

Hi.

A pause, a moment. Heart pounding I heard the only thing I needed
to hear my heart is pounding I could hang up now.

A pause.

A moment.

How's Paris?

It's good.

Everything you dreamed?

Don't know yet.

Behaving?

No.

I think about you there, worry about you.

I'm okay.

I miss you.

Same, though I try not to.

Why?

Because it hurts.

Yeah, me too.

How's San Francisco?

It's great.

Everything you dreamed?

Yes.

What are you doing?

Working at an investment bank, got a nice apartment in the Marina, go out once or twice a week, hang out with friends on the weekends.

Sounds nice, mellow.

It is.

We talk for an hour, I know the call will cost a fortune but I don't care. Every second of the call is wonderful, every second of the call hurts, hurts my heart and mind and soul and spirit, I can feel the pain seeping into my body, my bones, moving into every part of me, deep and heavy and real pain. We talk about books politics she gives me updates on friends from school tries to explain to me what she does at her job, I tell her about Shakespeare and Company and Maison de Gyros, sitting in cafés watching the world go by. We stick to happy cheery subjects avoid going into whether either of us is seeing anyone I certainly don't want to fucking know. She asks when I'm coming home I tell her I don't know she asks if I'm ever coming home I tell her I don't know. She tells me she's glad I called, and I tell her so am I, she says don't lose her number I tell her I won't. We avoid saying the words I know I still feel, when we say good-bye I hang up the phone and stare at it and bite my lower lip and let the tears run down my face I am not going to sob or wail or let the pain out I want it.

I want the pain.

I want the fucking pain.

It makes me feel alive.

Makes me feel something other than hate, other than hate for myself.

Love and loss and regret and sorrow mixed and swirling into pain.

I want it.

So I bite my lip and stare at the phone clench my fists and let the tears run down my face.

For an hour.

Two.

I don't know.

But at a certain point the tears stop.

The pain doesn't.

I miss you.

The pain doesn't.

*

The Alcoholic's Dilemma. We drink because we feel pain. The drinking kills the pain. When the drink wears off we feel more pain, so we drink more to kill it, which makes us feel more, so we drink more. And thus it goes until you either stop or die. But stopping hurts too much.

And so.

And so.

I go.

*

Polly for two straight days when it closes I sleep in a park around the corner I don't remember much though I do know when I walked in for day three Omer refused to serve me.

*

Bar to café to bar to café on rue Saint-Denis and du Faubourg-Saint-Denis I wake up in a doorway. I'm wearing pants but I can tell I'm not wearing underwear. I'm wearing socks but my combat boots are gone. My wallet is in my front pocket I take it out there is still money in it. The doorway is in the section of Saint-Denis where ladies of the night like to stroll I imagine I spent a minute or two with one of them last night before passing out. I don't give a fuck about losing my underwear, but I am bummed about my boots. I have had them for years they were beat-up and beautiful. I get up and walk to Les Halles I find a shop selling the same style same brand I buy a new pair. They'll need to be broken in, but so be it. I find a bar to get a drink raise a toast to my missing boots, and to a long friendship with my new ones.

*

Philippe wants to try a Long Island Iced Tea. He read about them in a magazine he pulled out of the garbage and figures I'll know where to get them. I don't generally drink Long Island Iced Teas, but I know a place near the Champs-Élysées where American businessmen go to drink fancy cocktails. Philippe and I go to the bar and I drink Long Island Iced Teas until I can't walk. Philippe carries me to a cab gets me into bed I wake up twenty-four hours later.

*

I vomit on a table full of people and full of food at the Texas Star. I get thrown out and permanently banned no more Texas girls for me, though there hadn't been any for a long time.

*

I buy a gram of coke and a half-gallon bottle of whiskey Louis is away
with a new boyfriend they're skiing in Switzerland. The idea of Louis
on skis makes me laugh I imagine he spends more time looking at ski
pants than he spends actually engaging in the activity of skiing. Either
way he is gone and he is happy and I am happy for him and I am
alone and I get fucked-up. At some point, I don't know when, I call
San Francisco. I suspect I do it more than once though I do not know.
When I wake up I see the phone off the hook and the number next to
it, I wait until an acceptable hour and I call again, I want to apologize
I'm embarrassed and ashamed I just want to apologize. A woman I do
not know answers the phone asks for my name though I suspect she
knows it already, when I tell her she says please do not ever call here
again, there is no one here who wants to speak with you.

*

Thanksgiving I get invited to a turkey dinner. It's at American
University in Paris I go with a couple students who occasionally
drop by Polly. The dinner is in the cafeteria even though I'm the
same age as some of the students, a year or two older than others, I
feel much older, feel like school was a decade ago. The cafeteria has
large tables formally set, a turkey and mashed potatoes and corn
and stuffing on each, white wine and beer to drink. I don't eat much
drink a fair amount but not enough to lose my mind. After dinner
people mingle around, talk about Christmas plans, about the end of
the semester, about school gossip who's fucking who, who's fucking
the professors. I meet a girl named Natalie from Los Angeles we
have a couple mutual friends we decide to leave and have a drink
elsewhere. Natalie has olive skin dark eyes long black hair long thin
elegant hands, she's wearing all black a button-down shirt opened
low, a skirt and black tights, black leather boots. She's smart and
funny and has read a million books, she's studying art history and

wants to be a curator. We go to La Rotonde she digs it there, I tell
her it's too fancy for me she laughs. We have a couple drinks talk
about art she tries to explain why I should dig Salvador Dalí, I'm not
buying it melted clocks don't turn me on. A couple of her friends
from school show up one of them has a boyfriend with her who
is a writer living in Prague, he went to Exeter and Brown and he's
published stories and he's won awards and he believes he's the next
great American novelist and he doesn't think much of me. For most
of the time we ignore each other, as I tell Natalie the story of how I
ended up in Paris he interrupts me.

You're a writer?

Yeah.

Where you published?

In the Seine.

That a magazine?

It's a river. The big one. Over there.

I point out the window. Natalie laughs, he does not, asks me another
question.

Did you study writing?

Nope.

And you're not published.

Nope.

So you're an aspiring writer.

If that's how you think of it, it's not how I do.

Publish a story you're a writer, until then, you're aspiring.

I'll never publish a story.

Why not?

I don't want to write little stories. I don't want to be in some dumb
journal no one reads with ten other people and their little stories.
I'm here to write books. Big crazy dangerous books that fuck people
up and change their lives.

Hemingway died a long time ago, tough guy.

I don't give a fuck about Hemingway.

Then why are you in Paris?

Because many of the best books ever written were written here, and many of the best writers who ever lived, lived here.

Prague is the new Paris. It's where everything cool is happening.

You're cool?

I'm a real writer.

You might have a fancy degree, and you might have published some preciously composed story somewhere, but you've got no chance against someone like me.

Oh yeah?

Yeah.

Writing isn't a competition.

Yes, it is.

No, it's not.

Then why do they publish a list every week telling people what place they're in? Why do they count the number of copies sold and the number of languages translated? Why do bookstores have special places for certain books, and why does history remember the winners and forget the losers? You might have a fancy fucking degree, and you might have skills I don't have, and you might live in the new hot place for writers to live, but you're never going to beat me. You can think you will, but you won't.

He laughs.

You're pretty cocky for a nobody.

Once or twice a generation some motherfucker burns the world down. This generation it's going to be me.

He laughs again.

Why do you think that?

I didn't finish school, and I walked away from everything I cared about when I came here, and I got nothing to lose and nothing to go back to. When you get scared and tired and lose your confidence and wonder whether you're doing the right thing, you got shit to fall back on. I got nothing, not one fucking thing except my faith and my belief and my desire and my rage, and you can't teach those things, and you'll never find them if you don't have them, and you don't. You might think you do, but I can look into your eyes and see you don't. You got no chance against me, man. None. You might as well give up now.

He laughs again.

You're out of your mind.

Yes, I am.

And you can go fuck yourself.

Been said before, I'm sure it will be said again.

He stands, looks at his girlfriend.

Let's get out of here.

She nods, stands, looks at Natalie, speaks.

See you tomorrow?

Natalie smiles.

Yes.

They leave we watch them go. When they're gone, Natalie turns to me, smiles, speaks.

He's a dick.

Yeah, but so was I.

I thought it was hot.

Thanks.

I want to fuck. Right now.

Wonderful.

How far away do you live?

Not far.

Let's go.

We leave walk Saint-Placide is about fifteen minutes away the entire time I think about what it's going to be like to kiss her, taste her, be inside her. We get to my building walk into the courtyard up the stairs it's tense in the best way tension can exist, each glance each touch each breath loaded. I take her hand it's warm the feel of her soft smooth skin turns me on makes me hard. When we get to the door, the red scarf is on the handle. I shake my head.

Fuck.

What?

We can't go in there.

Why?

My roommate is in there with someone.

We can find a café, wait.

Fuck that.

She laughs.

Got another idea?

We'll find somewhere.

We walk back down the stairs into the courtyard I see the mailroom. It's small and empty, it's late no one should be getting their mail now. I lead her into the mailroom there's a light switch on the wall when you hit it the lights go on for two minutes turn off automatically. I start kissing her, her tongue is soft and heavy it tastes like red wine I press her against the wall. My hands wander so do hers I open her shirt take out her tits lick them suck her nipples they're hard in my mouth. She reaches into my pants whispers I want you inside me I tear her tights, rip them off her legs there's nothing beneath them. There are two bins next to us for garbage and discarded mail. I lift her onto one of them she spreads her legs I step between them and move inside her deep, hard, wet, home. I kiss her, move slowly and go as deep as I can we interlock hands moan as both sets of our hips move, find each other, move. As we start to move faster, harder I hear the door click, the door

open, the lights go on. I turn my head, shocked, see a man step into
the mailroom. It is my old friend.

The Baker.

He looks at me I look at him our eyes meet I'm shocked. He sees
me, Natalie, what we're doing, he smiles, nods, speaks.

Bonsoir, monsieur.

I smile, the Baker who hates me, respond.

Bonsoir, monsieur.

He walks toward the mailboxes, which are against the far wall. I'm
still hard, still inside Natalie, I turn to her she looks shocked, slightly
confused, slightly nervous, slightly amused. I smile at her, shrug, she
laughs smiles back. I hold her hands a little tighter she holds mine,
it's a ridiculous situation nothing to do but smile. We both look
toward the Baker, who is casually opening his mailbox as if we aren't
there, or he hasn't seen us, or as if he often walks into the mailroom
to find people fucking on the trash bins. He takes out his mail, takes
his time looking at it, acts as if he doesn't know we're there, as if he
doesn't know I'm inside Natalie, as if her shirt isn't open, as if her
legs aren't wrapped around me. He separates his mail, one pile in
each hand, turns and walks toward us. He stops at the trash bin next
to us, opens it, drops his mail inside. Natalie and I watch him the
entire way, as if we don't believe what is happening. He looks at me,
nods again, speaks.

Bonsoir, monsieur.

I smile, respond.

Bonsoir, monsieur.

He closes the bin, pats me on the back, leaves, hits the light switch
on his way out. Natalie and I burst out laughing I'm still inside her,
her legs are still wrapped around me. I lean forward kiss her she
kisses me back and our hips start moving again, gradually faster,
gradually harder. When we finish we walk to a café on the corner

have a drink come back to the apartment the scarf is gone she stays
the night leaves before I'm awake.

*

The Baker is now my best friend. I walk into the boulangerie and
he greets me with open arms and a hearty *bonjour*. His wife smiles
at me. They give me a baguette straight out of the oven, crispy on
the outside warm on the inside, instead of one of the cold ones from
the bins. They ask me how I'm doing and we chat about the weather
for a minute or two. When I leave I say *merci*, they tell me they're
looking forward to seeing me tomorrow. I walk out and laugh, ahhh
the joys of Thanksgiving.

*

I go back to writing, drinking, writing, drinking, sleeping. I think
about the writer in Prague, wonder what he's doing, if he's in a café,
if he's reading, if he's looking at art, if he's working. I can imagine
the story he told his friends, other writers from fancy schools, young
and published, living in the new Paris. I imagine them all laughing
at me, poor fool, delusional idiot, drunk talentless shit-talker. I work
as hard as I have ever worked, drinking only to keep the sickness
at bay. I want to prove myself. I want to make him remember me.
I want him to walk into a bookstore and have to confront a book
with my name on the front of it. I want him to have to read it. And
I want him to hate it. And hate that I was right. And hate that he
remembers me. And hate that I won. A chip on my shoulder. Yeah,
there is, a big fat fucking chip. Whatever gets me up in the morning,
forces me to work, to take risks, to do the best I can do, to keep the
faith and the belief and the discipline, whatever it takes, I hope that
chip is there forever.

*

I write 75 pages in ten days. A book called *Waiting for Sarah*, a doomed romance, the book based on *Le Misanthrope* that I had put away, but came back to, with the new pages and the old I have 125 in total. I take a day off I want to walk to Sacré-Cœur but it's raining and it's cold, the rain is almost snow. I don't own a waterproof jacket and I don't want to get sick, so I take the Métro, rue du Bac to Abbesses. When I sit down in the charming old shitbox of a train car I look up and I see Katerina. She's in an ad for a chain of fancy clothing stores, she appears to be skipping down a street, she's wearing a cute dress and carrying a fancy bag and has delightful shoes on her feet, she's smiling wide her crazy beautiful hair flowing behind her. I laugh, I had been thinking about her earlier in the day, she had told me that the idea of turning *Le Misanthrope* into a novel was a terrible idea, I was wondering if I should find her and give her the pages and ask her if she was right. Life is weird. When you think about something and it appears in front of you. When you think about someone and they call you or you bump into them. When you want something and in some unexpected way you get it. Doesn't happen all the time, but it happens enough. I don't know why or how or if it's just luck or coincidence or if we only notice when it happens and don't when it doesn't, which is most of the time. But I notice today and I laugh and I look up at the roof of the charming old shitbox of a train car and I ask God if he's messing with me, playing with me, sending me a message of some kind, I don't know if anyone hears me or if I'm just a fool talking to a metal ceiling but I like thinking that seeing her wasn't just luck or coincidence but the deliberate act of someone who cares for me, or is sending me a message. I say thank you, God. I nod with respect. I look back at

Katerina skipping and smiling and beautiful, and I hope wherever
she is that she actually feels that way, that she's smiling, skipping,
that her beautiful red hair is flowing wildly behind her, that she's
happy and content, that God is watching over her.

*

I read the pages. I ask the Baker for a box he says anything for you,
mon ami! I find some rocks at square Boucicaut. I walk to Pont
Royal. Pages and rocks into the box. The box into the Seine. A big
nasty green and brown loogie after the box. It's easier the second
time. Like getting punched in the face. First time hurts the worst,
every time after it's a little less.

*

But it still hurts and I still deal with pain the only way I know how
to deal with it. I drink I wander I drink I pass out I drink I get into
fights I drink I wake up without knowing where I am or how I got
there I drink.
I drink.
I drink.
From a few minutes after I'm up until I descend into oblivion.
I drink.
December in Paris.
It's cold the temperature in the thirties.
There's rain and sometimes snow.
Louis goes home to see his family in Lyon.
Philippe to Beaulieu-sur-Mer.
The days are short I'm lucky if I am awake for three hours of
sunlight. Or graylight. Or whatever light there might be, it makes
me cringe I prefer the darkness.
I have a three-day blackout I was in a bar in Montmartre I wake up

on the sidewalk near place Jeanne-d'Arc I don't know what I did or where I went or why.

I go back to the apartment I'm cold and sick, I spend the day in bed I'd rather be cold and sick with weather than sick with withdrawal.

I call my parents they want me to come home for Christmas I tell them I can't afford it they offer to pay for it I tell them I love them and I appreciate it but I'd rather stay I don't want them to see me in the state I'm in.

Two-day blackout, day in bed.

Sick.

Vomit every morning with the first drink sometimes bile sometimes blood sometimes both. Vomit several times more every day sometimes bile sometimes blood sometimes both.

I spend Christmas alone I go to Maison de Gyros for a special dinner I go to Polly for a special drink the streets are empty so I wander I walk into Notre-Dame it's crowded with worshippers celebrating the birth of Jesus, I sit in the back row and I cry whatever I thought might happen when I came to Paris it wasn't this I'm sick and alone and I don't give a fuck about anything anymore and I don't know how to stop it, so I sit and I cry I stay long after everyone else is gone I sit alone in the back row and I cry.

Two-day blackout one in bed.

It snows an inch or two it stays on the ground it's cold I'm cold.

Two more days.

Blackout.

Bed.

Another day.

Blackout.

Blackout.

Black.

Out.

*

I wake up in a bed. It's not my bed. It's big and fluffy the sheets are white and clean. There are pillows tons of pillows I'm in them and surrounded by them they smell like flowers or detergent made to smell like flowers. I'm under a giant comforter it's heavy and it feels wonderful the crisp soft cover, the weight of it on my body, I open my eyes. I'm in a large simple bedroom. There are simple, modern nightstands made of pale wood on either side of the bed, lamps and glasses of water on each. There are stacks of books on the floor, stacks and stacks of books piled against the wall, on the edges of the room. The walls are covered with crayon drawings of flowers red and blue and pink and purple and green, prints of famous still-life paintings of flowers are tacked or taped next to the drawings. There are huge French windows the sun is streaming through them. I sit up, reach for the glass of water closest to me. I'm not wearing a shirt or socks but my boxers are on. The water is cold and tastes good, my mouth is dry I can feel it moving down my throat into my stomach, which is empty. My head hurts and the streaming sun makes it worse though it's beautiful, the sun, streaming, and it makes me smile. I don't know where I am or how I got here or how long I've been here, but this is the best place I can remember being for as long as my memory can take me right now. I finish the water put the glass back on the nightstand move over to the other side of the bed reach for the second glass. As I start to drink it I hear footsteps coming toward me, I watch the door the water moving down my throat into my stomach cold and crisp it's wonderful. Katerina walks into the bedroom. I lower the glass, smile, she's wearing white cotton pajamas with little flowers all over them, carrying two cups of coffee. I wonder, very literally, if I died and this is some version of Heaven. She smiles and speaks.
Hey, Writer Boy.

I smile.

Hi.

She walks to my side of the bed.

Move over, give me some room.

I move over, she offers me one of the cups.

Coffee?

I take it.

Thank you.

She climbs onto the bed, sits cross-legged facing me.

You're a real fucking dumbass, you know?

I laugh.

What did I do?

I went to Polly to see if you were around, wanted to wish you Happy New Year.

That's nice of you.

And I also kind of wanted to fuck you.

Even nicer.

Your pal Omer said you had been in earlier but had left. As I was walking away I saw you passed out in the little park in front of Shakespeare and Company.

Yeah, I sleep there sometimes.

It's fucking snowing, and you were in a pool of your own vomit.

Usually not like that.

You could have died, literally.

I'm pretty indestructible.

I thought you were dead when I saw you. I ran and got Omer, and he helped me get you back here.

Omer is a good dude.

I don't know why but he likes you.

I laugh.

I don't know why either.

She motions toward my cup of coffee.

You gonna drink that?

Yeah.

I take a sip, it's hot and strong.

It's good, thank you.

She smiles.

I've missed you, Writer Boy.

I missed you, Model Girl.

You're the first boy I've ever had in my apartment.

I'm honored.

When we leave you're going to have to wear a blindfold so you don't
know where it is.

I laugh.

Fine. Whatever you want. I'm just happy to be here now. Happy to
see you. Part of me thinks I'm dead and this is Heaven.

They wouldn't let you into Heaven.

Then this is the closest thing I can imagine to it. This bed and this
room and this coffee and you, you, you, Model Girl, you. Thank
you. So much. Thank you.

She laughs.

You're a fucking cornball.

I laugh.

Hard on the outside, soft on the in.

She smiles, sets her coffee on the nightstand, lies down facing me.

You wanna snuggle?

I smile, set down my coffee.

Yes.

Yes.

Yes.

Los Angeles, 2017

What's it like there right now?
Sunny, warm.
How sunny, how warm?
Not a cloud in the sky, about 78 degrees.
That way every day?
More or less. Sometimes a bit warmer.
Shorts and a white T-shirt every day?
Yes.
Adidas sneakers?
Adidas slides.
I always wanted to live in perfect weather.
You're still young.
Hardly.
You are.
We're not young anymore.
We're not old.
Getting there.
Go live somewhere warm.
Not going to happen.
Why?
Just won't.
Why?
Just won't.
Is there a particular reason?
A couple of them.
What?
I'd rather not say.
This isn't fair, Model Girl.
What isn't?

I tell you about my life, you never tell me about yours.

What do you want to know?

Where are you?

Oslo.

Is that where you saw me?

No, though I knew you were here. A couple times.

I came there because I hoped to see you.

I thought you might.

I did.

So I went to a reading you did in Stockholm.

I would have looked for you there as well. Anywhere I went in
Scandinavia. I looked for your hair in the crowd.

Ha.

Ha?

I figured that's what you'd do, so I wore a hat.

Smart.

Model smart.

Legit fucking smart. Way fucking smarter than me.

Different.

I wish we had seen each other.

Best that we didn't.

Why?

Just is.

How long have you been in Oslo?

Since Paris.

You left right after I did.

How do you know that?

Philippe.

Really?

We're still pals. He lives in LA. He and Laura got married, had three
kids, got divorced. And he's exactly the same.

You stayed in touch after you left?

Didn't see him for a couple years after, but when I did, I asked him about you, and he said you vanished not long after we saw each other.

I did.

Why?

Not why you think.

You sure?

Yes.

Really?

Yes.

Why?

Doesn't matter.

I've always wondered.

Really?

Always.

I came back for my mother and my brother.

How are they?

My mother passed away.

I'm sorry.

It was for the best.

Still sorry.

My brother is a fancy tech lawyer here in Oslo.

He owes you.

He's been a very good brother, and I love him.

You married?

I was.

To who?

A man here. Son of a wealthy banker. We were together for about ten years.

What happened?

I left him.

Why?

He was an asshole.

Aren't we all?

He was in the opposite way you are.

What do you mean?

**You pretend to be an asshole but you have a kind heart. He
pretends to be kind but has the heart of an asshole.**

Sorry.

Don't be fucking sorry for me, Jay.

That's my line.

It was mine first.

I stole it from you.

I just stole it back.

Kids?

We had one.

Just one?

Yes.

I always...

One. We had one.

Boy or girl?

**Boy. Sixteen. Loves hockey and soccer. Will probably be a banker
when he grows up. Lives half the time with me, half with his
father.**

Tell him I said hi.

He's read your books.

Does he know we know each other?

**I told him I knew you when I was young and crazy in Paris. I was
hoping he'd think I was cool.**

Did it work?

He didn't believe me.

You want me to call him?

I'd rather have you call me.

I'd love to hear your voice.

It's the same.

Will you swear at me and call me names?

Absolutely.

Send me your number. I'll call you right now.

I can't right now.

Why?

I'm at the hospital.

Fuck. Why?

I'm here for an appointment, but I'm here quite a bit because I became a doctor.

No shit! That was the dream.

I did it.

That's the best thing I've heard in forever. Sounds corny, but I'm proud of you, so fucking proud of you.

Thank you.

Doctor Girl. Your new name.

I like it.

My old pal Doctor Girl.

I need to go now. My doctor is waiting for me.

Good luck.

Thank you, Jay.

Let me know when you want to talk.

Soon.

Paris, 1992/1993

We spend the day in bed. Katerina gets out to get me chicken soup and white wine, the wine keeps the shakes away. I drift in and out of sleep. Every time I wake up and she's with me I smile. Her arms around me. Her hand on my hip or my stomach or my chest. When she kisses me, lightly, on my neck or cheek, lightly on my lips, when she teases me with the tip of her tongue. Sometimes when I wake up she's sleeping, sometimes touching me or kissing me, sometimes she's reading *Hunger* by Knut Hamsun, and that she's reading it makes me smile. Hunger indeed.

Hunger indeed.

It's a delirious day, between my sickness and my joy, between sleep and not, between not quite believing any of it is real and feeling like nothing in my life has ever been this real. I wake up and it's dark and she's gone and I get out of bed walk around the apartment. The floors are large wide hardwood boards two or three hundred years old warped and cold each step feels good on the bottom of my feet wakes me more. Out of the bedroom into the living room bookshelves overflowing, large French windows with sheer white silks hanging, a huge old comfortable pink couch with giant cushions, a small round table with one white chair and some roses in a vase. Along one wall there is a small kitchen, a mini-fridge an electric cooktop a coffee machine a sink, a drying rack carefully lined with clean dishes. I walk over to the bookshelves. Mostly novels, some are in French, some in English, some in Norwegian, a few nonfiction books, a couple travel guides, a book about applying for college. The walls are white, mostly blank, in a few places framed photos of her family, I walk over to one, her mother and father and brother and her, she's probably eight or nine, standing on a beach in winter, she has a huge smile, her hair longer and crazier, her eyes twinkling. She's holding her mom's hand

with one of her hands, her dad's with the other. The picture breaks
my heart. Because I know she was happy and her family was happy
and it all went to shit, and it all became pain, and it all became loss,
and it all ended. And if I could, if I were a sorcerer or had a time
machine or could somehow change destiny, I would go back to this
moment, this exact moment, this beautiful happy joyous moment,
and make sure that all of their lives were different, that they stayed
happy and together, that this little girl now a woman I love would
still smile like she's smiling in this picture, and not because she was
paid to do it, to pretend to do it, but because it was what was in
her heart, because there was true happiness in her heart. As I stand
and look and hurt and wish the door opens and she walks in with a
couple bags, I turn and smile she smiles back not as pure as it once
was but pure enough for me she speaks.

You're up.

Yeah.

Snooping?

A little.

Find anything good?

I love this picture.

Me too.

And I dig your place.

Don't get used to it.

I laugh. She sets the bags down on the kitchen counter, starts
unpacking.

It's New Year's Eve. I thought we could have our own little party.

Awesome.

She holds up a brown paper bag.

I got tacos. I expect you to teach me about tacos and whether these
taste like real tacos.

I laugh.

I can do that.

She takes out a bottle.

I got us some champagne. Not super-fancy, but pretty good.

Some bubbles will feel good.

She takes out a small box with a ribbon around it.

And I got a cake.

I smile, walk toward her she smiles I put my arms around her.

Thank you.

I kiss her, pull her in tight, lay my head to her shoulder she lays hers on mine, we stand there, breathing, our arms around each other, and as weak and sad and stupid and pathetic and fucked-up and lost and doomed as I have felt in recent days, I feel simple and strong and loved now, in this moment, now, I feel like the future doesn't matter, the past is irrelevant, that whatever dreams I had are real in Katerina's arms, that I could die and be happy, now. We stand holding each other. I smell her hair fresh, clean, some kind of fancy shampoo, her skin soft against mine, her body so thin too thin I can feel her ribs, her arms pulling against my back. A minute two I don't know how long she slowly steps away I start to speak she smiles and holds a finger in front of my lips speaks.

We still got rules, motherfucker, we still got rules.

I laugh she gets out a couple plates. I open the bag of tacos two steak two chicken two shrimp small plastic containers of guacamole and salsa and hot sauce. I put together the plates one of each for each of us, she opens the champagne pours two glasses motions for me to follow her we walk into the bedroom sit cross-legged facing each other on the bed. She raises her glass.

Happy New Year, Jay.

I raise mine.

Happy New Year, Katerina.

I'm happy I know you.

And I, you.

Rules or not, you're my dude.

I smile.

Rules or not, you're my girl.

She smiles we touch glasses each take a sip. I give her a lecture on tacos
as we eat. About the difference between American tacos, Tex-Mex
tacos, and true authentic Mexican tacos. These appear to be authentic
Mexican tacos, or as authentic as one can find in Le Marais of Paris,
France. They have soft corn tortillas, they are steak not ground beef,
the shrimp are large and heavily spiced, the chicken is shredded. There
is little or no cheese, the guacamole is fresh, the hot sauce is good and
fucking hot. I gobble about half of each taco, which is all my stomach
can handle, Katerina takes one or two tiny bites of each, I wish I
could get her to eat more but she's always respectful of my shit, of my
madness and my addictions, so I am respectful of hers. We're both
broken in some way, both in pieces. She seems to know how to put
mine back together. Hopefully I can help with hers.

We finish the tacos I clear the plates come back with the cake and
two forks, I sit on the bed set the cake between us. She smiles.

I'm a little disappointed, Jay.

Why?

One of the things I adore about you is your cheesy cornball
tendencies.

And?

I was expecting one fork.

And we could feed each other cake?

Dork-style.

I laugh, pick up my fork and throw it across the room, through
the doorway, somewhere into the living room, we hear it bouncing
across the floor. She laughs, cuts a piece from the edge of the cake,

which is a small round cake covered with red, white, and blue
frosting and the numbers 1993 on the top, lifts the fork.

Ready?

I am.

Here I come.

I smile, she smiles, she moves the fork and piece of cake on it toward
my mouth, into my mouth. I close around it she pulls the fork from
between my lips I let the cake sit on my tongue and melt, it's sweet
and soft and gushy and delicious I smile.

Mmmmmmm.

She smiles.

Good?

So fucking good.

I reach for the fork take it from her our hands linger as I pull it
away, I cut a piece of cake she watches me do it. As I lift the fork our
eyes meet pale green and light brown like cocoa our eyes lock. She
opens her mouth those pouty lips our eyes are locked I move the
fork into her mouth she closes around it I slowly pull the fork back
from her perfect beautiful lips.

Mmmmmmm.

Right?

So fucking good.

She takes the fork from me our eyes locked we go back and forth
feeding each other, staring, letting our hands linger, the tips of our
fingers linger. I always associated the word *intimate* with sex, with
the act of fucking, but fucking with love or emotion involved. I now
know I was always wrong. Intimate is touching someone's heart, and
touching someone's soul, with love, with deep pure true love, and
having them touch you back in the same moment, in the same way.
Doesn't matter if you fuck. Don't really even have to physically touch
each other. And this, right now, this moment, staring into Katerina's

eyes, our fingers lingering, eating cake, feeding each other cake, knowing I love her and knowing she loves me, knowing we'll never say it and knowing that it doesn't matter, alone on New Year's Eve, after having spent most of the day in each other's arms after not seeing each other for four months, and having that time not matter, and if anything having it make us closer because we missed each other, this is the closest I have ever felt to another human being, and this is what *intimate* means, what intimacy is, and is what I have always wanted to feel with another person, this, now, her, love true and unspoken, love real, eyes into each other, hearts and souls into each other, connected by the lightest touch of our fingers, love, intimate.

Halfway through the cake, she sets down the fork, smiles and starts leaning in I follow her and lean toward her our eyes still locked we start kissing each other. Long and slow our hands together alternating between light and heavy our lips and tongues kissing each other. I push the cake off the bed onto the floor we lie face-to-face, hands locked, feet entangled, kissing. Though we know where we're going, neither of us is in a hurry. We kiss slowly and deeply our eyes still open an inch apart hers are bright and beautiful full of life and joy and love, a serenity and a peace, an intimacy. Our hands start to slowly wander removing clothing exploring sometimes light sometimes heavy hands finding playing squeezing caressing she lies back pulls me on top of her our eyes are open as I move inside her. We take our time.

Kiss.

Stare.

Smile.

Whisper.

Laugh.

Slow and deep.

Fast and hard.

Slow and deep.

Hips in rhythm.

Hands locked.

Eyes into each other.

Bodies one body one.

We take our time.

It's cold but we sweat the sweetest kind of sweat the bed soaked.

We finish.

Together.

One body one.

Ecstasy desire joy pleasure passion bliss rapture peace God one body together.

I stay inside her as we lie side by side staring into each other's eyes still lightly kissing at some point the new year arrives our eyes close and we fall asleep, one body one still inside her.

*

I make coffee in the morning leave a hot steaming cup of it on Katerina's nightstand go outside walk through Le Marais until I find an open shop I buy flowers and bread and cheese and tomatoes and wine and a copy of the *Herald Tribune* a couple fashion magazines some candy bars walk back to her place I will keep the location secret I press the buzzer and I wait.

Part of me thinks she's not going to let me in.

I wait.

Thirty seconds.

A minute.

Ninety seconds.

I debate whether I should push it again.

I put my finger on it, but don't push.

Take it away.

Put it back.

Take it away.

Two minutes.

The bags are getting heavy.

I debate whether I should push it again.

I could actually imagine her not letting me back in.

Which would be kind of funny, and kind of amazing.

And very much like her.

And would kind of break my heart.

Or actually break it.

I wonder if she's still asleep.

Could be.

But I've been gone awhile.

I wonder if she went out to get me flowers and bread and cheese and tomatoes and wine and a copy of the *Herald Tribune* and a couple fashion magazines and some candy bars.

Maybe.

She's kind of sweet and amazing like that.

Three minutes.

I debate whether I should push the button again.

Bags are really heavy.

I put my finger on it, but don't push.

Take it away.

Put it back.

Take it away.

Fuck it.

I'm gonna push it.

Fuck it.

I do.

Firmly and with gusto and with the cheer and optimism of a new year.

I push it.

Let go.

Wait.

And then.

Then.

Then.

The greatest motherfucking sound in the whole wide world.

My heart leaps!

It leaps!!

Like a hare running from the big bad wolf it leaps!!!

The buzzer on the door makes its beautiful buzz.

Like a sound from heaven.

As if composed by Mozart.

And sent to me by God.

I hear the buzz.

My heart leaps!

And I go inside.

*

She opens the door wearing a fluffy white velour robe her hair in a
towel drops of water running from her forehead down her cheeks and
off her chin and her neck down her chest she's smiling and she speaks.

I was in the shower.

I can see.

I kind of wanted you with me.

I very much wish I had been here.

I step inside she closes the door behind me I walk over to the
kitchen start unloading the bags.

I got some supplies.

I see.

And I got you some flowers.

Thank you.

And if you don't want me here, I will absolutely respect that and take off.

I very much want you here, Jay.

I turn around she's leaning against the wall facing me, light is streaming through the windows cascading off her skin and lightening her eyes, reflecting off the drops of water running down her face and body, I stop breathing for a moment and I smile.

You are seriously the most beautiful girl I have ever seen in my life.

She smiles.

Thank you.

Can I just stare at you for a minute or two, or maybe thirty or a couple hundred?

She laughs.

Yes.

And I can compliment you in other ways while I stare at you, if you would like.

I would like that, I'm a fan of compliments.

You're smart, and funny, and cool as shit, and you have great taste in clothes and books and art and apartments and men.

She laughs again.

I'm not sure about that.

I smile.

The men part?

Yeah.

Yeah, you're probably right. I take it back. But I have others.

I'm waiting to hear them.

You kiss magnificently, you're cute as fuck when you're sleeping, you have wonderful breath, your tongue tastes like ice cream, and your lips are like pillows from heaven.

Laughs again.

You're laying it on thick, Writer Boy.

I start walking toward her.

Your eyes light brown like cocoa are windows into some kind of lost paradise, the tips of your fingers magic, the words you choose like the poetry of angels, your voice is that of a siren princess.

She's smiling, smiling like she did as a child, which is the greatest sight of my life, greater than any sunset, any painting, any vista, any photograph, any anything, any anything that I have ever seen, I stop in front of her, lean against the wall in the same manner as she's leaning against it, face her, smile.

And your pussy, your pussy is the sweetest most delicious most magnificent most delirious most peaceful calming inviting exciting incredible absolutely awesome and amazing pussy that has ever been on this earth in the entire history of existence, absolutely 100 percent glorious and astonishing and miraculous.

She laughs.

You are definitely going to be a famous writer someday.

Right now all I want is to be your boyfriend.

That's all I want you to be too, Jay.

What about your rules?

Made to be broken, right?

Made to be fucking smashed.

Then let's smash 'em, Boyfriend.

I smile step forward put my arms around her look into those eyes light brown like cocoa they are windows into some kind of lost paradise I start kissing those lips like pillows from heaven I taste that tongue like ice cream and feel the electricity as the tips of her magic fingers touch mine.

Don't break rules.

Fucking smash them.

*

We spend the morning in bed reading talking flirting joking laughing smiling staring touching kissing fucking staring. We eat lunch bread and cheese and tomatoes and wine. I need to go home get a change of clothes. We walk through Le Marais across Pont Marie and Île Saint-Louis into Saint-Germain we hold hands as we walk bump hips and shoulders I put my arm over her shoulders pull her in tight and kiss her. We stop at Flore for a coffee watch people walk past make up stories about who they are and how they live and love and laugh and hurt the stories get increasingly ridiculous until everyone we see is either a spy or an assassin or one of the long-lost Russian Romanovs. We walk to Saint-Placide I take a shower halfway through she gets in with me we kiss under the stream she tells me she likes me clean I tell her I like her dirty she laughs and says she thinks we can be clean and dirty at the same time, I suggest we test her hypothesis and she agrees and we test it and she is correct. I pack a bag some khakis, T-shirts, a hoodie she laughs at my pitiful clothes I tell her I am a simple man who likes simple things she laughs again and says I'm a broke writer who spends all his money on books and booze instead of clothes and once again she is correct. We walk back through Saint-Germain stop in a little bistro on rue de Buci eat dinner I have escargot and a steak she pushes a salad around we split crème brûlée and a whiskey. We walk across Pont Neuf stop at La Comédie, Petra is working she's surprised to see us together thinks we're cute we split another whiskey we go to her place climb into bed snuggle up. I kiss her and thank her for the best day I've had in Paris by a large margin easily the best day, she asks me if I'd like her to make it even better and I smile and say yes and we spend the next hour making my best day even better. We fall asleep together entwined boyfriend and girlfriend in love with each other though we won't say it we're in love.

I don't need to have any dreams.

The dream is in my arms.

Boyfriend girlfriend.

Love.

Los Angeles, 2017

I have been given so many gifts, so many blessings, so much grace. A beautiful wife, healthy children, a loving family and trusting friends, home work success, comfort beyond necessity, resources beyond requirement. And I am grateful. So grateful. I understand things could have gone another way. And that I have been so lucky, so incredibly lucky.

And yet.

And yet.

And yet.

I look backward. Think, reflect, and wonder. Not on all that has gone right and all that I have to be grateful for, but on the mistakes I've made, the hurt I have caused, the wreckage I've left behind. The pain I've created echoes across time and the years, it calls to me and I hear it, it sings a song of sorrow that lives within me, it cries and no matter how or what or why I can't make it stop. No matter how or what or why no matter how long I spend kneeling or how long I look to heaven I can't and it won't I hear it and it cries a song that never stops.

I love the sun of Los Angeles. The crystal-blue sky. The warm air drifting. But more than the sun I love the water, the looming black horizon of dense sea, the crash of repeating waves endless and eternal, the depths unknown and unexplored and unfathomable. When the song of the unfixable past comes to me singing and crying I go to the water. Drive a winding road lined with privilege and manicured green through the hills and down to the sand I park as far from anyone else as I can, I take off my shirt and my shoes I wear a pair of simple black shorts I am stripped as bare as I can be. I walk across searing black asphalt my head down I don't want to see anyone or speak to anyone all I want is to hear the song that brought me the echoes and the cries and the sadness and the sorrow and the regret, the days past that I cannot recall or change or fix or make better, I would give anything and everything if I could make them better. The sand moves beneath my feet I know when I'm closer I'm closer I am closer as the endless and eternal crashing rings I keep going until I am in one step two steps three steps I am in.

There is always a shock of cold. The Pacific vast and deep the Pacific graceful and terrible the Pacific never warms. The shock of cold with every step deeper as with so many things in life if you stop it will scare you and paralyze you so I keep going one step two steps three steps four. I shudder as the cold and the black move past my waist I shudder as they move past my chest and shoulders I shudder when I descend, diving into the crash and swimming through it and past it, I find the breaking point and go beyond.

And there I stay.

In the calm beyond the break.

It's cold and still and deep and black.

Unknown and unexplored and unfathomable.

And there I stay.

Listening to the song and the cries and the echoes, the voices and the words and the stories, the pain and sadness and sorrow and regret.

And there I stay.

Alone, floating, lost.

And there I stay, beyond the endless and eternal, before the horizon line, on my back, staring at the sky it's crystal blue and full of love and life and hope and absolution and paths changed and pain forgiven and mistakes corrected.

And there I stay, floating in the water and floating in my mind and floating in my past and floating in my heart and in my soul, floating in some kind of dream that I can somehow make everything okay, make myself okay, make everything right, make it easier to look in

the mirror, make the yoke lighter and the burden weightless and
make myself believe that I somehow deserve all that I have been
given because I don't believe I deserve it, I don't believe I deserve it,
I don't believe. But there I stay, hoping and dreaming that someday
I will.

I will be able to listen to the song and smile.

Hear the echoes and let them bring peace.

Listen to the cries and cry with them.

Make myself believe.

Make myself believe.

Paris, 1993

We fall into a routine as normal and beautiful and perfect and simple and easy and fulfilling as I have known in my life, new young true love. We wake up together I make coffee. We sit in bed drink the coffee talk about whatever, sometimes what we did the night before, sometimes the news, sometimes the day ahead, sometimes the books we're reading, sometimes art we've seen or want to see, sometimes we talk about the weather. Sometimes we fuck, we usually shower together, sometimes we fuck again in or after the shower. I keep clothes at her place, a toothbrush and some soap. Most days she has castings or fittings or meetings or shoots and she comes and goes as she needs and as she pleases. I work I'm writing a new book maybe the third time will be a charm. This one is about a teenage drug dealer who leaves home to ride around on trains with his girlfriend it doesn't have a title. Katerina gets me a fancy notebook to write in, a fancy pen, it feels kind of nice, makes me feel a little bit fancy, though the words I put on the fancy paper with the fancy pen are anything but. If she's around in the afternoon we go for coffee or a walk we go to the d'Orsay together, the Louvre, le Centre Pompidou. We walk along the Seine stop in the little book stalls and look at the old books, though I can speak French I can't read it, she teases me and calls me a dumbass it's hard to argue against her diagnosis. We look through the little art stalls at old paintings every single one made by someone like me with big dreams and big hopes and big ambitions and big expectations of being in one of the museums, now they're forgotten, lost to the cancer of time, whatever they made, and some of it truly beautiful, is being sold for a few francs in a little shed on the side of a river. We go to the pet shops at Quai de la Mégisserie and look at puppies oh boy they are all so cute, we talk about getting one of them we laugh we can barely take care of ourselves. We walk around

place Vendôme look in the windows of the jewelry stores Katerina
sees a necklace she loves in the window of an old fancy French jeweler
it's a heart-shaped diamond pendant I want to buy it for her don't
care what it costs her smile is worth more to me than every penny I
have. We watch break-dancers in Les Halles listen to buskers in front
of la Fontaine des Innocents have coffee in Faubourg-Saint-Denis.
Sometimes we stay in and fuck or nap or read or some combination
thereof. When she's out in the afternoon I often walk around Le
Marais and buy supplies for dinner, try to cook, usually with some
degree of disaster, simple things like pasta or steak or baked chicken,
neither of us actually eats that much, especially Katerina, though
she appreciates the effort and thinks it's cute, I give the leftovers to
homeless men who sleep in the streets and parks around le Centre
Pompidou I know I am not that far removed from their life and
their pain. Sometimes we go out for dinner, to one of the little
bistros in the neighborhood or in Saint-Germain, or we walk up to
Montmartre. On a night when we know she's free the next day we
go to Le Refuge des Fondus and have a proper date, I put on my
only decent clothes some khakis and a sweater she wears a cute little
black dress we drink wine in baby bottles and get crazy drunk and
make out in streets and alleys and bars as we walk back to her place
we spend all night kissing, licking, sucking and fucking, doing blow
and laughing, talking about crazy dreams, what-if situations, what
if she gets a Chanel campaign, what if I write a best-seller, what if
she gets L'Oréal, what if something I write becomes a movie they get
more ridiculous and more dramatic what if I win $100 million in the
American lotto and buy the biggest castle in France we hold hands
and walk to the Seine at dawn watch the sun rise sleep all day. Other
nights we go to the movies snuggle up in the back row, we do double
dates with Philippe and Laura, Laura loves Katerina and is happy
I'm mellower it keeps Philippe mellower. Some nights we hit the old

spots Polly, Stolly's, Bar Dix, nothing crazy just hang out and have
a drink or two almost every night we stop at La Comédie and have
a drink with Petra who thinks we're cute and kind of can't believe
how domesticated we've become, we share a whiskey or two a bottle
of cheap wine, I drink a beer she has a glass of champagne. We fuck
every night, and every night our eyes lock, deep and holding, our eyes
open and vulnerable and giving, our eyes our hearts lock our souls
lock intimate. I occasionally go home, maybe once a week to check
in with Louis who says he misses me but is happy alone and without
the mess and drama I often create. I stop in at the boulangerie my
friend the Baker says he misses me which makes me laugh his wife
smiles and offers me their best bread, best pastries. I check my money
situation. I came to Paris with $1,200 in cash and $18K in traveler's
cheques I have $10K left after almost nine months, I should be able
to stay at least another year, longer if I keep my alcohol intake down.
I don't ever want to leave Paris, I don't ever want to leave. Through
January and the start of February I live a life and I have a routine as
normal and beautiful and perfect and simple and easy and fulfilling as
I have known, full of work and books and art and food and joy and
new young true love with a smart cool badass woman beautiful inside
and out a woman I still can't believe wants anything to do with me, I
live I live I live. Fuck that machine. I don't need it. Don't care about
it. Don't think about it. Work save vote obey teach your children to
do the same pay your taxes die rot in a hole none of it matters I'm in
love.

Love.

Los Angeles, 2017

You never sent me your number.

I know.

Why not?

I've been thinking.

Thinking what?

I don't want to talk to you.

Wow.

Wow?

Yeah, wow.

Wow what?

Wow, that hurts, actually quite a bit.

It won't, when I tell you my other idea.

Which is?

I want to see you.

Wow again.

That hurt too?

No, that kind of makes me smile.

Good.

Actually makes me really smile.

Even better.

It's been way way way too long.

For good reason.

What's that?

I'll tell you when I see you.

When will that be?

When are you free?

I have a pretty mellow schedule.

Could you come to Europe?

Sure.

Soon?

Probably.

I'll figure a couple things out and let you know?

Cool.

Thank you.

I'm curious, though.

About?

Why all of a sudden?

You'll understand.

Tell me.

No.

Why?

Let me do this the way I want to do it.

So mysterious.

Always have been.

True.

You'll understand when we see each other.

Soon.

Yes, soon.

Katerina.

Jay.

Until.

Soon.

Paris, 1993

In the year 1400, Charles VI, the King of France, known as both the Beloved and the Mad King, issued an edict called *A Charter of the Court of Love*, which officially declared February 14 to be an annual celebration of love. He hosted a gigantic party that was attended by the royal court and included a huge feast, a jousting festival, poetry, dancing, and song competitions, and a royal mediator to settle any and all sorts of amorous disputes and disagreements. It is believed he chose the date because it is the date that St. Valentine of Rome, a Christian priest who married Roman soldiers and their girlfriends despite such unions being banned by imperial authorities, was buried in the year 273. So while most people in the world blame America for the orgy of flowers and cards and candy and dinner dates and presents and expectations and disappointments that Valentine's Day has become, the blame actually should fall on the French and their insane ruler. That being said, I dig Valentine's Day. If you're single, there is literally not another day of the year when you have a better chance of finding new love, whether that love lasts ten minutes or a lifetime, and if you're not single it is an opportunity to be as cheesy and as corny and as lovey-dovey as you please, to be as over-the-top with love and affection as you want to be, but without the possibility of mockery, or even with mockery, but also usually accompanied by a smile and some love returned. I want a big Valentine's Day. I truly don't give a fuck if Katerina gets me anything, or gives me anything beyond a true smile, a sweet kiss, and the privilege of falling asleep with her, and if I get one or two or all of those things, I will have a wonderful day. Her schedule has picked up, as Paris Fashion Week for the fall collections is coming up, which means she'll be wearing, with all of the other models, clothes made by the designers that will be for sale

in the fall, months and months from now. She has multiple castings
every day, she has fittings, meetings with companies that might be
interested in hiring her, with photographers and bookers. I offer to
go back to my place and leave her to do whatever she needs to do,
and come back when it's over, but she says no, that the best parts
of her day are when she can forget about all of it and just hang out
with me, even though I am, in her loving words, a half-grouchy
unemployed fuckboy, which is kind of true. I decide to make a big
bold statement. To try to show her what she means to me, how
much she means to me, to give her not only love but something
more, an outward expression of my love. We still haven't said it to
each other, and we don't need to because we both know, I know and
she knows, it's in our eyes, our touch, our kiss, it's in the way our
hearts beat when we see each other after being apart, the way our
hearts rest when we lie in each other's arms. And even though we
haven't said it, I want to show it, in some way more than day-to-
day expressions, in some way that will remind her of my love when
we're apart. So I go home and I get my stash of traveler's cheques I
put the entire stack into my pocket. I start walking rue du Bac to
Pont Royal across the Tuileries I know the stack will be considerably
smaller after I get what I'm going to get in place Vendôme. And I
am happy to do it. I am almost skipping on my way money doesn't
mean much compared to love, and I would rather be penniless than
without her, take whatever I have take it all, just let me be with her
let me be. I walk to the far corner of the place even the cobblestones
are fancy and perfect most of the other shoppers are men in suits
and coats I am rocking khakis a long underwear shirt a white
T-shirt over it combat boots and a black wool seaman's hat. I stand
in front of the door. It's tall and wide ancient oak, trim around the
top a half-circle above with the name in fancy old script. There's a
doorman in a red uniform opening and closing the door I walk in

and nod he smiles and chuckles at me. I walk past and inside there's
a security guard just past the door I nod and smile at him he stares
at me like he wants to shoot me. I walk around the store I know
what I am here to buy each room is filled with glass cases jewelry
on velvet displays I have no idea how much it is all worth but more
than every generation of my family has ever seen and more than
every generation will ever see. Rooms are organized by price level,
there is the expensive room, the very expensive room, the incredibly
fucking expensive room, the unfuckingbelievably expensive room,
there is a grand staircase leading to a second floor where your bones
have to be made of platinum to even start up the stairs. I go to the
expensive room where almost everything costs more than I have
ever spent on anything in my life. I look for the little necklace with
the diamond-studded pendant in the shape of a heart I find it. I
stand in front of it there are lights embedded in the ceiling they
make everything glitter and shine each bend of gold, each bend
of platinum, each and every diamond in every one of the rings,
necklaces, earrings, bracelets. A woman walks over she's wearing
lovely tailored clothing and a name tag that says CECILE, she's
probably forty undoubtedly elegant and sophisticated and fancy,
she asks if I need any help I smile and say yes, thank you. I point to
the necklace with the diamond heart pendant, ask if I can see it, she
smiles and says of course and takes it out of the case. There is a tiny
price tag on it I'm scared to look at it. Cecile sets the black velvet
display on the counter I stare at it Cecile watches me I don't move
she speaks.

You want to see it?

I'm scared to touch it.

She laughs.

It won't bite.

I look up at her.

I know, but I'm still scared.

She reaches down takes it off the display holds it up, a white-gold chain and the heart made of diamonds shining as light bounces off of it, glittering as it gently sways. I stare at it and my heart beats faster it makes me nervous.

For a girlfriend?

Yeah.

You must love her.

I smile.

She's pretty fucking badass.

She laughs.

That's kind of a wonderful compliment.

An easy one to make.

I can tell you she will love this.

I know.

Should I wrap it up for you?

I stare at it shining glittering swaying I don't know how much it costs I'm scared to look. I also don't really give a shit. Money comes and goes, comes and goes. I need it for food and books and booze and shelter, don't really care about anything else, don't care about clothes or fancy trips or cars or watches or rings or stereos or anything else money can buy I certainly don't care for them more than I care for Katerina it's not even close, not even fucking close. I look at Cecile, smile, nod, speak.

Yes, please.

She smiles.

Excellent choice.

Cecile turns with the necklace and display reaches under the counter for a box starts assembling my little present. My heart starts beating I'm nervous. Nervous to see how much I am going to spend, nervous about walking out of here carrying the necklace, nervous about seeing Katerina when I have this for her, nervous thinking about giving it to her nervous imagining her reaction I'm nervous. I watch Cecile as she puts the display into a red box with gold trim and gold lettering, as she wraps a red ribbon around the box, as she puts the box in a small red bag more gold trim and more gold lettering. There is a cash register behind her she rings it up I'm fucking nervous she turns and tells me the price $4,200 almost half of my remaining funds. I take a deep breath it's actually not as bad as I thought it would be, if I keep living the way I'm living less booze not much food borrowing Katerina's books instead of buying them, living as simply as possible in every way, my cash will last longer and I can look for some type of job, get paid cash under the table, work at a bar or a bookstore, I'll figure something out. And whatever joy the necklace brings to Katerina is worth whatever the cost, whatever joy it brings is worth far more worth more than everything I have, everything I own. I hand over a giant stack of traveler's cheques, Cecile counts them and gives me change in francs, hands me the bag, smiles.

She's going to love it.

I smile.

Hope so.

Thanks for coming in.

Thank you for your help.

I take the bag turn walk out nod to the security guard who probably thought he was going to get to beat me up, nod to the doorman who probably thought he was going to get to watch the security guard beat me up, walk into place Vendôme it's cold the sun is starting to go down I take rue des Petits-Champs until it turns into rue Étienne-Marcel until it turns into rue aux Ours I go back to the apartment press the buzzer my heart still pounds every time I do it she's not there. The little red bag is in my hand it makes me nervous my pocket is full of all of my remaining money, if someone tried to mug me right now I'd let them have the money before the little red bag they'd have to knock me out or kill me to get the bag away from me. I walk to La Perle order a coffee it's filled with fashion people you can tell by their clothes, their animated nature, they all look very busy and very stressed but don't seem in a hurry to go anywhere or do anything, they're just very busy and very stressed. I drink my coffee it's hot and strong a minor-league replacement for the charge of cocaine it should make me more nervous but it makes me less. Speedy drugs, and caffeine is a speedy drug, always calm me down, make me more lucid, it is the primary reason why I love them, caffeine cocaine speed they calm me down my hands are steady and true holding the bag the little red bag for her. I pay for my coffee walk back to her building push the buzzer. I wait ten seconds fifteen, I hear the world's greatest sound, yes it is the world's greatest sound the entry buzz, I open the door walk inside up the stairs the door is cracked I enter. She is sitting at her little table wearing her pajamas, there is a chair on the other side of it with a bow tied around the top of it. I smile she smiles it's a big true smile all I need in this world is some love and a smile. I hold the little red bag behind my back walk toward her we're both still smiling I speak.

Hi.

Hi.

How was your day?

Busy. You?

Mellow.

I lean over kiss her she smiles motions to the chair.

Happy Valentine's Day.

I smile, sit down, keep the bag behind my back.

My own chair.

You like it?

I love love love it.

Both real and symbolic.

A table for two.

No.

No?

Not a table for two, a table for us.

I smile.

The best present I have ever gotten in my whole life. Thank you.

She motions toward the table.

There's something else.

I look, see a small box, a black ring box, sitting.

For me?

Yes.

Are you proposing to me?

Not yet.

I laugh, reach for it.

Thank you in advance.

I open the box not sure what to expect I can't imagine wearing a ring I can't imagine her getting me one. I flip the top open there is a key sitting in the space where a ring would be, a small gray metal key upright in the velvet. I take it out stare at it, put it in the palm of my hand. It's light and cold and the most valuable thing I have ever held, at least to me. I look up, smile. She speaks.

You're my dude, Writer Boy.

And I can come and go as I please.

Open door, open heart.

Open door, open heart.

Yes.

Can't think of anything that would mean more to me, or that I would want more.

Me too.

Thank you

Welcome.

And now.

Yes.

I reach around for the little red bag.

For you.

I set it on the table. She looks at it, at me, back at it, back at me, smiles.

No shit?

No shit.

What is it?

Open it and see.

Are you proposing to me?

Not yet.

I'm nervous.

So am I.

You really went there?

I did.

They let you in?

Shockingly, yes.

She looks at the bag, picks it up, smiles.

Even if it's empty I'd be happy. That you made the effort.

It's not empty.

What is it?

I laugh.

Just open it.

She takes out the box.

It's not a ring.

Don't know.

Yes, you do.

Not telling.

She sets the box on the table, stares at it.

If this is what I think it is.

I don't know what you think it is.

She looks up at me, smiles, light brown like cocoa into pale green.

I went and looked at it after we saw it.

Don't know what you're talking about.

It's too much.

Don't know what you're talking about.

She smiles, takes off the ribbon, looks up at me looks into me, lifts the top of the box slowly lifts it, it comes away, she holds it for a moment, stares at it and smiles and moves it away there are no lights overheard but it doesn't matter. It glitters and shines, her smile wider wider wider, she stares at it and smiles wider.

I can't believe you did this.

She takes it out of the box, glitters and shines.

How did you pay for this?

I had some extra money.

No, you didn't.

I did, and I wanted to do this, and I want to see it on you.

She holds it up glitters and shines she smiles.

I want you to put it on for me.

My pleasure.

I stand walk around behind her she watches me smiles. I reach around she's holding the necklace in front of her neck, I put my hands on top of her hands intimate, my fingers entwined with hers intimate, I take the ends of the necklace white gold from her fingers intimate. I move it slowly down so it sits on her chest shoulders neck over her freckles, I bring the ends around she reaches up lifts her hair thick lustrous red, I open the clip slide the delicate little loop into the clip close it, let it go she lowers her hair. I move my hands around her neck down her shoulders arms find her hands entwined,

I lean over look at the glittering, shining heart on her neck glittering
and shining she whispers
It's beautiful.
I'm happy you dig it.
Thank you.
You're my sweetheart, Model Girl.
I...
I kiss her neck.
You don't have to say it.
I...
I already know.
Yes.
Yes.
Hands entwined I kiss her neck, lick her neck, kiss her lips softly.
Yes.
Yes.
Lips and tongues softly.
Yes.
Yes.
Glittering and shining.
Heart.
Happy.
Valentine's.

Los Angeles, 2017

How do you see the rest of your life playing out?

I don't know.

If you could write it, what would you write?

I don't know.

Yes, you do.

Yeah, I probably do.

Tell me.

I just want peace. To love my wife and kids, to do something that
makes me happy, to be able to wake up every morning and look
at myself in the mirror and not hate what I see. I don't give a fuck
about money or fame or any of the rest of it anymore. I did it and
it left me empty. I still love writing, the actual process of it, sitting
alone in front of a blank screen and spending the day or the night or
both putting words on the screen, so maybe I'll try to write a couple
more books.

About what?

I don't know.

No ideas?

Not really.

Why?

Don't know.

Yes, you do.

People always ask me how I write books. I always tell them I don't
really know. That I have books inside me, that they grow inside me,
that at a certain point I feel full with them and that my job is to
translate them. That the process of writing is just getting out what's
there, in my mind and my heart, in my soul, and doing it as accurately
and precisely as possible. I don't use outlines, I've never read any of
the books I've written, and except for the first book I've never allowed

them to be edited. I don't really know how it happens. I think and I feel and I put what I think and feel and what's already inside me into words on the screen and eventually there's a book. And I might have ideas but ideas don't do it. I have to wait for a book to be there. In its entirety. Before I start. And I don't have one right now.

Yes, you do.

I don't.

You're just scared.

Why do you say that?

I know you.

Maybe.

You want peace, and writing brings you peace, but everything you've done and everything you do creates chaos and pain.

Unfortunately.

You should have known.

Known what?

If you burn the world down, it's very likely you burn yourself in the process.

You've always been smarter than me.

Did it hurt?

So much.

Still does?

Every day.

We've never really talked about it.

If you have questions, ask.

What happened?

Complicated question.

Give me the truth, as simply as you can.

I wrote a book, it came out, I lied about it.

Simple as that?

No.

Tell me the real version.

I wrote the book. Obviously it was based on my life. I took all
kinds of liberties. Changed shit, made shit up. My only goal was to
write the best book I could, to break people's hearts, crush them,
to move them deeply and in ways they had never felt, make them
understand the pain and horror and rage and sorrow and self-hate
that I felt as an alcoholic, a drug addict. To make them understand.
To take them to hell. To make them understand hell. To show
them a way out. To change them in some way, the way books have
changed me. I wanted people to love it or hate it. To write it in a
way that it confronted them, offended them, delighted them, scared
them, forced them to take a position on what I wrote and how I
wrote it. I worked so hard on it, had so many dreams tied up in it. I
had this sign on the wall in front of where I wrote it that said BARE
YOUR SOUL, and I did, I fucking did. And I believed in it, so
deeply. I was in my 30s and my friends and family all thought I was
crazy. That it was time to give up. That I was a loser, a bum. That it
was time to end the *I'm going to be a famous writer* gig. But I didn't.
From the moment I started writing that book, I knew.

What?

That it was right. That I found it. That I was going to do it. So I
kept going. Wrote the fucking book. I remember when I finished it.
It was the middle of the night. I had been working on it for a year. I
was alone and tired and it was dark, probably 4 a.m. I wrote the last
word and I stared at it and I burst into tears. Just sobbed. Face in
my hands, for probably an hour, just sat and sobbed. I was the only
one who cared, the only one who believed, and after all those years, I
had done it, I had written a book that I wasn't going to light on fire
or throw in a river. From there I found an agent, and we submitted
it to publishers as a novel, a novel that told a version of the story
of part of my life. At some point someone thought it would sell as

a memoir, they asked me if I was okay with it as a memoir. I didn't
give a shit, just wanted it to come out, just wanted the dream to
finally come true. The publisher knew what they were buying. When
it came out I asked what I should do about the fact that not all of it
was true, they said no memoir is, just do the interviews. I was cocky
and proud and believed in the book, and I went along with it, I lied,
got swept up in it, and the book became hugely successful, and I
kept lying. I hated doing it, and hated myself every time I did, but I
didn't know how to stop.

I'm sorry.

Don't be. It was my own fault. I fucked up.

Still.

Still nothing. It was my own fault. I fucked up.

And the talk show?

A great gift and a complete fucking nightmare.

I can only imagine.

I remember when I found out. The producers had called my
publisher, said they wanted me to be on a show about addiction,
to which I said no. I considered myself a writer, not an addiction
specialist. I wanted the book to be seen as a work of art, not a self-
help book. So they requested a chance to talk, I figured why not.
The book club had been shut down a long time. I didn't really think
about it being a possibility. About two minutes into the call, the host
of the show got on told me she wanted to restart the club, that she
was waiting for a book she thought good enough to do it with, asked
me if I wanted to do it with her. I laughed and said yes. I thought it
would sell an extra million copies. My wife and I had just had our
first kid and she had stopped working and the extra dough would
be a great blessing. I went on the show. I fucking lied. The book
went crazy. Sold five million copies in America in 3 months, five
million more outside America. I couldn't walk down a street without

someone wanting my autograph or my picture, I got thousands and thousands of letters and e-mails, became some kind of poster boy for recovery, I fucking hated it. The book wasn't a book. It was some kind of gospel. People thought I had answers and I didn't. I'm just a writer. I wrote a book. Simple as that.

Until.

Until.

Until.

It blew the fuck up. In a way it was a relief, in a way it was a nightmare, in a way a dream come true. I didn't have to lie anymore, which was a relief. The media hated me and stalked me, the talk-show host screamed at me, I got five hundred death threats, and had nineteen lawsuits filed against me, which was all kind of a nightmare. I became the most divisive, most controversial, most polarizing writer in the world, which was the dream. And the book kept selling. Millions more copies, people didn't seem to give a fuck what was true or what wasn't. It was all surreal and weird and frightening and thrilling. And it reduced the book to what it was intended to be. A fucking book. Read it as it is. Love it or hate it. Cherish it or throw it in the fucking garbage can. Judge it as a work of art designed to break rules and conventions and traditions, judge it however you please. And it freed me to do and write whatever I want. And I did, and the books all sold shitloads of copies and got shitloads of attention and they were all divisive and controversial and polarizing. But the freedom to do them came at a cost. It was painful and embarrassing and stupid. And I never realized how much it hurt to have people hate you and hate what you did, how much it hurt to have them call you names and say you're a piece of shit. I never realized that the dream had a second side, which was the nightmare. I never imagined the toll it would take. And the wreckage it would cause. With the publisher, people who were going to make it into a movie, people who had believed in it and believed in me, with the talk-show host. And it was all avoidable. I didn't need to lie. I shouldn't have lied. I was wrong to have lied. It was a huge fucking dumbass mistake. One I deeply regret. One I would change if I could. One that haunts me every day.

You ever see the talk-show host again?

I've bumped into her a few times over the years. She smiles and she's very gracious, but I can tell she fucking hates me, and I can tell she regrets having ever fucking met me, and I can't really blame her.

We all make mistakes, Jay.

And we all wish we could go back in time and fix them.

Maybe you'll get the chance.

Nice to think about, but it doesn't happen. And that's what sucks about getting older. The mistakes pile up, the regrets pile up, the wreckage piles up. And my piles are all pretty big. And I can't do a fucking thing about any of it.

You never know.

I do, though, I do.

You don't.

Your turn.

My turn what?

Write the end of your life.

Ha.

Ha?

No.

Why?

Not today.

Why?

I'm tired.

Tell me.

Soon, Jay. Soon.

I keep the key in my pocket come and go as I please. Katerina's busy it's Fashion Week she's walking in seven shows taking meetings in between she's up for two big campaigns she's stressed and nervous not eating and doing blow. When I see her she's tense speaking fast telling me about shit I don't really understand walk-styles goody bags comp-cards exits first-looks call-sheets go-sees run-of-show dressers stylists bookers makeup artists she's simultaneously incredibly excited and completely miserable. She runs around all day from show to meeting to appointment to fitting, at night she goes to parties with other models other fashion people they go to clubs dance, drink, snort cocaine, go crazy. I keep to myself let her do her thing I read and write and walk and wander, sit in cafés look at books at Shakespeare and Company go to Polly have a drink or two or three or four. Omer is happy to see me, the other regulars are drunk and they don't seem to notice or care. I'm usually asleep when Katerina comes home, she's happy and drunk and wants to make out and fool around, she tells me how much she missed me and gives me the highlights of her day, I listen and smile and try to be enthusiastic and supportive I tell her I'm stoked for her and proud of her she's the #1 supermodel in the world as far as I'm concerned.

I dig Katerina's apartment but miss mine, even though it's a dump compared, she stops in during the afternoon gives me a quick kiss tells me she has a big night ahead won't be home until very very late maybe not until morning. I tell her I'll probably stay at my place I haven't been there in weeks, she says cool gives me another kiss runs out the door I leave and walk home. Louis is there drinking wine with a couple of his friends, I take a shower clean up change clothes join them. They drink much better wine than I do, they know about the various regions and vineyards and producers and vintages, whatever they give me is red and delicious, all I know is if it has alcohol in it I'll drink it. They're going to Banana say it's going to be a huge night Louis says that Fashion Week is like the gay French Super Bowl, except it lasts a week and happens twice a year. They want me to come with them I have nothing else to do it's cold and sleeting we pile into a cab and cross the Seine.

There's a huge crowd outside of Banana, people spilling out into the street, the music is loud the bass thumping, as much work as some people put into getting dressed for Banana on normal nights, they seem to have put in more tonight, sequins ball gowns Carmen Miranda hats ten-inch platform shoes it's a feast for the eyes, for the senses, ridiculous and magnificent. We move through the crowd Louis says one of his friends has a table we find them, there are five of us three empty seats, bottles and glasses everywhere. Louis hands me a glass of champagne I stay standing, watch the joy and exuberance and celebration unfolding around me. There are people talking and singing, dancing hugging kissing, at tables on platforms on the bar everywhere. Louis introduces me to his friends all of them work in fashion one of them asks me if I'm Katerina's boyfriend I laugh and say yes. He says you just missed her, she was here with a man named Jean-Luc who runs an Italian fashion brand, they were with a group of people who work for him and a bunch of other models. Jean-Luc was teasing her about her new boyfriend, a penniless American writer named Jay, Katerina was teasing him back, telling him he was just jealous. I smile, tell him I'm bummed I missed her, though I'm actually not. She's doing her thing, with her people, I don't want to intrude, seem like I'm trying to watch her or find her or check on her or control her. I want her to have a fun night. She's been working incredibly hard and needs some fun, some stress relief, to blow off some steam. She's doing her thing with her people, I'm doing mine.

I have two or three drinks do a line of blow in the bathroom it's good, pure, finely chopped cocaine my heart rate increases, I become happy and chatty fashion people have good drugs. I see my former make-out partner Stijn he asks me if I want to make out again I laugh and say no, he's with my other former make-out partner Melanie she asks if I want to make out and I say yes but I have a girlfriend now and would feel like a dick. She laughs and says if and when you break up come find me it was fun last time, I thank her and agree it was indeed fun, indeed fun. I see Louis he's found a beautiful young design assistant named Karim he has dark hair and olive skin Louis is drunk and wired he tells me he's in love. I laugh and tell him I'm happy for him he asks me if he can have the apartment, I have Katerina's key with me I say of course. I have two or three more drinks no more blow I want to read for a while go to sleep wake up tomorrow feeling human. I thank Louis for taking me out tell him I had fun slip away into the night it's dark and cold no moon, I slip away into the night.

Banana is near Le Marais so it's a short walk ten minutes maybe fifteen I open the door to the building walk up the stairs open the door to Katerina's apartment step inside. The dress she was wearing when I last saw her is sitting on the floor a few feet away, a man's suit lying next to it. I can hear them in the bedroom. Hear her moaning, hear a man speaking French. My heart starts pounding pounding pounding, I feel immediately fucking sick, like I want to put a bullet in my brain, I want to go to sleep and never wake up. I know I should turn around and walk out, but I walk forward, toward the bedroom, I want to see whatever is happening, I'm already broken my pounding heart is broken I want to be destroyed I know I need to see I walk toward the bedroom.

I step inside her bedroom, my entire body is shaking, my hands legs arms shoulders, I can feel my thighs shaking my lips shaking my heart is shaking, my broken heart is beating out of my chest. I step inside her bedroom. She's lying on her bed her legs spread. There is a man on top of her he's facing me his face is between her legs I can see his lips and tongue on her and in her. Her face is between his legs I can see her mouth moving up and down taking him into her mouth licking and sucking. I stare I can't move I'm shaking my entire body is shaking I can't believe what I'm seeing but I know it's real, I'm shaking my entire body is shaking. The man senses me, looks up and smiles at me. He knows who I am. I have seen him before. However many months ago he was at the Musée d'Orsay with her I made fun of him because he didn't know shit about *Olympia*, I have seen him before. He smiles at me I'm shaking. I want to kill him but I'm too hurt to move, too broken too shocked and too destroyed he smiles at me I shake. I reach into my pocket take out Katerina's key, the key she gave, the key I thought meant she loved me, I take out her key. As he moves down looks me in the eye and licks her I hear her moan I want to kill him. I drop the key on the floor. She hears it hit the metallic clink I see her look around and see me as I turn and walk out of her bedroom, I hear her call my name as I walk through the living room, I hear it again as I walk out the door I hear her call my name as I walk out her fucking door. I move quickly down the stairs I don't want to see her or talk to her none of it matters anymore nothing fucking matters I hear her door open behind me I hear my name Jay Jay Jay.

I step out of the building Jay I step into the night Jay it's dark and cold no moon I hear my name Jay I slip away.

It's dark and cold.

No moon.

None of it matters anymore nothing fucking matters.
I hear my name.
Jay.
I slip away.
Into the darkness.
Into the night.

Los Angeles, 2017

Sitting alone in my little barn, or cottage, or studio, whatever you want to call it, on the back of our property, away from the house, away from the noise, away from people, away from the world, staring at the blank screen. I can feel something it's there though not as it usually is or how it has been before. I have always waited, waited until it was all there, until I knew or felt and could sense everything, beginning to end, the entirety of it, I have always waited. I open a browser go to Facebook pull up Messenger click the name. I didn't recognize it the first time. Jente Paenbenk. Didn't know what it meant, or who it was, or why they were writing to me. Jente Paenbenk. I read everything every message every conversation beginning to end I read everything. It makes me laugh, smile, it hurts me, I feel sadness joy regret elation. I read all of it. It makes me think, smile and remember, think and smile and remember. I normally wait until I feel all of it. Beginning to end. I have always waited until I felt all of it, beginning to end. This time I don't know. But I want to do it. I want to start. I want to fill the blank screen with words. I want to tell a story. A story from life. To write a book. To think and smile and remember. And to put those thoughts and that joy and those memories on paper. I take a Sharpie from a cup filled with pencils and pens and markers I take off the cap I can smell the ink I lean forward toward the white wall in front of me. In large black letters I write Bare Your Soul on the wall. I smile. I think. I remember. And I start. With two fingers I type.

Los Angeles, 2017

It started with a message request on Facebook. Someone named Jente Paenbenk. No picture, no friends. A blank profile. It started again. After twenty-five years.

Do you ever think of me?
I responded:
Maybe.

And so it went.

I think of you every day.
Good.
Sometimes it is, sometimes it's not.
That's life, right? Sometimes it is, sometimes not.
Yes, Jay, that has certainly been the case. For both of us.
Who is this?
I want you to think of me every day.

And so it went.
And so.
It.
Went.

Paris, 1993

I go to Philippe's apartment in the 8th arrondissement. It's a long walk I stop in a liquor store and buy a half-gallon bottle of cheap whiskey I drink it as I go. I replay everything in my mind, the images stay. Walking up the stairs, opening the door, seeing the clothing on the floor. Walking into the room seeing them together seeing her with another man seeing his lips and tongue seeing her head moving up and down. I'm still shaking. Shaking as I walk shaking as I bring the bottle to my lips shaking as I light and smoke cigarette after cigarette shaking. I see him look up at me and smile and go back down. I watch the key drop I see her look around at me I hear her calling my name I'm still shaking.

I think about walking in front of a car or truck it would be easy to do. I think about jumping off a bridge it would be easy to do. I think about finding a knife and cutting my throat it would be easy to do. Our heart is an organ that pumps our blood moves our blood through our body, but our heart is also an organ that fills that blood with whatever we are feeling and the blood, the blood, the blood moves through every part of us, every fiber of us, every cell. All I feel is pain. Deep overwhelming soul-destroying pain. In every part of my body in every drop of blood in every fiber in every cell. Pain. And as joy and love kept me away from alcohol, or at least allowed me to use it with some modicum of control, pain takes me back to it. In every drop of blood, in every fiber, in every cell. The whiskey burns as it goes down, burns my mouth burns my throat burns my stomach I don't care. The physical sensation of pain takes me away from the other pain. I get drunk quickly. I had a head start at Banana a few drinks like the kindling that ignites an inferno, I was lit before now I'm fucking burning. The images stay. The pain lives in my heart, in my blood. Walking up the stairs opening the door seeing the clothing on the floor. The pain walking into the room seeing them together pain. Seeing her with another man pain seeing his lips and tongue on her and in her pain. Seeing her head moving up and down pain. I see him look up at me and smile and go back down I think about walking in front of a car or truck or jumping off a fucking bridge it would be easy to do pain. I hear the key drop and see her look around pain. I hear her calling my name pain pain pain fucking pain fuck you I'm in so much fucking pain I want to fucking die I want to make it end fucking die. My heart. My blood. In every fiber every cell. And I would rather die than feel what I feel pain.

And so.

And so.

And so.

I drink.

Halfway to Philippe's and half the bottle is gone. I'm dead fucking drunk I throw up on the sidewalk at place de la Concorde. When I'm done heaving I sit down there are cars moving around the circle, the obelisk and the fountain are both lit, there is a small amount of water on the road everything is shimmering and beautiful and there are people in the cars going somewhere in Paris, I imagine they're happy or at least not in pain. I take a long draw from the bottle. The whiskey burns my mouth, throat, and stomach, I lean over and throw up again throw up on the ground between my legs I don't give a fuck. I take another long draw this time it stays down. I take another stays down. I light a cigarette the vomit smells I don't give a fuck everything hurts I'm in pain. I take another draw. I stare at the obelisk and the fountain. At shimmering lights. At the cars full of happy people or at least not me pain. I take another draw.

I stay until the bottle is gone. When I stand I vomit again I can hardly walk I'm on the edge of the blackness the edge of oblivion,

but my mind won't let me go there. The images flashing endlessly
flashing images of her and of him and of the two of them together
the images keep me conscious, or some version of conscious. I
know Philippe's address know where the apartment is but I stumble
around lost, I stumble around I can't find it, it should take fifteen
minutes it takes ninety. When I do find it I press the buzzer wait,
press it again wait, press it again. The door opens Philippe is in his
garbageman uniform he's getting ready for work he looks at me
speaks.

What the fuck, Jay?

Hi, Philippe.

What happened to you?

Can I stay here?

What happened?

I just need somewhere to stay.

You okay?

No.

What happened?

I just...

I start to cry.

I just need...

I cry.

Somewhere to stay.

Cry.

Philippe puts his arm around me leads me into the building I can
hardly walk through the small courtyard I'm crying and I can't walk
up a flight of stairs to his family's apartment. Philippe asks me what
happened asks me what's wrong I'm crying and I can't tell him, I ask
him if he has anything to drink and somewhere I can sleep, he gets
me a bottle of vodka and leads me to the guest room. He knows I'm
fucked-up and in pain he helps me take off my combat boots and

my jacket, he helps me get into bed I start drinking the vodka I'm
still crying. He gets a glass of water and sets it on the nightstand I
can't stop fucking crying. He leaves and softly closes the door the
images are flashing in my mind there is pain in my blood I can't stop
crying.

When I hurt.

I drink.

I drink to make the hurt go away.

Though I know when I wake it will only hurt more.

I don't give a fuck.

I can't stop crying.

I want blackness.

Oblivion.

I drink.

I find it.

*

I wake up in the middle of the afternoon and for a second or two I
don't know where I am I don't remember.

And then.

It all comes back. Like a fucking hammer to my soul. Like a fucking
building dropped on top of me. It all comes back and I can't actually
believe any of it even though I know it happened and it's true I saw
her and I saw him and I saw the two of them together. I sit up and
I take a sip from the glass of water, the bottle of vodka is empty. My
mouth is dry the water feels good moving down my throat I can
feel it in my stomach. I don't remember the last time I ate and I'm
not hungry. I just hurt. Everything hurts. And I want it to go away.
I stand and walk into the living room Philippe is reading the paper
and drinking coffee. He says hello I nod, he asks me if I'm okay I say
no. I ask him if he'll go to the liquor store with me he asks me what

happened I ask him for a drink he gets a bottle of wine and opens it
and hands it to me. I drink the bottle and I tell him what happened
and even though I want to cry and I almost cry, I don't. When I'm
done he stands and gives me a hug and tells me he's sorry. I ask him
if he'll go to the liquor store with me and he says yes and we go to
the nearest one and I spend every cent I have on bottles of cheap
whiskey and cigarettes. We walk back to his house and I ask him if I
can stay for a couple days I tell him I probably won't leave the guest
room and he says yes, you can have anything you want, you can stay
as long as you need. I go back to the guest room and I drink until
the blackness comes, I drink until oblivion takes me.

*

I stay at Philippe's for four days I'm either dead fucking drunk or
asleep the entire time on the fifth day I sleep for twenty-four hours.
I wake up and though my mind isn't clear, it is clear enough to know
what I'm going to do. I take a shower go back to the apartment
Louis and I share, I pack my shit, I leave Louis a note thanking him
for his love and for his friendship and for his generosity, I leave him
a thousand dollars in an envelope to cover rent and bills for a couple
months, I want to give him time to find a new roommate, I love
Louis and I hope our paths cross again someday, I hope our paths
cross again.

*

I stop by the boulangerie the Baker smiles and asks me where I've
been he says he's happy to see me his wife waves to me says *bonjour*
tells me the pain au chocolat is delicious today. I thank her ask for
one, tell him I've been busy staying at a friend's place, that I might
not be around for a while he asks me why and I tell him I think it's
time for me to go. He walks around the counter gives me a big long

hearty hug I slip $100 into his apron pocket I thank him for all the
tasty treats he laughs I wave to his wife as I leave I eat the pain au
chocolat it is indeed delicious thank you old French baker people,
thank you.

*

I take all my books to Shakespeare and Company. They offer to buy
them I don't want money I want them to sell them to people who
will love them I want whoever reads them to love them as much as I
do. As I walk away I smile at the sign and say thank you Shakespeare
and Company, thank you.

*

One last sandwich at Maison de Gyros I'm more or less sober this
time the crispy bread the spicy lamb meat the fresh lettuce and
tomato hot fries spicy red sauce tangy white sauce it is the most
delicious combination of edible delights in the entire world thank
you Maison D, thank you.

*

Sitting in front of *The Gates of Hell*. Torture and ecstasy. Writhing
bodies. Beauty and love and terror and eternity, men and women
screaming, reaching, kissing, begging, crying, being tortured by love
and pain, being tortured by regret and sorrow. I sit on the bench
where I was sitting when Katerina and I met. It's cold and gray and
raining the Musée Rodin is empty there are no tourists in Paris at
the beginning of March. I have been here for almost a year. I came
seeking and searching, lost and hungry, desirous of and desperate
for books and art and madness and love, desperate for life for life for
life desperate. Money didn't matter to me still doesn't, achievement
didn't matter to me still doesn't, success didn't matter to me still

fucking doesn't. I didn't want to be part of that machine, another cog in that machine still don't. And though I'm leaving Paris and leaving France what I have seen and felt and read and written, the art and books and buildings, the sidewalks and streets and parks and bridges, they will never leave me. Won't matter where or how old I am or what I end up doing, what I learned here what I came here to learn is that it's possible, to say fuck that machine, to live as you please, to love as you please, to believe as you please, to eat drink sleep think fuck as you fucking please. To say fuck you to that big dumb soul-destroying machine. To defy it. To have a dream and chase it. To not give a fuck what people think of you and what you have in your heart and your mind and your soul and what you dream about to absolutely not give a fuck. To do everything feel everything experience everything. What I learned here in the most beautiful, most civilized city on earth is that I don't have to work vote save obey pay my taxes join the homeowners' association smile at Christmas parties kiss my boss's ass get sick die and rot. I don't have to do any of that bullshit and I won't do it, I fucking won't. I don't know how many times I have sat here in front of *The Gates of Hell*. Staring thinking feeling dreaming I don't know how many times. I didn't understand what I was looking at until now. That for me and for all who came before me every writer and every artist, *The Gates* aren't to Hell, *The Gates* are to Freedom, that the torture and ecstasy, the beauty and love and terror, the addiction and disaster and exuberance, are the price we pay to find it. I'm happy to pay. Whatever the cost, I don't care. Take everything I've got none of it fucking matters. All that matters is that I was here, and I saw, and I felt, and I loved, and I believed, and I lived.
I lived.
I lived.

*

I call two friends who are living in London ask them if they need a roommate. London's expensive they say they'd be happy to have me I get their address and tell them I'll see them soon. I call the airline there are flights every hour tickets are cheap I can buy one at the airport.

*

Philippe comes home I tell him my plan he laughs and says he'll miss me but thinks it might be a good idea, a good idea for both of us. We decide to have a night. A final night. He takes a shower rids himself of his occupational smell puts on some decent clothes, I wear my uniform khakis long underwear shirt white T-shirt we go out. A drink at Flore. Dinner at Lipp. Sangria at Bar Dix. Absinthe at Polly Omer isn't there I leave him a note of thanks, tell him I love him, a note of thanks. Vodka on ice at Stolly's, walk past La Comédie without stopping. Philippe has given me so much, paid for so much, I take care of everything this time. And everywhere I go I think of Katerina. I see her even though she isn't there. I hear her. I feel her. I remember times we had things we did conversations laughs and smiles, a kiss. Every woman I see reminds me that they aren't her and that she's somewhere in Paris and that I'm never going to see her again. Every woman I see makes me hope that I feel about someone else the way I feel about her it will take time if it happens at all, so much time. I see hair reminded freckles reminded little black dress reminded Adidas sneakers reminded a smile reminded, I hear a laugh or a funny word or a smartass remark reminded. And so with every drink Philippe has I have two or three, and as the night goes on I move closer to darkness and closer to oblivion I don't want to be fucking reminded.
Philippe wants to go to Les Bains Douches. He says it's my last

night we should do it right, I'm happy to go along. It's a short walk
to rue Sainte-Avoye to rue du Bourg l'Abbe to the old bathhouse
turned into the fanciest nightclub in the world. There's a large door
like a hotel entrance, a carved marble Bacchus above it, spotlights
illuminating red carpet the thumping beat of dance music filling the
air. There's a line at the door menacing doormen standing guard.
Philippe walks up to them says hello they smile and shake his hand
pat him on the back they shake my hand and usher us into the club.
I ask Philippe how he knows them he tells me he picks up their
garbage every morning the doormen are usually still there. We walk
inside labyrinthine rooms, all former baths, a large pool still filled, a
black-and-white-checked dance floor, couches bars waitresses a huge
crowd of beautiful people, men women gay straight French Italian
English American German nationality doesn't matter, style does I
have very little of it. Philippe finds the manager who gives him a hug
and takes us to a velvet sofa, a small table in front of it, the room
is dark and loud and crowded, lights flashing and moving, people
talking drinking dancing.

I look at the menu figure fuck it it's my last night, I order a bottle of
champagne Philippe laughs. We watch the crowd Philippe gets up
and dances with a group of three girls all tall thin and beautiful, he's
a great dancer unselfconscious and uninhibited, a surprising amount
of rhythm, a huge amount of enthusiasm and gusto. I finish the
champagne order another bottle, ask for a bottle of vodka as well.
Philippe comes over to our sofa with the girls they sit with us, drink
with us, talk with us, laugh with us, flirt with us. They're all models
in their late teens or early twenties, two American one French.
They're cool, smart, funny, gorgeous they simultaneously make me
remember and make me forget. We go through three more bottles of
champagne and the vodka one of the Americans looks like the most
beautiful California surfgirl in the world she has a vial of cocaine

asks if we're interested. I say yes we go to one of the bathrooms close
the door cut lines on the lid of the toilet with a credit card get wired,
it feels good so good, the first stimulant since, the first thing I've
done to bring myself up since it feels good so good.

We open the door step out Katerina is standing in front of me. I'm
too surprised to speak or move my heart was already pounding from
the blow, it immediately feels like it's going to explode. Surfgirl
walks away I stand in front of Katerina she's wearing a pink dress, a
black sweater, hair pulled back in a ponytail, the necklace I gave her
glittering and shining around her neck it hurts me to see it she stares
at me speaks.

That was quick.

What?

Over me already.

Fuck off.

You fuck her in there?

No.

You sure?

Here with Philippe, just met her, she had some blow.

I wouldn't blame you if you did.

Heart pounding I feel like I'm going to throw up, I still love her even
though she makes me fucking sick, the glittering and shining heart
around her neck makes me fucking sick. I start to step around her, I
want to walk away. She reaches for my arm.

Please.

What?

I'm sorry.

Doesn't matter.

I'm so sorry.

Doesn't matter, Katerina.

It does.

Fuck off.

I step around her start to walk away, she steps in front of me.

Please, please talk to me, for five minutes, please.

Why?

I need to explain.

There is really no fucking need to explain anything.

I step around again, she reaches for my arm.

Please.

I turn to her she looks like she's going to cry. Her brown eyes wet, lower lip quivering.

Please.

She motions to the bathroom the door is open she steps in I follow, she closes the door it's small and we're close, she locks the door.

I'm sorry, Jay.

Stop saying it.

I was drunk and high and he and I have a history and I'm up for a job with his company and...

Who you here with tonight?

Why does that matter?

Him?

No.

Who?

Some girlfriends.

He's here.

He was, I don't know if he still is.

You meeting him later?

No. No. Never again. No.

I don't have anything to say to you, Katerina.

Please accept my apology.

I loved you. I still love you. I thought you loved me.

I do.

Yeah?

Yes.

That's why I saw you with another man's cock in your mouth and his tongue in your pussy.

I'm sorry.

You want to apologize, cool. Can you erase my fucking memory too?

She puts her hands on my chest.

I'm sorry.

She starts to cry.

I'm so fucking sorry.

She cries I let her, she puts her head on my chest keeps saying

I'm sorry.

Over and over I know she's being genuine and true, I know she's sorry. I still love her and hate to see her hurt or cry I hate that she keeps saying

I'm sorry.

And as much as I hate her hurting and crying, it doesn't make me hurt any less or make me forget or make me anything other than feel fucking awful. I hate this bathroom hate this club hate this night I just want to fucking leave. I start to move Katerina off of me gently push her away, she lifts her head, looks up at me, her eyes into mine light brown and pale green it breaks my heart, it breaks my fucking heart, she looks into my eyes. I push her away she says

No.

Pushes me back against the wall.

No.

Her eyes into mine light brown pale green what was once intimacy is sadness pain and regret, she moves her hands behind my head pulls me toward her kisses me. And I taste her. Her lips her tongue her breath. And I kiss her back. And it is fast and immediate and passionate, the taste the desire the longing the loss our lips and

tongues and hands fast immediate passionate. My hands move
up her dress pull off her thong her hands in my pants take me
out we're kissing breathing she pushes toward the toilet the seat
is down I sit on top of it she sits on top of me. I'm inside her I
feel joy and pain extreme pleasure and extreme sadness, there is
nowhere I want to be more and there is nowhere I want to be less,
I never want to leave I want to get the fuck away. Her hips move
slowly and deeply I pull her against me I don't want to look in her
eyes for the first time since I've known her I don't want to look
into her eyes. I don't want to see love and I don't want to see pain
and I don't want to see hope I don't want to see regret. I close my
eyes to her to myself to the world I hold her against me she moves
her hips slowly, deeply. We cum quickly, powerfully, I feel her
body shake I hear her moan, I pull her tighter against me I throb
inside her throb. We stay for a moment two, don't move don't
speak I'm inside her she's sitting on my lap I'm holding her. Her
head is on my shoulder my face buried in her hair it smells clean
fresh and beautiful. She starts to cry. To cry on my shoulder sob on
my shoulder I pull her tighter she's so thin and frail in my arms, I
don't want her to cry it hurts me more to hear her cry, to feel her
cry, to know she's hurting, it hurts me more.

I'm sorry, Jay. I'm sorry.

It's okay.

It's not.

Don't cry, Katerina.

I'm sorry.

Don't.

I start to cry. Not sobbing but tears running down my face I couldn't
speak if I needed to speak, quivering lips quivering hands. We sit
with each other, each of us crying for our own reasons, but in the
same place we were together strong and true, now we're broken, and

what was will never be the same it's broken. Someone starts banging
on the bathroom door I pull her tight whisper
We gotta go.
She kisses me my neck my cheek my lips stands up moves off of
me straightens her dress. I stand up put myself together button my
pants there's more banging on the door. Katerina speaks.
What do you want to do?
I reach up, wipe the tears from her cheeks.
I don't know.
Let's go home.
I'll never step foot in there again.
Let's go to your place.
No.
What do you want to do, Jay?
I don't know.
More banging on the door I step around her open it. I step out
there's a man, a woman, a man dressed as a woman, the man says
thank you I step around them, Katerina follows me. We walk to
the edge of the club music lights people dancing and drinking she
reaches for my hand I pull it away.
I'm going to find Philippe and get out of here.
When will I see you again?
I don't know.
What are you going to do?
Get out of here.
Please let me make this better.
I don't want to talk about it anymore.
She looks like she's about to cry again, I reach out put my arms
around her pull her close, pull her tight she whispers
I love you.
I don't respond just hold her she whispers again

I love you, Jay.

I say

I love you too.

I let her go and walk away I don't look back I can't look back if I do look back I won't be able to keep going I don't look back I walk away. I find Philippe the girls are dancing he's drinking a glass of champagne on the sofa, I tell him I'm going to leave he says cool I'm ready to go. I get the check five bottles of champagne and a bottle of vodka in the fanciest nightclub in the fanciest city in the world the bill is enormous I don't give a fuck I just want to leave. I pay the bill my money is almost entirely gone, enough left to get to London and get a start, Philippe and I walk out he says good-bye to the manager and the doormen I don't look back.

He wants to go to Laura's he gives me the key to his place. When we split I give him a hug tell him thank you for being such a magnificent friend, Paris wouldn't have been shit without him. He laughs says it was fun, come back someday. He goes to Laura's I go to his place drink another bottle of wine go to sleep. I wake up the next morning write another note of thanks leave him my friends' phone number and address in London tell him to stay in touch. I leave his key on top of the note. I pack my meager belongings into a backpack take a train to the airport buy a ticket fly to London.

Good-bye, Paris, I love you.

Thank you.

Love.

Los Angeles, 2017

I want to see you.

Great.

I need to see you.

You okay?

I've been better.

What's wrong?

Can you come to Zurich?

Zurich?

Yes.

Why Zurich?

It's where I'm going to be.

When?

When could you come?

It'll take a day or so to get there. I could leave whenever.

What will you tell your wife?

The truth.

What will she say?

She knows about you.

What does she know?

Everything.

Everything?

Yes.

Will she think it's weird?

Probably, but I'm not coming there to fuck you, or to start some
affair with you.

No, you're not.

And it's happened before. More than once. My friends all know if
they need something and I can help them, that I will. If they need to
see me, I'll come.

I don't need your help, I just need to see you.

Why?

You'll understand when you get here.

You're kind of freaking me out.

Haven't I always?

In so many ways, yes, though most of those ways were pretty wonderful.

Hopefully this will be as well.

Yes.

Three days from now, Writer Boy.

I can make that happen, Model Girl.

Send me your travel when you have it. I'll send you info on where we'll meet.

Cool.

À bientôt.

Busting out your French?

Oui.

À bientôt.

London, 1993

My life here is simple. I live with two women both great friends they share a bedroom I sleep on the couch. It's a big couch soft and comfortable when I lie down I sink into it and it swallows me. I have a warm comforter and giant pillow. The place is on a little street called Tamworth near a cemetery and a Tube station, a store on the corner sells beer and cigarettes and candy bars. We keep it reasonably clean a small kitchen, a table and four chairs, my couch, a television. My friends Anna and Amy both came to avoid the machine in America, both have working papers, both have simple jobs in offices. They were both here for their junior year of college and wanted to come back, neither will stay forever, for now they're happy to go to work they go out after work they have fun together, they laugh and smile and raise their glasses, they aren't interested in much beyond having a good time. I have a job working as a PA at a film company. A friend from America hooked me up it's off the books I get paid in cash at the end of every week, it's not much but enough. I spend my days getting producers and directors coffee, serving them lunch, making deliveries. It's simple and easy and mindless I go where I'm told, I do what I'm told, for now I'm cool with it. I write at night, usually for two or three hours before I start drinking. Some nights the drinking is at home a couple bottles of cheap wine or a few beers, some nights I meet Anna and Amy at a pub I laugh and smile and raise a glass with them, some nights I go out on my own I found a bar that sells MD 20/20, known in America as Mad Dog, known by me as a Purple Ticket to Hell, some nights I punch that ticket and meet my old friends Mister Darkness and Mister Oblivion. London is a good town to be an alcoholic. There are pubs everywhere they all close at 11:00 p.m. You can wander around all night and everything is closed, except for the big clubs in Central

London, which do not interest me. I get drunk and I'm in bed by
11:30, I can wake up the next day and go to my dumb job.
I think about Paris constantly. Think about the places I love, the
people I love, the streets I love, the air I breathed in Paris the air that
gave me life, the air it gave me life. I think about Louis bellowing
at the sky, I think about Omer snickering at the drunks in Polly,
I think about Philippe picking up garbage and having dinners
with Laura and occasionally sneaking out and getting hammered.
I think about Bar Dix and Stolly's and Shakespeare and Company
the beautiful books and the beautiful lost people who pass through
those doors. I think about *The Gates* and *Olympia* the film of Picasso
painting and the dumbass motherfuckers taking pictures of the
fake *Mona Lisa*, I think about coffee at Flore and sandwiches at
Maison de Gyros and steaks at Lipp. I think about the bridges and
the parks and the monuments and the squares and the churches
and cathedrals, I think about the Seine, slow and heavy and eternal,
silent and looming, utterly and absolutely dominant, seemingly still
but not, filled with 2,300 years of hopes and prayers, of love and life
and death, unfortunately filled with several hundred pages of my
writing. When I think about Paris, I think about Katerina. I wonder
where she is, what she's doing, if she's happy, if she's smiling and
laughing I hope she is.
I imagine her reading in bed.
Making coffee.
Walking through Le Marais.
Rushing to a meeting or casting, strolling home.
I imagine her looking at a painting, some odd awesome unexpected
opinion on the tips of her lips. I imagine her looking through
magazines at the newsstands, books on the quay, art in the stalls. I
imagine her drinking champagne and chatting with Petra, I imagine
her sitting in a café making smartass remarks, I imagine her red hair

in the breeze, I imagine her sitting on the Métro singing a song to herself. I imagine her smile, the smile I saw the most beautiful thing I saw in the most beautiful and most civilized city in the world, I hope she's smiling now, and I hope that smile is big and happy and true.

And as much as I hope someday she finds happiness and joy and whatever peace she seeks, right now I don't want to think about her. I want to forget her. I want to let go of the memories I can still taste her and smell her and sometimes I wake up looking for her next to me. Every time I think of her it hurts me. Every time she comes into my mind it hurts me. Every imagination I have of her hurts me. And as many as I have that are good and pure and beautiful and sweet, they are balanced by the one that is and will always be burned into my fucking mind, the one where her head was moving up and down and he was looking up and smiling at me. It comes to me when I wake, it comes to me as I fall asleep, it comes and goes throughout my day it comes when I'm sober and it comes when I'm drunk, heavy and hard and crushing it comes to me again and again, again and again it comes.

My life here is simple.

I work and I write and I get drunk.

London is big and beautiful and vibrant and filled with art and books and music and life, but not for me.

Maybe in another life or at another time, but not in this life or in this time.

My heart is broken.

Won't be forever it is now.

Probably time for me to go.

Not sure where there's nothing for me at home.

But it is.

Home.

So I'll go, figure it out, roll the fucking dice, I can do there what I'm doing here, and I'll be farther away, and though they say wherever you go there you are, I call bullshit on that, being farther away will be better for me, across an ocean, thousands and thousands of miles, it will be better for me.

Time to go.

Roll the fucking dice.

Los Angeles, 2017

Got a flight.

Thank you.

Nonstop from LA to Zurich.

Great.

Leave tomorrow.

I'm here already.

I take off at 7:20 p.m., land at 3:15 p.m. the day after.

Long flight.

I'll read, sleep.

Some things never change.

In the old days I would have gotten drunk.

Thankfully that did change.

Need anything from America?

Just you.

I'm not one of our finer products.

The only one I need, though.

If you change your mind, let me know.

I won't.

See you in a couple days.

Text me when you land, and I'll tell you where to go.

London And Paris
And London And America, 1993

Phone rings I answer it, it's Philippe.

JayBoy Motherfucker.

I laugh.

What's up, Phil?

You gotta come back here.

You miss me?

A little, but that's not why you gotta come back.

I'm going back to America, man. I'm not coming back to Paris.

You owe me.

I probably do.

Katerina's on the warpath. Going berzerko. Going to all our old spots, hassling people, says she needs to see you.

Tell her you don't know where I am.

I did.

And?

She laughed at me and called me a fucking liar.

She's smart.

You need to come back. Just for a day. Deal with her.

No.

I'll give her your number and address in London.

Please don't.

You owe me. And this is your mess. Come clean it up.

Kind of funny hearing that from a garbageman.

He laughs says please come back he wants to be able to go to bars and drink in peace I tell him I'll come for a night find out what Katerina wants calm her down ask her to leave him alone. We hang up.

Two days later it's Saturday I wake up around noon and I take a shower go to the airport there are cheap flights every hour. I fly to Paris take a train into the city walk from the gare I love French gares I walk from the gare to La Comédie. I walk in and I sit down Petra is working she pours me a whiskey smiles and speaks.

Hi.

Hi.

I thought you moved.

I did.

Back for a visit?

I heard Katerina is looking for me.

Haven't seen her much lately.

Why?

She's doing her thing, I'm doing mine.

You get in a fight?

We had a philosophical discussion that did not end well.

Sorry.

It happens.

Do me a favor?

Maybe.

Let her know I'm here.

Sure.

Petra turns walks to a phone on the wall behind the bar picks it up dials speaks for a moment hangs up. She walks back over.

She'll be here in a few minutes.

Thank you.

Need anything else?

Glass of champagne for her?

She laughs.

Sure.

She pours a glass it isn't fancy but does have bubbles, she sets it
in front of the stool next to me. I sip my whiskey and wait, I'm
nervous and I'm scared to see her, my hands are shaking and my
heart pounding I wonder what she wants what's so important. I love
her but I'm not coming back. I don't want to get back together my
hands are shaking and my heart is beating, I sip the whiskey but it
doesn't help.

I hear the door open I turn she walks in sees me smiles, it's a sad
forlorn smile she raises a hand. I smile sad and forlorn and raise a
hand I watch her walk toward me. She's wearing jeans and sneakers
a big white warm wool sweater, no makeup, her hair in a ponytail it
hurts me to see her emotions flood back, love and lust and pain and
hurt, how funny she is, how weird and interesting, her confidence
and intelligence, how much more beautiful she is without makeup.
She turns her stool toward me, I turn mine toward her, she sits and
speaks.

Hi.

Hi.

I got you a drink.

She pushes it away.

I'm good.

Really?

Really.

I heard you're looking for me.

Philippe or Louis or Omer?

Philippe.

I didn't know who knew where you were, so I went to all of them.

Only Philippe.

You still in France?

No.

Where?

I'm here now, to see you. What do you need?

I don't know how to say it.

Yes, you do.

I don't.

I'm not sure I've ever met or known anyone who knows how to say what they want to say as well as you do, Katerina.

She smiles.

Thanks.

So say it.

She looks at me, smile fades, I can see her struggling to speak, lip quivering, looks at me, looks into my eyes light brown like cocoa and pale green into me it hurts, she speaks.

I'm pregnant.

I'm speechless shocked thrilled scared.

I'm just over two months pregnant.

Light brown into pale green into me, her eyes and her words into me.

I want to keep the baby.

I smile subdued and shocked of all the things I expected to hear and considered I might hear a child, a pregnancy, a baby a life created by us the two of us together was not one of them. I'm not sure whether to hug her or scream with joy or cry or yell or run, I look at her eyes locked into each other I speak.

How?

I don't know.

I thought you never...

I didn't, I don't.

When?

That last night. When you walked away.

You sure?

Yes.

What about...

I never fucked him. Or I haven't for a long time, not since that day we saw you in the museum, and even then I thought about you when we did.

I laugh.

I'm not sure that actually makes me feel any better about him.

I'm sorry, Jay. I'm so sorry.

You don't need to apologize again. It's done, it's past.

Thank you.

And I think we have other things to worry about now.

She laughs.

Yeah.

And you're sure, you took a test, all that?

She reaches into her pocket, pulls out a small white plastic stick about four inches long, sets it on the bar, I look down at it. On its face there are two words in French short lines symbolic of the results after the words.

Enceinte II

Pas Enceinte I

There is a small opening next to the words where the results appear, there are two lines II in the space two lines II *Enceinte*. I take a deep breath, look up, Katerina is smiling, clearly nervous, light-brown eyes wet and hopeful and happy. I smile, my eyes wet and hopeful and happy, speak.

Fuck.

She laughs.

Yeah.

What are we gonna do?

I don't know.

I was gonna go home.

Home America home?

Yeah.

You still can.

I'm a shithead, but not that much of a shithead.

She laughs again, looks at me, speaks.

Can I have a hug?

I smile.

Yeah.

We both stand I put my arms around her hold her tight, she puts her arms around me pulls me in holds me tight, we stand don't speak holding tight together we're having a baby, having a baby. I can feel hear her start to cry I hold her tight we don't move whatever I thought is irrelevant we're having a baby life just changed, life just changed in the most magnificent shocking wonderful terrifying way possible, we're having a baby. She pushes me away tears running down her cheeks I wipe them away she smiles speaks.

Thank you.

I smile.

For what?

I wasn't sure how you'd react.

Like I said...

She interrupts me.

You're a shithead, but not that much of a shithead.

I laugh.

Yeah.

I'll be right back.

Cool. She kisses me turns walks away. I sit down look at my whiskey debate whether I should take a sip of it or not things are going to have to fucking change with me. As I debate Petra walks over, speaks.

Hey.

I look up.

Hey.

She tell you she was pregnant?

I smile, nod.

Yeah.

She's never going to speak to me again, but I can't let her do this.

My heart drops.

What?

Drops.

She's lying to you.

I can't believe the words shocked stunned I can't believe.

What?

She's lying to you. She's not pregnant.

I stare at her shocked stunned confused unable to respond to speak respond.

She misses you. She wants you to come back. She loves you and knows she fucked up. In a month she'll tell you something went wrong, but you'll be back together and she thinks she can make everything right.

No fucking way.

It's true. It's why we're in a fight. I think it's fucked-up.

No way, no way. She'd never do that, it's too fucked-up.

No?

No.

If that's what you think then you don't know her very well.

No fucking way.

Believe whatever you want, but don't say I didn't warn you.

She turns and walks away, I'm shocked stunned confused unable to speak or move my heart pounding I feel like I'm going to vomit. I reach for the whiskey drink the entire thing it burns my mouth, my throat, my stomach I want another. I hear the bathroom door open

Katerina is walking toward me smiling. I look at the test sitting on the bar *Enceinte* II. I look back at her walking toward me smiling she sits speaks.

Hi.

Hi.

I look at the test, *Enceinte* II. She can see something has changed, I've changed, shocked stunned confused it's on my face.

What's wrong?

I look up. Into her eyes, she's nervous, scared.

You sure you're pregnant?

Shocked stunned confused, both of us.

Yeah, I'm sure.

Really?

Yes.

You're not lying to me?

Her shock is replaced by hurt.

No, no fucking way.

I motion toward the test on the bar.

Let's go get one of those, right now, and we can go to your place and you can take it in front of me.

Fuck you.

Why is that a problem?

Fuck you for not believing me.

If you're actually pregnant I don't see the problem.

Fuck you.

It'll take five minutes.

I fucked up once, Jay. I've apologized over and over. I need you to believe me on this.

Five minutes.

Fuck you, you piece of shit.

Fine.

She picks up the test *Enceinte* II puts it in her pocket she's shocked stunned confused enraged we both are. She looks at me.

If you won't believe me I'm going to get up and walk out that door.

Five minutes, Katerina.

And you will never fucking see me again.

I'm not going to stop you.

Fuck you.

I heard you the first four times.

She picks up the glass of champagne throws it in my face, I don't move or react she turns and walks out the door, I watch her go don't say a word don't try to stop her. When she's gone I put some money on the bar Petra is helping another customer I stand and walk out don't say good-bye I just want to get the fuck out. Shocked stunned confused enraged. I go back to the gare take a train to the airport I get on the last flight of the day back to London. Shocked stunned confused enraged. I quit my job stay in London for two weeks I'm fucking drunk the entire time whatever happy memories I have of Katerina are gone shocked stunned confused enraged. When I am sober enough to make phone calls I start contacting people in America looking for a place to go one of my friends has a family vacation house in South Carolina that needs a caretaker. I can live for free write get another job to eat and live, I get on a plane to New York take a bus to Charleston.

I start smoking crack two days after I arrive.

There are three roads in life that a crackhead can take. A road to death, a road to prison, a road to sobriety.

I'm in rehab in Minnesota three months later.

Zurich, 2017

I land Katerina sent me an address while I was in the air. The flight was long I read for a little while slept for most of it. Airport is clean modern efficient as beautiful as an airport can be, customs is quick simple and easy. I find a cab start into the city.

Zurich is beautiful. Clear clean bright-blue sky a ring of distant mountains. Buildings out of a fairy tale mixed with glass and steel monuments to money and discretion. It's cold and the air is crisp I sit in the cab and stare out the window. I'm nervous and excited it's been so long almost twenty-five years so long. I wonder what she wants what she's like if she's the person I remember if she's the person I imagine if she's the person in my mind the person in my heart the person who became and is part of my soul. I wonder if her hair is still long if she has aged at all I doubt it, I wonder if her eyes are still bright how I'll feel when they look into mine. We pass restaurants cafés banks houses apartment buildings shops hotels churches traffic isn't bad I'm in the car for thirty minutes. Taxi pulls up to a small house amongst other houses and shops, a café on the corner. I pay the driver thank him get out of the car there's a short walk to the front door I push the bell wait.

A man answers. He's probably my age clean-cut in pressed khakis a button-down tucked-in shirt he has a stethoscope hanging around his neck he smiles.

Hi.

Hi.

May I help you?

I'm looking for a friend.

Your friend's name?

Katerina.

Are you Jay?

Yes.

Come in, she's waiting for you.

He opens the door I step inside. The house is simple humble uncluttered there's a central hallway a living room a small dining room a staircase up. Man leads me down the hall toward the back of the house past rooms with closed doors he stops at a door at the end of the hall motions toward it I step forward knock. I hear her voice

Who is it?

It is still the same I smile, still the same I hear her voice and smile respond

Jay.

Come in.

Heart beating smiling slightly confused by the house and the man, I reach for the door turn the knob step into the room. Room is large and bright, two comfortable chairs, a small bed a nightstand next to the bed a glass of water two cups sitting on it, a huge picture window with a view of Lake Zurich it's stunning and serene and peaceful and beautiful. Katerina is sitting in one of the chairs. She's gaunt, rail-thin, jaw and cheeks heavily defined. Her hair is gone she's wearing a silk Hermès scarf on her head, which makes me smile. Her arms are gone so thin so fragile she has a blanket on her lap. Her eyes though, her eyes are alive and bright and flashing, light brown like cocoa, and her smile is big and wide and true. She's clearly sick, clearly incredibly and terminally ill. My heart simultaneously leaps and breaks it has been almost twenty-five years her eyes are flashing her smile big and wide and true, but she's dying. My heart simultaneously leaps and breaks this is not what I expected in any way, at any point, she's still so beautiful but clearly so sick my heart leaping and breaking she speaks.

Been a while, Writer Boy.

I laugh, bite my lip, stop myself from crying, my hands shaking.

Hi, Model Girl.

She motions to the chair across from her.

Come sit with me for a while.

I nod, bite my lip, stop myself from crying, my hands are shaking I sit down. She smiles and our eyes lock light brown and pale green. We sit silently and stare at each other, into each other, into our hearts and souls and spirits, into our history and our past, into this moment, into our love, I still love her and still feel her love and she can see it in my eyes and I can see it in hers. We sit and stare. A minute two three four five I don't know how long but it feels like forever, and it feels like a forever that I would happily and joyfully take, it feels like a forever that I lost somehow and I have now found, forever. I don't move or look away, don't need to, I see her eyes and I know she sees mine, and right now, it's all I want or need, her eyes. Five minutes six I don't know she smiles and takes a deep breath and reaches for my hand, her hand is so frail, so thin, all bone and skin, she speaks.

Thank you for coming.

I'm happy to be here.

Yeah?

A little confused, but happy. And suddenly, also incredibly fucking sad.

I reached out to you when I got sick.

What's wrong?

Cancer.

What kind?

The bad kind, the terminal kind.

I laugh, she smiles.

I'm still funny.

You are.

I'm sorry I didn't tell you.

It's your right.

When I wrote you I didn't know if you'd respond, or if you'd tell me to fuck off, or if you were still angry with me, and once we started I didn't want to taint our talks. I wanted them to be pure, to be true, I wanted you to think of me the way you held me in your memory, I wanted you to think and smile and remember.

I did, I have, I do.

And?

And what?

Good or bad?

I smile.

So much wonderful, so much truly, truly wonderful, very little otherwise.

Except.

Forget about that dumb bullshit.

We all make mistakes.

We surely do.

Another one of the reasons I wanted to see you.

How many were there?

Reasons?

Yes.

I wanted to look into your eyes, and see if you were still the same behind them.

You most certainly are.

As are you.

Your eyes have always been my favorite part of you.

She laughs.

I don't believe that.

It's true.

It wasn't what you paid the most attention to.

I laugh.

I was young, frisky.

Didn't know any better?

No, I absolutely did.

She laughs.

Can we stick to my reasons?

Sure.

I wanted to say good-bye.

I don't want to do that.

You're going to have to.

No.

Yes.

She reaches into her shirt pulls out the necklace, it's still glittering, still bright.

I wanted you to see this, and to know I've worn it for most of my life.

I smile, big and true.

Look at that.

Right.

Still all shiny.

She laughs.

It's the nicest thing anyone ever did for me.

I don't believe that.

You didn't have any money, you couldn't afford it, we were already together so it wasn't going to get you anything, it was pure, and done for no other reason than that you loved me.

All of that is true.

She takes it off.

I want to give it back to you.

She holds it out to me.

No.

Take it.

It was a gift, pure, because I loved you, I'm not taking it back.

She takes my free hand, drops the necklace the glittering heart inside my palm, closes my hand around it.

I want it to be part of our family history.

My heart simultaneously leaps, breaks.

What do you mean?

Leaps and breaks, she wasn't lying.

I think you know.

Leaps and breaks.

You had a baby?

Yes.

Our baby?

Yes.

Petra...

When you first left I had the idea. I would find you and tell you I was pregnant and you would come back. I told Petra and she thought it was the craziest thing she had ever heard me say, and I used to say some crazy shit. When I actually was pregnant, she didn't believe me. When you asked me to take the test I was pissed at you for not believing me, and at her for telling you, and at myself for everything that happened before, and I just wanted to get away. I left Paris and went home. And I had a baby. Our baby. Our beautiful baby. My mother helped me and in many ways it saved her, at least for a while. I got married and had another baby. They were raised together, though they knew the first had a different father, someone from my past that I wouldn't discuss.

Leaps and breaks

I'm so sorry.

Leaps and breaks

Don't be.

Leaps and breaks

I always wondered, and I tried to find you.

I know you did, and I hid myself well.

I'm so sorry.

We were young and we fucked up, both of us.

I'm still sorry. So so sorry.

I told our baby, our beautiful baby, who is twenty-four now, who you are recently. I gave our baby the choice of meeting you, the choice of knowing you, the choice of having you be part of our baby's life.

Leaps and breaks

Boy or girl?

If you want to find out you will.

I do.

She smiles.

I thought you would.

I do.

Do you know what this place is?

I think so,

You do.

Yes.

It's legal here, and it's time for me, there is no hope, and it is only going to get worse.

No.

I have said all my good-byes. You're my last one. You are going to give me a hug, and if you want, a kiss, and you're going to let me look into your eyes one last time, and you're going to leave me.

No.

I'm going to get into that bed and take those two cups of pills and move on to wherever we go next.

No.

And if you want to meet our baby, you are going to leave here, and walk to the café on the corner, where our baby, our beautiful baby, is waiting to meet you.

I start to cry.

I do.

I love you, Jay. I believe, deeply and truly, we'll see each other again, wherever it is we go next, and we'll be friends, and we'll laugh about old times, and you'll give me updates on the life of our child.

I cry.

You ready?

No.

I am.

No.

Come.

She stands and the blanket falls away I see how frail she is, how sick, how close to the end. I stand and step forward and put my arms around her, gently pull her in, gently hold her, I can feel her heart beating against my chest, I hope she can feel mine. I listen to her breathe she puts her head on my shoulder, her head on my shoulder the way she did when we were young, when we were in love, when we believed, when we had hopes and dreams, when we had our whole lives still in front of us, our whole lives still in front of us. She steps back slowly puts her hands on my cheeks and looks into my eyes light brown like cocoa into pale green, we look into each other, our eyes locked one last time, one last time, one final time. She smiles, leans forward and whispers

I love you, Writer Boy.

And I smile, and whisper

I love you, Model Girl.

And she kisses me softly, lightly, sweetly on my lips, softly lightly

sweetly. She steps back and smiles again and motions toward the
door.

Go.

I start to cry.

There is someone waiting to meet you.

Tears running down my cheeks.

Our beautiful baby is waiting to meet you.

I bite my lip, nod, let the tears run, hold the glittering diamond
heart in my hand it is still in my hand.

Go.

I walk to the door she walks to the bed. I open the door I see her get
into the bed slide under the blankets, I stand at the door and watch
her, she looks up at me and smiles.

I loved you, from that first moment, all the way through, I loved
you, I still do.

I cry.

Me too, so much, so much.

She smiles and points.

Now go, Jay, or I will get out of this bed and kick your ass.

I smile, bite my lip, nod, let the tears run. I step back, I see her
reaching for her pills, I don't want to see her take them, I close the
door, stand staring at it, not believing what just happened, what is
happening, what she's doing, what I'm going to do, meet our baby
as she dies, meet our child as Katerina dies. I stand staring I want
to go back in and say more, apologize more, make her hear me
more understand how sorry I am more, but I know she wants to
go her own way. She always did. Go her own way. So I step away
slowly, I move down the hall staring at the door until I reach the
end, I take a deep breath, bite my lip, nod, let the tears run, stare
at the door, and I turn and step out of the house. The sky is clear
and clean and bright blue. I see the café on the corner. She's going

her way. Someday I'll go mine. And I believe, deeply and truly, we'll see each other again, wherever it is we go next, and we'll be friends, and we'll laugh about old times, and I'll tell her about the life of our child.

The life of our child.

I'll tell you, Katerina, about the life of our child.

Thank You

Thank you Maya, I love you, I love you. Thank you M and E and M, I love you, I love you. Thank you Eric Simonoff, for everything, but mostly for just being my friend. Thank you David Krintzman, for twenty years of guidance, friendship, and rocking in the free world. Thank you Guymon Casady, my new pal. Thank you Jenny Meyer, my old pal. Thank you Sylvie Rabineau and David Stone. Thank you Jen Bergstrom and Alison Callahan for a new home, I hope I get to stay awhile. Thank you Patrice Hoffman, and thank you Roland Philipps, my motherfuckers over the sea. Thank you Brad Weston and Pam Abdy, my West Coast BFFs. Thank you Todd Cohen and Greg Ferguson, Matt Jordan and Alie Rivier, for your friendship, your hard work, your opinions, and your tolerance of my music and my moods. Thank you Will Cotton for your art and your gift. Thank you Sarah Lazar for your design. Thank you Aimée Bell and Jennifer Robinson and Meagan Harris. Thank you Lisa Litwack and Jaime Putorti. Thank you Brita Lundberg and Max Meltzer. Thank you Gary Urda and Liz Perl and Wendy Sheanin and Jennifer Long and the sales and marketing teams at Simon & Schuster. Thank you Father Peter Walsh and Pastor Martha Klein Larsen and Father Justin Crisp. Thank you God, for your blessings, and for your peace, and for your love. Thank you to the pew in the third row for allowing me so much time, so much time. Thank you Terry and Chris at Zumbach's for my daily dose. Thank you Nicorette for keeping me calm all day. Thank you Jonathan Schiller and Josh Schiller. Thank you Richie Birns and Sheera Gross. Thank you Jazmine Goguen and Taylor Rondestvedt. Thank you Alexandra Jacobson and Nathaniel Lovell-Smith. Thank you Jim Raggio and Aileen Gorospe and Kristi Eddington. Thank you Regi Cash and Angelo Pullen for the years ahead of us. Thank you Robert Rubin and Michael Davies and Joe Blake, thank you Lauren Santo Domingo and Elizabeth Faulkner. Thank you Dr. Jonathan Fader and Ryan Holiday. Thank you David Genovese for my windows, I'm going to miss them. Thank you Matthew Drapkin. Thank you Nils and Suzi, Carter and Charmaine. Thank you Dawn Olmstead and Elise Henderson. Thank you Sam Taylor-Johnson and Aaron Taylor-Johnson, my English BFFs. Thank you Melanie Laurent. Thank you Boris and Priscilla for hanging around with me while I work and everyone else is asleep. Thank you Jag and Peg and Amar and Elizabeth and Abby and Nick. Thank you to our great friends in NC, you know who you are, you deserve your own page, thank you thank you. Thank you Mom and Dad, Bob and Laura and Jonathan, my blood, my blood. Thank you to readers and booksellers around the world who support my work and allow me to continue to do it, thank you for this gift, thank you. Thank you Marvelous Marvin and Auguste and Charles and Arthur and Henry for showing me the way, for showing me the motherfucking way. Thank you Philippe Faraut, the best motherfucking friend a motherfucker could ever hope to have in life, no I didn't forget you, thank you, thank you. *Merci aux gens de France et de la Nation de France, merci aux gens de Paris et de la Ville de Paris, tu vis dans mon coeur, chaque jour je respire, tu es vivant dans mon coeur, merci, merci, je vous remercie.*

James Frey is originally from Cleveland. He is the author of *A Million Little Pieces, My Friend Leonard, Bright Shiny Morning,* and *The Final Testament of the Holy Bible,* all international bestsellers. He has sold more than twenty million books and his work is published in forty-two languages.

Photograph by Matt Jordan

KATERINA

James Frey

This readers group guide for Katerina includes an introduction, discussion questions, and ideas for enhancing your book club. The suggested questions are intended to help your readers group find new and interesting angles and topics for your discussion. We hope that these ideas will enrich your conversation and increase your enjoyment of the book.

Introduction

In 1992, a young writer named Jay arrives in Paris, ready to live the bohemian dream. Against a scene filled with bars, drugs, and sex, he meets a young model on the verge of fame. Both are reckless, impulsive, and deeply in love. Twenty-five years later, Jay is rich, famous, and numb, reflecting on the exciting life he once had, when he receives an anonymous message that draws him back to the life, and possibly the love, he abandoned years prior. Percussive, propulsive, and powerful, *Katerina* is a love story oscillating between memory and reality that will give readers much to discuss.

Topics and Questions for Discussion

1. For decades—centuries, even—Paris has been a city that represents creativity and the bohemian dream. How does that idea link up with Jay's experience? How is it different?

2. Jay's life in 2017 is very different than the life he leads in 1992. How might someone's expectations of later life differ from the reality? Have you ever had something turn out differently than you expected?

3. How are young Jay and old Jay's outlooks similar? Different? Do you identify with one or the other? Both, to some extent?

4. "Life is waiting" is a phrase repeated throughout *Katerina*. Do you think it's a helpful or hurtful reminder to the narrator? The reader?

5. Though we don't spend much time seeing Los Angeles as a place, how are the moods of that city and Paris similar or different? Do they each have a specific impact on Jay's lifestyle?

6. What other books (or writers) does *Katerina* (or James Frey) remind you of? Does this novel join a canon of others about the artistic experience?

7. Discuss the way Jay approaches women, sex, and relationships at the different stages in his life. Does it change over time?

8. Katerina is a young model when she and Jay meet, and they have a lot in common: they're reckless, artistic, in search of something bigger—and it's obvious that they have a lasting impact on each

other. Do you think that one great love shapes who we are and how we approach life? Can young love be lasting love?

9. A recurring theme throughout *Katerina* is memory, and how truth and fiction both factor into it. To what extent do you think Jay's story line in Paris, and his relationship with Katerina, are based in fact? In nostalgia? How does that inform his mental state as an older man?

10. Throughout the book, Jay links his creative capabilities with dysfunction—the more he experiences pain, the better he thinks his work is. Do you agree with this mind-set? Are there other writers or experiences you can think of that support or disprove this belief?

11. In *Katerina*, the structure is split between transcript/quick messages (2017) and longer, narrative prose (1992). Which did you enjoy more? Which is more effective in conveying the story's emotion and tension, and the relationship at the story's core?

12. While in Paris, Jay has a group of friends—Greg, Kevin, Philippe—who play a large role in his life. What role does each friend play? Which one did you relate to the most?

13. Would you get in touch with your first love? In your opinion, what are the pros and cons of connecting with former relationships, and what do we—and Jay—learn from them?

14. Think about and discuss the final scenes of *Katerina*. What did you think? Does the reality of Katerina live up to the memory?

Enhance Your Book Club

1. Henry Miller's *Tropic of Cancer* plays a huge role in Jay's life. After reading *Katerina*, read Miller's classic and see if you can compare, contrast, and discuss the influences it had.

2. Plan a real or imaginary trip to Paris, or other parts of Europe mentioned in *Katerina*. Which of Jay's favorite spots are on your itinerary?

3. Think about a period of your life (like the early 90s, for Jay) that impacted you most. Have everyone bring a photo or a memento from that time, and share some memories with one another about how your life changed because of it.